Ghost Town

Cherie Claire

DEDICATION

To Jim Grant and Emilia J. Bellone, two fellow warriors in hurricane recovery who taught me about Masaru Emoto and the power of positive thinking. I relish our drives from Lafayette to the front lines, and even more so our friendship.

CHAPTER ONE

"If there is magic on this planet, it is contained in water."
— Loren Eiseley, *The Immense Journey*

Only hell could be hotter than Louisiana in summer, brutal heat indexes topping one hundred and a stifling stillness to the air that suffocates even the hardiest among us. Thunderstorms roll in violently from the Gulf of Mexico and offer a temporary respite, but temperatures quickly resume like the steam seeping up from the banquet, or what we call in New Orleans a sidewalk.

I look out on to my patio that only one month ago was ablaze in color and full of hope. Now, my poor plants are wilting, gazing back in agony.

"I'm sorry," I whisper, as much to apologize for the intense heat as to the fact that I'm not braving that swelter to water them.

As if on cue, my neighbor's cat scratches at the back door, demanding entrance. He's really the neighborhood cat, belonging to no one, but we all feed him whenever he shows up. I managed to have him neutered and you would think he would consider me an enemy for life but he returns daily for my cans of cheap cat food. Honestly, I don't get it — if I were a cat, I wouldn't eat the stuff — but these days, I welcome the company.

When his scratches become insistent, I know it's ungodly hot outside. I open the door and he jets off towards the bathroom where I keep the food and there's a nice stretch of cold tile to sleep upon.

"Nice to see you, too," I say to the orange, yellow and white streak darting through my tiny living room.

I live in what my mom lovingly calls a "potting shed," the mother-in-law unit of the big house in front. My landlord, Reece Cormier, took pity on my soul when I showed up one month after Katrina destroyed my hometown of New Orleans, asking him if he would rent out the back unit. Reece was renovating the front house at the time, ignoring the rear apartment, so I hoped for a vacancy considering that there were no rentals to be had in Lafayette due to the influx of Katrina evacuees.

After I had inquired, and mentioned that I had arrived in the town two hours west of New Orleans when the National Guard dropped us off here, the man started crying. He stood in his front yard, power drill in his enormous hands, and cried, big manly tears falling down his sunburned cheeks. He grabbed the top of my arms and silently nodded, then walked me back toward the unit and introduced me to what would become my little haven.

And the key to opening my prison door.

The storm blew away my excruciating newspaper job, covering the cops and school board beat in St. Bernard Parish on the edge of the civilized world — well, at least to a New Orleans city girl like me. So, even though I call Katrina a bitch, she gave me a chance to follow my dream job, that of being a freelance travel writer. And this tiny rent-free apartment is helping me do just that.

The unit needed work when I moved in, but it was livable, the toilet flushed and the shower released enough of a water stream that I would never go dirty, even if I had to hold the bathtub release with my toe to keep the water flowing down the drain. After I paid my electricity deposit, the lights worked too. I connected to Wifi and the outside world and happily started my new career.

Two years later, I'm still alive and traveling, although the current recession is keeping me up at night.

Stinky — my name for the orange tabby — turns to me when he finds what I have left him and lets out a pitiful cry.

"Sorry dude," I tell him. "I'm broke."

The sound only gets worse, as if he's being de-balled all over again.

"That's what you get for visiting a writer, you idiot. Try

the Broussards down the block. It's a double lawyer household."

He doesn't relent, so I open the front door. "Take it or leave it."

The cat gets the message. Either that or eating crappy cat food from the Dollar Tree is preferable to being outside in Louisiana. He heads back to the bathroom.

Before I shut out the humidity invading my air-conditioned oasis, I notice Reece on the back porch of his house. He's standing catty-cornered from me with the patio and swimming pool in between. I instinctively raise my hand to wave, then catch myself and pull the door close. I'm mad at him right now.

I check my watch. Fifteen after twelve. Late as usual.

I glance around, evaluating for the umpteenth time to see if everything in my meager apartment looks right. I moved here without furniture — hell, without anything — so there's no consistency, no color scheme, no master design. The table came from the Johnston Street Goodwill that offered free items to those with the right New Orleans area codes. The two accompanying chairs, that of course don't match, I found outside my door one night. The mattress I bought from Sears with my credit card, although the sheets hail from Salvation Army and are topped with blankets culled from various travel press trips. Because we're in the dog days of summer, I'm using my Gulf Shores beach towel and a throw that sports "Shreveport – Louisiana's Other Side" as bedspreads.

In my work as a travel writer I get invited to join press trips with other journalists. We're flown to various locations, put up in hotels and wined and dined in the hopes of us generating great press for their destinations. It's a dream job, yes, but it's also hard work. And it doesn't always pay well, hence the squeaking feline in the other room.

I love my little abode, even with the tacky swag I bring back from the Southern cities I visit, including the rug with the cheesy photo of Gatlinburg and the picnic basket from Georgia with plastic plates and utensils that I dine on every night. They not only remind me of the places I have visited since Katrina washed away my job with the New Orleans Post but of escaping my overbearing family and ex-husband back in the city.

As soon as that thought flits through my mind, I hear my mother and sister approaching.

"Vi lives here?" my sister Portia says incredulously. "Are you sure we're at the right place?"

"This is her *dream* house," my mother answers, and you can cut that sarcasm with a butter knife.

I try to swallow that ball of hurt that lodges in my throat every time my attempt to garner family approval fails. It sits there, blocking my air, when I open the door and smile as if nothing is wrong.

"You made it," I say pleasantly but the words come out hoarse and weak due to that lump that refuses to move.

"No thanks to the Baton Rouge traffic," my mother says entering the apartment. "I don't know how you can stand that Basin Bridge."

Portia follows, gazing around my living room — which is really one big room serving as dining area, sleeping quarters and work space — as if she's afraid to touch anything for fear of catching some awful disease. My mom runs a hand across the one nice piece of furniture I own, an antique desk some other generous Lafayette resident placed at my door.

For months the items kept coming, no doubt because Reece had spread the word about the Katrina refugee — god, I hated that word — who landed on his doorstep after spending two days on her roof before being rescued to the Cajundome, Lafayette's version of a domed stadium. Despite what my mother calls my apartment, there's an actual shed behind my place that now holds all the donated items I received since that bitch blew away my hometown.

"Isn't that pretty?" I ask my mom, because I can't stop appealing for their approval. "Some anonymous neighbor gave that desk to me."

"How do you know it was a neighbor if they were

anonymous?"

Give it to Portia to be literal. My older sister graduated high school at fifteen and passed the bar at twenty-one. She's a card-carrying Mensa member and constantly reminds me of that fact.

I decide to change the subject.

"Y'all want something to drink?" I head to my dorm refrigerator in the makeshift kitchen and pull out the fresh lemonade I made for their visit. Neither one seems interested.

"I thought we were going to that weird festival you mentioned," Portia replies.

My mom glances at me, and even though she's probably ready to bolt as well, she asks for a glass. This gives me hope although neither woman moves to sit down.

"Y'all relax and take a seat," I say, but the two stand awkwardly in the center of my potting shed, looking like two Evangelicals at a death metal concert.

I hand my mom her lemonade in the cup that promotes Blue Bell ice cream. Before she takes a sip, she gazes at the little girl and her cow gracing the outside.

"I got that in Brenham, Texas," I explain with a goofy smile. "Got to sample the ice cream right off the factory line."

I love Blue Bell ice cream, and tasting that creamy concoction before they froze it was the highlight of my Texas press trip. And, I must admit, I'm bragging about my new job, hoping my family will be as impressed as my friends are.

"Get this," I continue, my voice still struggling through that ball that won't disintegrate. "We asked the owner if he was struggling through the recession and he said they actually make money in hard times. That people eat more ice cream during recessions."

I thought that fact was interesting, something fun to write about in a year that was causing me to rethink my new career. The recession wasn't hitting Lafayette and Louisiana as hard as the rest of the nation, thanks to the booming oil industry and the money rolling in for hurricane recovery. But magazines and newspapers were on the decline and the recession only gave those companies ammunition for cutbacks and layoffs. So far, I lost two clients, took a pay cut on one of my best publications, and had three people insisting the check was in the mail — three weeks ago.

The current recession was one reason I had asked my mom and sister to visit. That and the rising over Blue Moon Bayou.

"Are you eating more ice cream?" my mom asks me and I wonder if she sees through my veiled invitation.

I sip my own lemonade from a cup that quotes Henry Miller: "One's destination is never a place, but a new way of seeing things."

Okay, so I bought that one.

"My favorite is Millennial Crunch," I say. "It's Blue Bell's latest since they just turned one hundred."

I'm so their demographic. Even though my lights might be cut off tomorrow, I have ice cream in the freezer.

"I can tell," my mom says, looking me over. "Just because they feed you on those trips doesn't mean you have to eat everything."

It never ceases to amaze me how family members pick the scabs off vulnerable sores. Yes, I've gained a few pounds. It's what I do under stress. And yes, I don't have to eat all that's put in front of me on press trips, can bypass the open bars and the dessert trays. But I live on mac and cheese when I'm home, since writing remains such a high-paying profession. Who wouldn't indulge whenever possible?

I pull my blouse down over the belly that's been growing consistently post-Katrina, although I'm not as thick as all that, considering that hurricane took off close to twenty pounds two years ago.

"You shouldn't be drinking lemonade," Portia adds. "That has so much sugar in it."

I close my eyes and instruct myself to breathe. How the hell will I be able to ask these middle-class women, who live in perfect houses and afford gym memberships, for money?

Mom hands me back the cup, while Portia pulls her purse tight over a shoulder, her hand resting on top. Neither says a word or looks at me, so I get the message.

"Ready to go?" I ask, trying desperately not to feel disappointed that they didn't like my meager little home, the one I created from scratch along with my new career with nothing in the bank but a FEMA check.

Both women immediately head for the door, my mother asking Portia where she got that snazzy new purse and Portia replying with a lengthy discourse on the pros and cons of Northshore shopping, post-storm; Portia moved across the lake after Katrina damaged her Old Metairie home. I follow behind, feeling disappointment lingering behind my eyes, demanding release in a good old-fashioned cry.

As Portia and my mom head down the brick walkway to their car, I turn and lock the door. Just before I do, I spot Stinky in the hallway licking the remnants of that awful cat food off his paws, bless his little heart.

"Man the house," I tell him, and he looks up ever so briefly and winks, that weird cat thing that makes you wonder if they know what you're thinking. Because for a moment, I believe he does.

I wonder about a lot of things these days, mainly if I'm as intuitive as my aunt claims I am. I had been born with "the gift," according to her, but over the years repressed my ability to speak with the dead. People tend to do that, considering how conversing with the deceased doesn't go over well with friends and family members. Over time, I ignored cousin Harry with the hole in his head from the time he went fishing, got drunk and fell overboard and into the path of the outboard motor. Or poor Mr. Stanislos, the former second grade teacher who walks the halls of my elementary school reciting times tables.

No one believed I saw them anyway.

By sixth grade, I was done being polite to the little old lady with hair worked up into a bun who would call to me from the porch of my neighbor's house like that crazy woman in *To*

Kill a Mockingbird. In college, when the frat boy who committed suicide appeared at my dorm room door, I slammed it in his ethereal face.

I convinced myself it wasn't real, that I was imagining things, and over time those spooks disappeared.

Katrina blew that psychic door wide open, however, but now I only speak to those who have died by water. I'm called a SCANC, a stupid abbreviation that stands for "Specific Communication with Apparitions, Non-entities, and the Comatose." In other words, I can only speak with those related to my trauma. In my case, it's water.

"Where are we headed again?" Portia asks when we climb into the car, me in the back seat.

"Blue Moon Bayou." A shiver rolls across my shoulders, considering the town a half hour away from Lafayette complements a water source. But then, I have never had ghostly experiences in this quaint south Louisiana town known for antiques, boutiques and a world renown zydeco brunch.

"And what's this festival you are so anxious for me to see?" my mom asks.

Deliah Valentine taught Shakespeare at Tulane before the storm and, even though the New Orleans university cut staff after Katrina and my mom makes due with adjunct classes at Baton Rouge Community College, she's still considered one of the country's foremost Shakespearean scholars. Ask my mom and she might say the world. It's why my sister was named Portia from *The Merchant of Venus* and my twin brother and I Sebastian and Viola from *Twelfth Night.*

"It's called Blue Moon Rising and it's quite the thing," I tell her. "There's a legend that upon the rising of the blue moon, the first person you will see is the one you are destined to fall in love with."

I thought my mother would eat this up. Reminded me so much of a Shakespeare comedy, like *Midsummer Night's Dream.* We're closing in on the summer solstice, so the timing is perfect.

"That's ridiculous," my mother answers.

I lean forward between them. "Imagine it. What if the person you wanted to see is suddenly called away when the moon rises and another person takes his place. You'd fall in love with the wrong person."

"If there was such a thing…," Portia adds.

"Better yet, what if, as in the case of this year when we have two blue moons within three months, you see the wrong person the first time and the right person the second?"

Portia huffs and starts spouting off how legends such as these keep society stupid but I see the wheels turning inside my mother's head. My mom is all scholar, always preferring the Shakespeare tragedies to the comedies because the latter were created, according to her, to humor the masses without brains. But I know her anthropologic mind finds this local tradition fascinating.

We park near the bayou and head toward Café des Amis, a restaurant located in a former coffin factory next to The Mortuary Bed and Breakfast. Annie Breaux sticks her head out the front door of the B&B and yells my name and waves. I wave back. Annie is one of the people I've met writing stories for national publications about my new home in Cajun Country.

"That place used to be a mortuary and is supposed to be haunted," I tell my sister and mom, although the ghosts are thankfully people who have died without the assistance of water so I can't see them.

"They all say that," Portia says. "Every hotel and B&B in Louisiana has ghosts now."

"Most of them do," I answer and Portia rolls her eyes. If only she knew.

We enter the restaurant on the tail end of brunch, with Curley Taylor and Zydeco Trouble rocking down the house on an impromptu stage in the front alcove. There are tables for eating but most people visiting today flood the makeshift dance floor, bopping up and down like a heartbeat, not caring that they run into each other regularly.

I can't listen to Cajun or zydeco music without moving — or smiling for that matter — so I immediately begin swaying to the vibrant tunes as we saunter up to the maître d'.

"Viola Valentine, table for three."

"Do you want to sit up front and dance or a quieter table in the rear?"

I look back at my family with hopes that we will enjoy this unique-to-Louisiana wild ride that people from around the world come to see, routinely packing this restaurant every Saturday, but my mom and sister reply in unison, "In the back!"

We follow the maître d' to the back room and mom insists on the table in the corner, as far away from the zydeco as we can get. I'm sad to miss Curley Taylor but equally disappointed that my family, once again, fails to appreciate what I'm offering. The waitress arrives, asking for drinks and appetizers in a sing-song Cajun accent. When we ask for three unsweetened teas — I'm not about to ask for anything with sugar — both my mom and Portia turn serious.

"What?" I ask, behind my water glass.

"This silly festival isn't why you asked us here," my mother begins.

I swallow the gulp of water lingering in my mouth. "What do you mean?" I answer as innocently as I can.

"What do you need, Viola?" Portia asks.

I need two thousand dollars to meet bills, replace my faulty brakes on the Toyota and buy groceries, but I don't know how to ask the two biggest critics in my life. Instead, I lie.

"I'm doing great. My new career is taking off. Reece still won't let me pay rent. What do you mean, what do I need?"

My mother gets right to the point. "How much?"

I place my water glass on to the table and sigh. "I started this business with nothing, you know. Most people who become freelance writers — especially travel writers — have savings in the bank. I was doing really well until this recession hit. Not many people can say that."

"Is this why you haven't divorced TB?" my mother asks.

My ex-husband who's legally still my partner married me years ago when I became pregnant at LSU. We barely knew each other, let alone considered it true love, although TB insists he loved me then and loves me still. When my sweet Lillye died of leukemia, my heart died with her, and TB and I lived a lonely, distant existence until Katrina pushed us on to the roof, washed away our jobs, and I found myself in Lafayette with the opportunity to start over. One of the first things I did following the storm was file separation papers. But that was before I really thought things through.

"We're staying married for the time being so I can share his health benefits," I say.

Portia huffs at this and I'm reminded how much I really hate when my sister does that.

"It makes great sense," I say in my defense.

"What would make great sense," my sister replies smugly, "is if you moved back in with him and did your 'freelance' in New Orleans."

Only thing I hate worse than her huffing is when she uses her fingers to mimic quotes. Who started that ridiculous gesture, anyway?

I grind my teeth. "I'm not moving back in with TB."

Portia crosses her arms about her chest. "Well, I'm not giving you money because you're too stubborn to make the right move."

"I don't need that much."

"Which will make moving back home that much easier for you."

I can't move back to New Orleans. Remember all those ghosts who have died by water?

I gaze over at my mother who's staring down at her lap.

"Don't ask Mom," Portia says sternly, and just like that, the conversation's over.

The waitress returns, we order crawfish cornbread and crab cakes for appetizers and I pick the pecan-crusted catfish although how I will be able to enjoy it knowing my newfound career is to crash and burn in the next two weeks is beyond me. Portia launches into how her two children are driving her crazy, their private school's depleting her disposable income and the new housekeeper is unreliable, which means she must search for a replacement ASAP, preferably one who speaks English. My poor sister, they will only be able to spend one week in Cabo this year instead of two and Christmas will be tight.

I glance over at my mother who's usually full of piss and vinegar, chiming in about her own shortcomings and lack of vacation time since she lost her plum teaching job, but for a change she's not talking. Since Katrina, I've suffered through hours of these conversations, listening to horror stories about disaster repairs and renovations, even though Portia lived far from the levee breaks and only had six inches of water and my mother had a tree damage part of her house. Neither lost their homes, nor had floodwaters to their attics. And I haven't had a vacation in years.

As usual I say nothing and nod and express sarcastic outrage over the fact that Portia can't buy a new BMW until Frederick, her husband, gets that raise, which has been pushed back until next year because his company's still rebounding from the storm. My mom sends me an evil eye for that one.

We eat lunch, me barely touching my fish, and then the bill arrives, which Portia grabs.

"Do you want me to help?" I ask.

"Yeah," Portia says, placing the bill in my hand. "You asked us here so you pay."

I look down and notice that the bill is thirty dollars more than what's in my checking account. I bite the inside of my cheek wondering what to do next when Portia grabs the bill. "Just kidding."

After planting her gold American Express on the table, Portia heads to the bathroom. My mother places a hand on my arm when she notices I'm about to let my façade slip and cry right there in front of Curley Taylor and the tourists from

Australia.

"Why don't you come home?"

I shake my head. How can I convince my mother New Orleans holds too many ghosts, not to mention all those bad memories of losing my precious baby girl, the one person who's passed I'm *not* able to see.

"I can't," is all I manage to whisper.

"Don't you miss us?"

There's pain lingering in her gaze I haven't seen since dad left. Something is amiss here and the hairs on the back of my neck rise. I briefly think to inquire but that old defensiveness remains.

"I love it here, Mom. I finally have a chance to do what I've always wanted to do. Can't you all understand that?"

She squeezes my arm and that sadness lingers. "We miss you."

My mother is a tough cookie, one of those professors you both admire and dread for getting an A in her class means giving up sleep for five months. She's been nicknamed the "Bard Bitch," although my mother secretly loves it, wears the title like a badge.

Underneath, however, when the mom side emerges, she's all heart. She was my rock when Lillye died.

I place my hand over hers. "I miss you, too, Mom. But I need to be here right now." That lump emerges again because those tears have never left their starting line and are waiting for the gun to go off so they can turn me into an emotional mess. "This is my dream," I manage to whisper.

Mom's about to reply and I pray it's about loaning me money when Portia arrives and barks for us to leave. We travel through town for the remainder of the day, shopping at antique stores and Portia buying new clothes at two of the swanky boutiques. We pause for coffee and dessert, then head for the bayou's edge when the sun begins to set. Moonrise is scheduled for seven thirty-six so by the time we reach the bayou park, the place is swarming with people.

Portia still rebukes the festival, my mother says nothing

and I'm quaking inside about how I will make it through another week when I spot Reece on the far side of the crowd. Portia follows my line of sight — and no doubt wonders why my mouth is hanging open — and mutters, "Who's that gorgeous man?"

I don't answer. I'm too busy watching my sexual fantasy laughing at a woman with silky blond hair tossed back over her shoulders, lips full and pursed like Julia Roberts and telephone poll legs falling gracefully into fashionable high-heel pumps. This woman exudes perfection. Tailored dress. Coiffed hair. A girl and a boy equally adorable and well-dressed at her side. It was a like a mother-of-the-year advertisement.

"Do you know him?" my mom asks.

"He's my landlord," I manage. My hero in a storm. My hope for love at last.

At least until he decided to get back with his wife.

The crowd teeters and I look to the horizon. There's too much sunlight for us to spot the moon but the mayor begins the countdown on the loudspeaker. Portia huffs, my mother gets a phone call and excuses herself to the car, and I can't help looking longingly at the man of my dreams, hoping he might glance my way. When the mayor reaches one, noting the moon is rising over the bayou, Reece looks lovingly at his wife so I cast my eyes to the ground. No use confusing fate. Obviously, Reece belongs with his wife, the mother of Dick and Jane.

As the mayor mouths the final moment, I hear someone call my name. I look up to find a young girl dressed in a simple pair of overalls and flannel shirt watching the event curiously from the bayou's bank. She's a stark contrast to Mrs. Louisiana: uneven cut hair that sticks out beneath a ragged cap, dirty shoes with holes in the sides, bruises and mosquito bites on her legs. She senses me watching her and looks my way, eyes squinted as if not expecting anyone to notice her.

"Can you see me?" she mouths and I'm so startled this

may be a ghost standing before me that I say nothing, merely nod.

"Vi?" comes the voice again and I turn to find my ex-husband, staring at me as the girl had done only this time with a love-sick gaze.

"What are you doing here?" I ask.

TB grins that goofy smile that has always driven me crazy, one that reminds me of our uneven relationship and fills me with guilt.

"Portia told me about the festival. And guess what? You were the first person I saw tonight."

I glance at Portia who's laughing her ass off.

Just then my mom arrives, announcing to Portia, "We have to go."

It's rare to see my mother not in control but something has happened and I feel a buzz deep in my soul akin to when a ghost arrives. I glance back at the girl by the bayou's edge but she has vanished. I look around the crowd but find her nowhere.

"Let's go Portia," my mother says sternly and that chill turns into a full-fledge shiver that rocks me up to my chin.

Mom kisses me on the cheek, places two twenties in my hand and offers a polite but brief greeting to TB, and the two head off to the parking lot.

"What on earth is that about?" I whisper to Portia as she walks past.

Portia pauses, stalling as if she's unsure of what to reveal. Finally, she whispers, "I'll explain later."

And in that instant, all chills disappear, replaced by a foreboding that stills my heart and fires up my temple. I stand there by the bayou's edge with enough funds to buy food for the week but still in dire straits, TB is gushing love into my ear like a high school freshman and the girl appears once more, shaking her head as if she's heard the entire conversation.

CHAPTER TWO

My head's pounding and TB won't stop gushing about his love that was meant for me, making me wonder if Portia was right about these legends being fodder for the ignorant. Of course, I feel guilty thinking that about my simple-minded ex-husband which intensifies the pressure building in my skull.

I can't help it. Even though the man loves me, has supported me through the toughest experiences in my life, never has a bad word to say about anyone, and practices that rare gift of unconditional love, I can't get past the emptiness I sense behind those puppy dog eyes.

Not to mention that deep down I don't love him.

I need more intellectual stimulation and less emotional release. When Lillye died, TB fell apart and I retreated. Call it what you will, but we all grieve differently and I saw no purpose in crying on people's shoulders and explaining to counselors how bad I felt because the most precious being on earth was taken by leukemia at a young age. Seriously, what is there to say?

Katrina amplified the problem, and then I began to see ghosts who have died by water. My Aunt Mimi believes there are no accidents in life, that those in the beyond are here to serve me as much as I them, including helping me move past my grief. Forget moving on; I'm confident that my newfound abilities will help me to connect to my baby.

How TB fits into this is beyond me.

"What are you doing here?" I ask him for the millionth time as we drive back to Lafayette.

"Portia said you might need me." He sends me a hopeful look.

I feel that burning sensation eating up my stomach liner, the one that appeared when the recession started and *Happy Traveler* magazine cut my assignments in half.

"Did Portia say something about your mom?"

I don't want to think about my mother at this moment, let alone discuss her dismissal of my financial problems. I would imagine TB feels the same since my family routinely called him a disease.

TB stands for T-Bubba, a combination of Cajun and redneck. In the South, the youngest man in a family might sport the same name as his dad but be differentiated by the word "little." For instance, John Junior might be called Little John. In French South Louisiana, the tradition translates to *Petit* John and is shorted to 'tit-John, then just T-John. TB's father's name was Thibaut Boudreaux, but folks called him Bubba. Naturally, his son became T-Bubba, and then TB shortened it even further.

It's one reason why I don't want to remain married to my husband. Why anyone would want to be known as TB is beyond me. The man is even proud of it. I tried introducing him as Thibaut (a lovely French name pronounced T-bow) but he would inevitably launch into the history of his nickname and I would stand there watching his audience gaze upon him like he's a circus attraction.

"You have to own your uniqueness," he would later argue in the car on the way home.

"Only if that uniqueness is worthy of attention," I countered.

"Vi," TB calls out, bringing me back to reality. "What did Portia say about your mom?"

"We're here."

Thankfully, we arrive at the Saint Streets, a group of avenues in staunch Catholic Lafayette named for a variety of saints. I live on Saint Francis Street, in the heart of it all, embraced by towering live oak trees standing sentinel over the Craftsman cottages and World War II-era homes. Driving down my quiet street with its line of blooming crape myrtles in the neutral ground and my headache lifts. I love my new town, an oasis amidst chaos.

"Can I come in?" TB asks, a question I've been dreading since Blue Moon Bayou. But then, I still need two thousand dollars.

I wince, feeling that guilt pinch my stomach once more. "Sure."

Unlike my mother and sister, TB enters my apartment and checks out everything. He loves the Walter Anderson print I picked up in Ocean Springs, Mississippi, and the antique desk with the brass pulls and the cool secret drawer where I deposit the forty dollars my mother has slipped me. TB doesn't find the kitchen rug with the brazen "See Rock City" advertisement cheesy and relaxes in my Papassan chair with a glass of lemonade, a drink he claims is the finest he's ever tasted. I frown and give him a "yeah right" look and he shrugs.

I expected Stinky to go flying out the door when we arrived, but instead the tabby hangs around, sniffing out TB, then settles into his lap while TB falls asleep and I head to the kitchen to make dinner.

"Traitor," I admonish the feline.

I have a strong *envie* for Alesi's, a Lafayette landmark that still contains a neon sign out front and serves up pizza with a variety of meats, cheeses and those tiny mushrooms that probably come out of a can but I love them anyway. I can devour one of those pizzas all by myself.

But I can't use that forty for pizza tonight, need to save it for cheap cat food and groceries. I pull out the familiar box of mac and cheese and begin boiling water, wondering if tuna and peas might help improve the meal I've come to detest.

As I stand there watching water boil, I think back on the scraggly girl by the bayou's edge. It's not unusual for me to spot ghosts, especially near a water source, but conversations with the deceased, known as intellectual hauntings, are rare. I wonder what her story is and if our meeting was planned by some divine source, hoping I'd help this girl move to the next realm. So far, I've assisted nearly a dozen people climb the ladder, as my friend Carmine likes to call it.

When my gourmet meal is ready, I kick TB's foot and he snorts awake, sending Stinky flying. I hand TB a plate and then open the door with my free hand; the apartment is tiny enough for me to do that. Stinky disappears into the night and I pull out a chair at the table while TB joins me and we indulge in mac and cheese with glasses of milk to thankfully wash it down.

After a few moments of silence, I brave the question.

"TB, can I borrow some money?"

He looks up without speaking, staring at me with that vacant look that always drove me crazy. "Huh?"

"I have to get my car fixed. I'm late on bills because clients aren't paying on time. It's a temporary thing. I'll pay you back."

TB wipes his mouth on the Visit Tuscaloosa dishtowel and leans back in his chair. For a moment, I think he's going to insist on me moving back to New Orleans like Portia did, even though TB knows about my ghostly abilities and understands how New Orleans with its plethora of watery deaths is off limits for someone like me.

He shakes his head sadly. "I'm sorry, Vi, but I don't have any. I just spent every dollar I saved to fix the front porch. And I don't get paid again until the end of the month. If you can wait three weeks, I can give you a couple hundred."

That hole in my stomach rears its ugly head when I realize TB said give and not lend. I've wished with all my heart that I loved this man, this generous, sweet, lovable person with his adorable smile, head full of ash blond hair and vibrant chocolate brown eyes. I'm not only giving up someone who could grace a romance novel cover but the best sex I've ever had.

Add to this picture the fact that he's slowly renovating the house we lived in for years, the one once submerged under twelve feet of water when the levees broke. I took one step inside that putrid mess of a house when they reopened New Orleans for visitors and swore I would never return. TB, on the other hand, cleaned out the fridge, gutted the walls, removed the pungent mold covering everything water touched and restored the house piece by piece as money became available. I still own half although I want none of it, not even a second mortgage to save my ass at present. I don't deserve it.

"It's okay, TB. I'll figure something out."

Just what, I can't imagine. The idea of returning to a newsroom to vomit news copy on a daily basis is totally out of the question.

A light goes off inside TB's brain and the sudden change startles me.

"I almost forgot," he says excitedly. "I've been working renovations on the new Courtyard chain of hotels and one of the managers I met the other day said they were hiring, that they are looking for people to travel around and review hotels."

I shake my head, not following.

"Like mystery shoppers."

TB reaches inside his pocket and pulls out a card and hands it to me. "Call him. Might be a fun job."

"Reviewing hotels?"

TB shrugs and continues eating. "It's a job. Might tide you over for a while."

I look down. *Jacob Yarbrough, Courtyard Hotels.* Could work.

It's late when we finish eating dinner, followed by Blue Bell, of course, then cleaning the plastic plates adorned with Georgia peaches. TB hovers, sliding his palms down his pant legs nervously.

"Of course, you can stay."

The light goes on again, but I extinguish it with a look. As much as I would love to have those delicious hands working magic on my body, something I haven't experienced in months, I know it's not a good idea to give this man hope.

We watch *The Daily Show*, laughing at Jon Stewart's quirky view of the news, then sleep together on my Sears queen mattress, me pulling out the giant throw I obtained from my trip to California, the one with the redwoods, a bear and a snow scene which looks so incredible this time of year. It barely covers us and I wonder if it's time to purchase a real bedspread.

"It's fine," TB mutters just before falling asleep, as if he reads my mind. He drapes an arm across me and I let him. Before twilight overtakes me, I actually believe it is.

I awake to the sound of Stinky demanding entrance once more and slip out of bed to open the door. Reece and his children are splashing in the pool so I command myself not to look his way, but, of course, I do anyway. Beauty queen is lounging in the morning sun in a fashionable bikini while Reece instructs the kids about water safety.

I can't help but stare. He's a tall drink of water, dark complexion and midnight eyes and he sports this adorable Cajun accent that cracks me up. He was off limits for months when I first moved in and started fantasizing, but he split with his wife and we started dating, if you could call it that. He showed me around Lafayette, invited me to parties, and we watched movies together. I know he's interested, enjoyed a few sensual kisses during those sweet months, but his kids are young and he and his wife were only separated so it was mostly hands off the gorgeous landlord.

In the past month, Reece agreed to attend counseling with his wife and the fun ended. Once he made the move to reunite with Mrs. Perfection, I retreated to my potting shed to pine in silence. He acts like nothing's happened and we can continue as before, sans the delicious kisses, but what's the use?

Reece looks up and waves but I merely grab the newspaper and turn away. It's then I notice that TB's truck is gone from the driveway so I dart back inside and call his name to be sure. He's left a note on my desk, explaining his work schedule — he's working a job in Lafayette but only for the day — and for me to call him.

"PS," the note reads, "I believe in legends and you're the first person I saw last night when the moon rose so you're going to see more of me. You can't get rid of me this easily."

I hang my head knowing that he doesn't make needless

claims and will be a royal pest and I wish I had a press trip lined up to get out of town. Then I remember the card he gave me and the possibility of a job traveling to review hotels. Just before I pick up the phone to call Jacob Yarbrough, there's a knock at my door.

Two African Americans stand at my door, a man and a woman, the man in a suit and the female dressed in what I would call gypsy attire.

"I'm sorry," I tell them, "but I'm not interested."

The man puts out a hand as I attempt to close the door. "It's not what you think."

"Pray for me if you want. I could use all the help I can get," I tell them. "But trust me, I don't have any money."

The woman laughs which gives me pause, lightens my heart with its lyrical sound. And that's all it takes for the man to slip his foot over the threshold. I look down in amazement. I've only seen this move in cartoons.

"Ms. Valentine?" the woman asks.

I'm still in my pajamas and I'm beginning to think this might be serious, so I cross my arms over my chest to cover my bra-less bosom. "Yes?"

"We're from Lake Lorelei, up near Alexandria," the man explains.

"We need your help," the woman says.

Now I'm back to being suspicious this is all about religion.

"For what?" I ask, moving back a step, glancing down at the doorstop that is this man's foot.

"We're having a problem with ghosts," the man says, then removes his foot.

Both look up at me anxiously and I have no idea how to respond.

"Why don't you let us come in and we'll explain," the woman says.

I'm still dumbfounded, so the man reaches into his breast pocket and pulls out a card.

"My name is Elijah Fontenot and I'm the librarian and mayor of Fontus Springs, a little town that skirts the lake.

This is Sirona Harmon and she helps out with city matters."

I look at one and then the other and figure they're harmless. I open the door wider and the two saunter in.

"Excuse my place," I tell them. "It's only a mother-in-law unit. I do have two chairs by the dining room table."

They don't laugh at the reference to dining room so I give them kudos for that. They make themselves comfortable and I grab my robe.

"And excuse me for not being presentable. I was up late."

That's only partly true. Since I work from home I sometimes spend all day in my pajamas.

Elijah waves his hand. "Of course, we should have called first but we thought this might not be the kind of conversation to have over the phone."

I grab a wooden box I use to haul groceries from my car to the apartment, turn it over and sit down. Elijah immediately rises, like the Southern gentleman he is, but I wave him off.

"What's this about ghosts?" I ask to keep him from insisting on giving me his chair.

Sirona leans forward, her hands tightly folded across the table. She bites her lip and glances at Elijah.

"Go on," Elijah encourages her. "Tell her."

Her eyes narrow when her gaze moves to me, but there's kindness lingering behind them. "First, there's something we heard through the grapevine and I need to know if it's true."

"Shoot."

"Is it true you can see ghosts?"

This is a new one for me. Until now, the only people privy to my weird ability was TB, my Aunt Mimi, a few people I've helped with apparitions in their midst and a couple of friends, mainly Winnie Calder in Mississippi and Carmine Kelsey in Dallas, other travel writers and dear friends. Carmine is also my mentor in SCANC life, explaining to me phenomenon when I'm confused, and walking me through the scary stuff.

I decide to be elusive. "Depends on who's asking."

Elijah smiles and leans back in his chair. "We're friends of

Winnie Brown, although she's a Calder now. She's a cousin once removed through marriage. Plus, we went to Ole Miss together."

We're all related in the South, and tying up people is like handing someone a resume. These two pass muster.

"I do sometimes see apparitions," I admit.

The two look at each other and smile, and suddenly knowing other people own my secret makes me uncomfortable so I quickly add, "But I'm not broadcasting this so keep it to yourselves."

The smiles fade and Elijah turns so that he's facing me directly. "We have a problem in our town."

"We've been seeing ghosts," Sirona inserts.

"More than usual."

"Lots more than usual."

"And we're really unhappy about it."

Believe it or not, most people I've met with ghosts in their midst don't mind the lights flickering or the radio turning on in the middle of the night. They laugh off the weird noises or the cabinet doors opening and tell their invisible guests to behave. And the ghosts usually do.

Take Annie Breaux in Blue Moon, for instance. Several folks have refused to check out of her Mortuary B&B and she doesn't hesitate to let her guests know of these wandering spirits. Most of her guests are thrilled to be able to experience the supernatural, although a few have run screaming from the building.

Something in Sirona's countenance makes me wonder if something else is at work here.

"Why are you unhappy?" I ask, dreading the answer. I've never experienced anything evil or demonic and I hope to never do so. I'm on the fence about whether something that horrific exists, but until I know for sure, I don't want to travel down that road.

Sirona swallows and her eyes enlarge. She leans across the table so that we're only inches away and whispers, "They're too many of them."

Cajuns call it the *frissons*. My Aunt Mimi in Alabama relates it to a skunk running over your grave, although how anyone would know that is beyond me. But the feeling overtakes me, violent shivers traveling up from my toes to the back of my neck and it takes me several moments to shake it off.

"Shall we start from the beginning?" Elijah asks.

I nod but offer coffee first — all Southerners must make sure their guests are comfortable and without want — and once we have our cups of java with milk, sugar, and what my friend Winnie calls pink packets of cancer powder, Sirona begins the tale.

"It began last spring, right before the state showed up to check out the old resort site."

"Fontus Springs used to be quite the place years ago," Elijah inserts. "People came from all over to soak in the hot springs besides the lake. Was said to cure a number of ailments, especially arthritis."

Sirona touches Elijah's hand and for a second I wonder if these two are a couple. "We're not supposed to make those medical claims, remember Stan?"

"Right. Delete that," he tells me with a grin. "But the town was something to see in its heyday."

"Now, it's just a blip on the map although we still attract visitors to the lake," Sirona says. "And because we have enough residents year-round — barely — we have a mayor and city council and a nice-sized library we're especially proud of."

"Kids go off to Boyce for school, though," Elijah adds.

"And the ghosts...?" I insert, hoping to get them back to the point.

Sirona inhales and lets out the air in a rush. "They began showing up around Easter."

"It was one or two incidents at first," Elijah says. "Mostly locals complaining about weird noises and seeing things out of the corners of their eyes. By Memorial Day several people at the lake houses were calling the police claiming that intruders were in the house. When the police arrived, there

25

was no one there and no signs of intruders inside or outside the homes."

"How do you know they're ghosts?" I ask. "Maybe it's kids playing around."

Sirona pales and looks away.

"We've seen them," Elijah says. "More than one."

"More than once or more than one ghost?" I ask.

At this Sirona looks back and I notice tears on her lashes. "Too many," she whispers.

Now it's Elijah's turn to take her hand. "They've taken over the town," he softly says to no one.

I've heard of more than one ghost per household but an entire town?

"I'm confused. What do you mean by taken over?"

Elijah lets go of Sirona's hand while Sirona looks out the window at my dying plants, wiping the tears from her cheeks in the process. "I think you need to come visit."

Now it's my turn to exhale. "I would love to help, Mr. Fontenot...."

"Elijah, please."

"Elijah. I would love to help but...."

Sirona turns back to me with a rush of emotions. "You have to help us," she says as more tears emerge. "We can't live like this."

Now, there are two pleading gazes my way.

"You don't understand," I say. "I only see ghosts that have died by water."

Elijah shakes his head as if that comment never happened. "You're the only one we've found who can help us. And Winnie was certain you can."

"I'm also broke," I add. "I have to find a job right away or I'm going to be a ghost in this tiny apartment after starving to death."

"We can pay," Elijah says. "Of course, we will pay you for your time."

No accidents.

I'm still confused but I shake my nod in agreement

anyway. We discuss payment, Elijah insists on writing me a check right there and then for our consultation, enough to pay my monthly electric bill, and I'm given directions on how to find the former hot springs resort on a lake in the epicenter of Louisiana. We agree to meet the following morning at Hi Ho's general store and bait shop that apparently serves coffee and breakfast in the back and the couple leaves me to wonder what the hell I have gotten myself into.

As they cross my threshold and turn to follow the brick walkway to their car, Stinky arrives and pauses a few feet away, staring at the couple intently. Sirona pauses and leans over, offering a hand to the stray cat.

"That's my bud Stink," I tell them. "He's harmless."

Sirona leans closer. "Hey, cutie pie."

Stinky suddenly hisses and growls and the orange hairs on his back reach sky high. Sirona jerks her hand back and rises.

"Stinky!" I admonish him, wondering what the hell got into my sweet cat, but he continues to hiss, then darts away like a cat out of hell.

Sirona appears wounded and I'm afraid she's going to cry again.

"I'm so sorry about that," I tell her. "I've never seen him act that way."

She doesn't say anything and hurries down the pathway, while Elijah offers me a grim smile, then catches up with her and places an arm about her shoulders. I watch them get in the car and hurry off, then turn back toward my fuzzy feline.

Stinky hides in the bushes off the patio, still hissing at the spot where Sirona once stood, and looking as if he witnessed the devil on his doorstep.

CHAPTER THREE

I'm driving north up Interstate 49 listening to NPR's Michelle Norris interview Wall Street experts, trying to decipher who is responsible for this economic downturn, when my cell phone rings. I had put a call into Jacob Yarbrough the day before, leaving him a long message about my background as a travel writer and how I had heard he had job openings in the hotel review department.

"Viola Valentine," I answer because I'm hoping the Los Angeles number is Yarbrough.

"Ms. Valentine," a friendly voice replies. "Jacob Yarbrough from Courtyard Hotels."

We begin with silly small talk, him asking if Louisiana is really that hot in summer and me assuring him it is, but the climate goes well with our spicy food, ha, ha. Then we get down to business. Since I got the Fontus Springs gig and the money situation isn't as bleak as the day before, I'm feeling cocky and that confidence wins him over. We have a long conversation about my views on what makes a good hotel and, since he's read my travel stories from the links I sent him, is confident I'm a good fit. He agrees to a trial run as opposed to an interview. I'll meet him in Dallas on Thursday where he'll train me, then let me loose over the weekend and evaluate me after the first review.

I hang up optimistic, a feeling I haven't felt in months. This could be the answer to my problems. The pay's not great but it's enough to keep me afloat. I'll send the lake ghosts packing, catch a plane to Dallas, and by next week I'll have new brakes on my ailing Toyota.

I travel down two winding stretches of country road, then a turnoff toward the town before I spot Lorelei Lake. Its enormity surprises me. I never knew this place existed, and being a travel writer I've been to pretty much every corner of Louisiana. Why the big secret?

There are signs to a county park that takes RVs, the requisite Baptist church, and a place selling homemade signs such as "Proud Marine Lives Here" and one sporting a crazed man in overalls that announces, "Avoid folks that begin a sentence with 'Hey y'all, watch this!'"

Downtown in Fontus Springs, if you can call it that, resembles a Stephen King novel: empty storefronts, rampant vines covering buildings and abandoned cars, and literally no one in sight. If there was a creep factor compass, the needle would be spinning wildly.

At the end of the three-block town, I spot several cars in the gravel parking lot of a concrete block establishment. There's an old-fashioned gas pump in front, a collection of propane tanks for sale, two giant dumpsters on the side — one sporting a misspelled sign that reads, "No RV sewerige allowed," — and several boats in trailers out back. A pretty inconspicuous place save for what looks like a giant nutria holding a beer on top of the building. I know this must be Hi Ho's, but I can't help staring at the hairy creature looking down on me as I park the car.

A knock on my window scares me so much I jump, spilling the contents of my coffee thermos.

"Sorry," Elijah says.

I emerge from my Toyota with a lovely brown stain fronting my blouse, a designer cotton number I nabbed in the discount bin at Goodwill. My heart sinks thinking I may have ruined this rare discovery.

"I'm so sorry. Let me get you a towel," Elijah continues, then hurries inside.

I follow and pause at the threshold to take in the scene before me: aisles and aisles of lures, lines, fishing poles, and items smelling acutely of fish. Some of those signs I witnessed on the road are lining the walls and I have to laugh at "A balanced diet means two fried chickens and four beers."

"They're all waiting out back," the man at the counter instructs me in a thick Southern accent. Go above Ville Platte in the middle of Louisiana and everything turns from Cajun to Gomer Pyle in a heartbeat. I gaze over to find Counter Man surrounded by everything from aspirin and toilet paper to numerous types of whiskey and condoms.

I head to where I hear a cacophony of voices, a large dining area that one enters after moving down two steps at the door. I realize that someone has attached a double wide on to the back of the store and cut a wide entrance into the side. On the walls of this "café" are several stuffed fish that I assume are bass, a couple of deer heads and a portrait of Ronald Reagan with a bald eagle flying behind. Gazing at the former president, I can almost hear *The Star-Spangled Banner* playing.

Elijah greets me with a box of baby wipes and appears genuinely distressed. "I am so sorry."

"No worries," I say accepting the wipes but as Elijah turns to make introductions, I grab a paper napkin off the Aunt Jemima napkin holder and blot the oblong stain that stretches to my navel. I hear my name mentioned so I look up, soiled napkin in hand, and am greeted with several "Nice to see you's."

I nod, answer in kind, and Elijah holds a chair out for me.

"What will you have," he asks. "And please let me get you a fresh cup of coffee."

I look around to the half dozen or so men, and notice many of them eating plates of eggs, grits and toast. I remark with a smile that I will have what they are having. No one gets the reference and an older, sunburned man in an LSU T-shirt yells my order to someone in the kitchen. And I mean yell. A skinny teenager almost immediately appears and places a cup of coffee before me, along with individual creamers and a large bowl of sugar. No pink cancer packets, I notice, wondering if women are allowed in back of the Hi Ho.

As I raise my cup to my lips, I notice the nutria starring back.

"Who's this?" I ask, pointing to the image on the side of my cup.

"That's Hi Ho," LSU explains. "He's our mascot."

"Used to be," Elijah clarifies, thankfully sitting down next to me. I feel more comfortable having him close now that several pairs of male eyes are staring at me as if *I'm* a ghost. "Years ago, we had a school in Fontus Springs before they started busing our kids to Boyce."

I examine the creature holding a beer and I still can't figure out what he is.

"He's a beaver," says a burly man to my left. "Some Coonass from Ville Platte did the artwork and left off the flat tail."

Elijah sends Burly a harsh look, no doubt on account of him using the derogatory name for Cajuns. There was a time when people uttered that expression freely, even Cajuns adopting it as their own, but political correctness changed all that.

"Excuse me, ma'am," the man says. "Meant no disrespect."

"I'm from New Orleans." I don't know why I blurt that out, since I hate that disparaging word for Cajuns. But something about this place so foreign to my upbringing makes me want to connect with these people, not feel so awkward among them.

I also don't ask why a school mascot is drinking a beer.

"So, about these ghosts in town…," I begin.

Immediately, the atmosphere shifts. All those gazes looking my way suddenly find other items of focus. The conversation ceases and I can hear the teenager in the kitchen slamming pots on the stove. I look at Elijah for encouragement but he's not meeting my eyes either.

"That is why I'm here, right?"

Finally, LSU straightens and gives himself a shake, like he was covered in dirt. "I don't know what Elijah's been telling you but I, for one, don't believe in all that nonsense."

This brings the group to life. A chorus of hemming and hawing ripples through the crowd as if on cue.

"Now, Pete," Elijah says, standing, "we already discussed

this."

"Don't matter what I discussed," Pete answers, also standing. "I'm not going to believe in all that woowoo stuff just because a bunch of people in town are hallucinating. I told you, it's probably something in the water."

This brings my own set of shivers.

"I doubt our drinking water is making people see ghosts," Elijah insists.

There's a buzzing in my head and the word water seems significant somehow. For a second, I wonder if someone's trying to tell me something until I realize that water is my forte, so to speak. Of course, it's important. As soon as I shake that thought away and focus back on the men, I feel — hear? — a sigh akin to a child being disappointed. I can't help but dart around to see if someone's there, but there's no sign of Lillye.

My inattention to the men and sudden focus on plain air stops the conversation.

"Did you see something?" Elijah asks, and I turn to find all those gazes back on me.

My disappointment in not seeing Lillye burns through me from the depths of my soul all the way to the lump in my throat. I shake my head and try to speak normally. "I dropped my spoon."

Elijah glances at the empty floor, then at me, and I wish I had talked him out of this assignment. I know he's doubting my ability, wishing he had his deposit back that I've already handed over to Lafayette Utilities System. And, once again, all eyes are back on ghost hunter Vi.

"Why don't you all start from the beginning," I say. "And may I please have another cup of coffee."

Asking for something ordinary helps. LSU jumps up and brings me a pot to refill my cup and the men start chatting about fish, the lake's level, and how soon fall will arrive. The air around us feels infinitesimally better.

Elijah, however, remains dour. When he raises a hand, all talking stops once more.

"My grams, Miss Bessie, over near the springs, said it all started Easter weekend," he says. "Old man Wallace Tate, the first mayor of Fontus Springs, came walking through her yard like a zombie."

"Your grandmother, in all due respect, is close to one hundred years old," says a guy in overalls with what looks like bad dentures.

"And sharper than you, Melvin," Elijah fires back. "What are you? Eighty-eight?"

"I ain't saying," Melvin replies with a smile and the group laughs, which helps break the tension.

"Martha at the bank saw two people one night in her house," Elijah continues. "And they disappeared into the wall. Shirley, the teenager who helps us stack books at the library, said there's a Confederate hanging around the park by the lake." Elijah runs a nervous hand across his forehead. "And that's just a few."

"My wife insists our bedroom is haunted," a man next to me says softly.

"She just don't want to go in there with you," a voice says and laughter emerges again. "Can you blame her?"

My neighbor smiles good-naturedly so as to not lose face among these men but I can sense he's disturbed as much as Elijah.

"I still think it's something in the water," LSU mutters and I listen for the buzzing, but it doesn't return.

"Has the water been tested?" I ask.

LSU wags a finger at me. "See, I'm not the only one who thinks we need to get the state up here."

Elijah shakes his head.

"I'm not saying it's the water but it would rule that out." I touch Elijah's elbow. "Where does your drinking water come from?"

It's the first time this morning that Elijah looks at me, really looks at me. I feel a deep sadness in those intense brown eyes.

"The springs," he practically whispers. "Goes through the

plant north of town."

"I've been saying all along those springs are probably contaminated," LSU says. "We should be tapping into the lake. After all, it's a reservoir."

"It's manmade?" I ask.

"One of the most perfect engineering feats in Louisiana."

Once again, the talking stops and we all turn toward the door. Standing on the threshold is a man in uniform with the state of Louisiana over one breast, hand on one hip as if he owns the world, and a countenance that insists that he does. He's not bad looking either and that part of me that hasn't seen action in ages wakes up.

"Speak of the devil," Melvin says. "We were just talking about you."

"That's so odd," the man next to me utters, as if this uniformed person is a ghost as well.

Elijah rises from his chair and greets Mr. Uniform, shaking his hand. "I called him here, you fools. I knew you would have questions about water quality."

Mr. Uniform takes in the room full of men and finally rests on me but says nothing, as if the crowd he has come to address doesn't concern me.

"Y'all know Matt Wilson from the State Department of Water Quality."

Elijah motions for the skinny tattooed girl in the kitchen to bring out another cup and pulls out a chair for His Highness. Matt nods to the men in front of him and sits.

"I think I know most of you here," he says, although he doesn't look back at me.

"This is Viola Valentine," Elijah says. "She's here to help us with our haunted problem."

"Alleged haunted problem," LSU adds.

Matt still doesn't look my way, offers up a smirk, and I instantly dislike him, no matter his good looks. I spent years covering the police beat in St. Bernard Parish, following around uniforms like him, men who wouldn't give me the time of day because one, I was a journalist, and two, a lowly woman.

"So, tell me, Matt," I say to his back. "How does drinking water cause people to see dead Confederates walking around?"

"It doesn't." The man is insufferable, still refuses to look at me. "I think what you have here is a case of the hysterics." He offers up a smirk, then sends Elijah a harsh look. "Or maybe it's just the women being hysterical."

Some of the men laugh but not Elijah and the man to my right, the one with the haunted bedroom. They both glance at me, waiting for an appropriate response, something astute. I'm so busy being pissed at women being called hysterical for the five millionth time in history that I'm rendered mute.

"As for the water quality of the springs and the reservoir," Matt quickly begins, "we've tested it time and again and found nothing. Just random minerals, which is why this place was a resort to begin with. Hell, people came from all over to drink this stuff. You have nothing to worry about."

"Then why...?" my neighbor begins.

"Then nothing." Matt leans back in his chair. "Someone saw their shadow one night and now the whole town's imagination is soaring. Just people wanting attention."

This riles my neighbor and he's about to retort but Elijah places a hand on his shoulder and squeezes. My neighbor thinks twice about replying but I can see him gritting his teeth.

There may be nothing to the hauntings of Fontus Springs and there may be nothing I can do about it if there are ghosts here (unless they truly died by water), but now I'm royally ticked. Cocky macho men burn up my last nerve. I stand and say loudly, "Okay, then. Elijah, how about you give me a tour of the town since you wonderful men asked me up here especially for this" — I hold up my fingers to make quotes — "'imaginary problem.'"

Elijah rises and some of the men appear uncomfortable but I don't care. I want this conversation to be over and I want to be rid of this arrogant man who hasn't the courtesy to give me the time of day. LSU rises, bless his heart, and shakes my hand, offers me some encouragement, as does the neighbor with the haunted bedroom. They even walk me to the door and wish me well.

Once in the parking lot, it's just me and Elijah and the latter looks as frustrated as I feel.

"Sorry about that. Matt is a bit of a jerk."

"I noticed." I pull out my keys and try to tame the anger burning in my chest. "Where are we to now?"

"Want to take my car?"

I think about my faulty brakes and the rolling hills around the lake. "Sure."

We climb into Elijah's SUV and start back toward the ghost town, no pun intended. After several minutes a calming quiet descends upon us. Now that my adrenaline has subsided, I decide I need to clear the air once again.

"Elijah, I only see ghosts who have died by water."

He nods solemnly. "I know."

"Then you do know that if these people died some other way, like a Yankee bullet for instance, or the mayor dying of natural causes, I'm not going to see them."

We're at a stop sign on the main thoroughfare but no one's coming so when Elijah pauses and looks at me solemnly, I let that gaze sink into my soul. Something's amiss here that goes beyond my ghost-hunting talents and the water testing by the state of Louisiana, but for the life of me I can't guess what.

"Maybe I shouldn't have asked you to come."

This is not what I was expecting. "I don't understand."

Elijah glances back at the road in front of us, where a lone dog saunters across the empty highway.

"There's something very strange happening here," he whispers. "I hate to get you involved in this but I don't know who else to turn to."

That buzzing returns and I feel like the universe is demanding I focus — but on what?

"Why don't you start from the beginning," I offer.

Elijah nods and takes a right down a one-lane road in bad need of repair. As the SUV bounces through potholes, I look up at the trees dripping their branches over us, as if to shelter us from the world. I usually enjoy the comfort trees give, especially in sweltering Louisiana, but today their shadows give me the *frissons*.

We continue through the woods, twisting and turning as our path curves and Elijah dances around even larger potholes. We descend about one hundred feet until the road ends at the lake, a tiny bright blue in a mess of overgrown bushes and trees.

"I take it this is Lorelie Lake," I ask when Elijah says nothing, simply stares ahead.

Elijah quietly turns off the engine, then exits the truck, and not knowing what else to do I follow along. We walk a few feet until the brush becomes thick and stare out on to a gorgeous lake and a picture-perfect sky. The juxtaposition between the water and this creepy stretch of road — not to mention Elijah's mood — is striking.

"Do you know the history of this lake?" Elijah finally asks.

"It's a reservoir. I take it the state created it for recreation or to provide water to the town."

Elijah smiles grimly. "No, it was always here, just not as large."

"Then, why did that man say it was man-made?"

Elijah wipes his hands on the front of his jeans, that sad smile lingering. "That's the million-dollar question. Everyone, including the state, kept saying the lake started when the dam was built. Over time, everyone started believing it."

He moves to head back to his truck, saying over his shoulder, "Come on. One more stop."

We travel down an obscure road that skirts the lake this time, another fine example of Louisiana transportation. Just before my teeth come loose from the endless bumps in the road, Elijah pulls over alongside property with trespassing signs everywhere. Through the dense brush, I spot deserted buildings in various states of ruin but mud roads that appear better than the ones we've been riding on.

"Fontus Springs," Elijah tells me. "What used to be of it, that is. This was once a popular destination after the turn of the twentieth century with a hotel, pool, restaurant — you name it. Springs date back forever, of course, but Europeans founded this spot as a resort in the late 1800s."

I peer through the windshield to what looks like the remains of brick buildings inside the overgrown brush. There's a chimney to the right, what's left of one, and a lone wall behind a line of trees.

"Hard to imagine anything of note existing in this desolate place," I say.

Elijah leans over the seat and grabs a file box from the back, then hands it to me.

"This is everything I could find on the springs. The library wanted to publish a commemoration booklet when the springs turned one hundred in 1989 but the City Council voted it down. Not enough funds, they said. When I started at the library I found this box hidden in the back of a closet. The previous librarian told me where it was, said to keep it close and to not leave it about the library for just anyone to access."

I've used libraries in my work and their mission is to disseminate information, not hoard it. "That's weird."

Elijah nods. "Got my curiosity up. I started researching the springs and the lake and have been adding to this over the years."

I peer into this box filled with letters, articles and brochures advertising the springs and its healing powers, then glance back at my employer. "What is it you want me to do?"

Elijah pulls off the side of the road and heads back to town.

"Read it."

I pull into my driveway as the sun sets behind the main house, still trying to make sense of the day. Elijah spent hours giving me a tour of the entire lake, introducing me to several people who had reported seeing ghosts. Again, these hauntings appear to be of those who have not died by water, but I recorded their stories on my tape recorder and made copious notes anyway.

The auto shop worker had witnessed a bearded man in overalls carrying an ax with half an arm missing so we all assumed he had perished from a wood-chucking accident. Shirley, the teenage library intern, swore she saw a man in a Confederate uniform at the city park, a tall man with a large dark stain over his chest, his eyes glazed and confused. And my breakfast neighbor, the one with the haunted bedroom, a man named Jack Branford, was standing on the porch when we drove up as if he couldn't wait to introduce us to his wife, Margie. I sensed her fear the minute I crossed the threshold.

Margie's nightmare began at two in the morning the Monday following Easter when she woke to crying from the corner of the room. She rose on her elbows and peered through the darkness to see what appeared to be a young woman staring at her, terrified.

"This jolt of fear ran through me," she told us. "I knew she wasn't real but I felt her pain as if she were me, as if I were being tortured by someone."

This had stopped me cold. "Why do you think she was being tortured?"

Elijah started shifting his feet then, and when I looked his way he gave me a hard, knowing stare. Meanwhile, Margie leaned in close to me as if the walls had ears.

"There were rumors, you know, that the resort had prostitution in the back and the mob ran the place."

This was news. "But torture?"

"During the Depression, women who came here were pretty desperate," Jack piped in. "It's been said that powerful men came from all over because of the unique services the women offered. Those who didn't do the acts required of them were beaten or they simply disappeared."

I looked over at Elijah, wondering if this was what he dug up in his research, and he nodded. Still, it was another example of a death that didn't concern water.

"Where's the room?" I asked.

Jack led me down a long hallway that was creepy in and of itself and I couldn't fathom why. He stopped at the threshold of the master bedroom but didn't walk through.

"Have you seen this woman?" I asked him.

He shook his head and refused to move. "No, to me it just feels wrong. But if my wife says it's a ghost or something evil happening here, then I believe her."

I walked into the room which appeared more like a guestroom. Everything in its place. Bed nicely made. No items of use such as eyeglasses, reading materials or clothes off hangers anywhere. I assumed the Branfords had moved into another part of the house.

I walked to every corner of the room. I peered into the closets. I checked the master bath. Nothing. I turned back toward the door to tell Jack as much but Elijah stood there waiting, gauging my reaction.

"I don't see anything, feel anything," I whispered to Elijah.

He nodded, then leaned closer and whispered back, "You need to come back when the sun goes down."

And that was where we left it. After several more interviews, I took the box that Elijah gave me and headed back to Lafayette. I'm totally confused as to what to do, thinking I can't help these people if they died by gunshot, beatings, and assorted farm instruments. But then, I wonder. Have I developed my intuitive skills enough to see ghosts who have not died by water? Has this accidental meeting happened to prove to me that I can see beyond my SCANC abilities?

A fire of hope burns in my belly. There was that girl at Blue Moon Bayou, now a town full of non-watery haunts. If I can see and address those who have not died by water, I might be finally able to reach Lillye, my precious angel on the other side.

As I pull up the emergency brake on my Toyota — always worried the brakes will really fail and my car will slide into the massive drainage ditch outside my apartment — I spot TB's pickup truck.

"What the…?" I ask no one, grab the box and head down the walkway to my mother-in-law unit.

I'm immediately greeted by Reece.

"Hey."

I pull the box against my chest, feeling defensive. "Hey yourself."

He pulls back slightly, as if struck by my comment. I wonder if I sounded harsh.

"I was checking to see how you are."

"I'm fine."

I can now hear the curtness in my voice.

"Are you mad at me?"

"How's your wife?"

My gorgeous, easy-going landlord who I've never seen angry or upset at anyone, deflates. I had vowed to be obtuse about my feelings regarding Reece, but I just spewed them all over the front of his shirt.

"I'm sorry," I quickly retract. "That came out wrong."

He smiles grimly. "No, it didn't. Vi, I thought you understood…."

"That you and your wife are staying together for the kids. Yeah, I got it. I didn't expect you to look so happy at the Blue Moon rising, that's all."

Reece rubs his hands on his thighs and looks away. "What did you want me to do in front of my kids, argue and be miserable?"

I hadn't really thought about that. Still, we were dating — sort of — and the next minute he's off to resume marital bliss. "Of course not, but…."

"You don't know. Life gets complicated when you have kids."

This comment sails straight through my chest and I feel like I've been stabbed. In the grand scheme of things nothing is more complicated and painful than the death of a child.

Reece instantly realizes his mistake. "Vi, I'm sorry. I didn't mean to insinuate...."

"It's okay." I pull the box closer to my chest and step back. Having lost my child I know how valuable time is with children, would understand more than most his desire to make things work. And yet his comment and instant dismissal of our relationship stings sharply. "Go back to your wife and do your duty," I say a bit harshly.

Behind me I hear the door opening to my apartment.

"Oh hey, Vi. I thought I heard you out here."

Reece glances at TB and then back at me, waiting for me to make introductions but I'm dumbstruck, caught in a hypocrisy.

"I'm TB," my ex-husband finally says, stretching out his hand, which Reece shakes. "I'm Viola's husband."

I cringe at the words, while Reece gives me a smug look. I dance a Michael Jackson moon walk backwards to the door and slip inside, wishing there was a big hole somewhere to swallow me up. TB lingers outside, however, and I hear the two men talking about carpentry and sports like old friends. What on earth is he doing here anyway?

Stinky rubs up against me and I'm thankful for a friend. I throw the box on to the bed and plop on the floor so I can give Stinky some real attention. He purrs his approval of my massage techniques, then looks at me with a wink.

"Why do you cats do that?" I ask, like he's going to answer.

Stinky sashays to the front door, which is still half open, and rubs his back against it like he did my leg. The door falls shut with barely a squeak and the sound of the men talking disappears. Stinky then returns to my magic hands, slipping an ear underneath to make sure I get the hint.

"Thanks." Did that cat just do me a favor?

I shake off the crazy thought and resume petting, although I reach over and grab the box, leaning against the bed to make myself comfortable. On top are the notes I took interviewing the residents of Lorelei Lake and it doesn't take me long to see a pattern. First, most of the interviewees are women, although that's not too surprising considering that women are more intuitive than men. Still. Second, for what I can assume, none of the ghosts have died by water.

I grab my cell phone and call the one person who knows everything about SCANCs.

"Hey darling," Carmine answers on the first ring.

It's so good to hear a fellow travel writer and SCANCy ghost hunter that I almost burst out crying. "Hey Carmine."

"What's the matter?"

He also gets me like no one else.

"What isn't? I'm broke, my press trips have dried up, my family's being a pain in the ass and my ex-husband is outside talking to a man I have sexual fantasies about."

Carmine laughs. "Is that all?"

"Oh, and I got a job cleaning an entire town of ghosts and for what I understand none of them have died by water."

"Okay, back up and explain the last one."

Carmine is a SCANC like me, someone also prone to seeing the dead at an early age but who ignored it growing up, especially since his feminine traits caused him enough trouble around schoolmates. Why add ghosts to the mix? He was beaten close to death by a group of boys threatened by his lack of masculinity and now, Carmine sees ghosts who are gay. Granted, he's not bothered as much as I am since apparitions batting for the other team lack numbers, but he did meet Oscar Wilde in Paris, an experience of which I'm eternally envious.

I explain it all — the Blue Moon rising, the girl by the bayou, Matt the asshole and the weird ghost town with its juxtaposition of gorgeous lake and resort ruins.

"Do you think this means I'm evolving? That I will see ghosts who have not died by water?"

I'm so hopeful, waiting to hear my good friend and SCANC mentor insist that my time has come, that I've developed my intuitive gift, and that the heavens will open up and I'll see my darling girl.

Instead, he laughs. "Hardly. I've never known a SCANC

43

to go beyond their specific abilities. That's why it stands for 'specific communication with apparitions, non-entities, and the comatose.'"

"But you told me once that it's possible that people can develop their intuition."

"Well, yeah, but what I meant was you can sense something that's outside your specialty, like something amiss in a place or something bad about to happen. Psychic skills, not seeing other types of ghosts."

My heart plummets but my mind refuses to give up the ghost — this time, pun intended. It can't be. It just can't. I know this assignment has been given to me for a reason.

"But what about the girl at the bayou?"

"She probably died by water."

"She was so real, Carmine, down to the button on her overalls. She talked to me like a regular person."

"So did that masseuse in Eureka Springs."

The first time I realized I had this ability was on a press trip to Arkansas and it was Carmine who had explained it all. During that trip, I saw several ghosts there, two of which were intellectual hauntings, or those who could communicate to me in some way. But there was one person who kneaded the knots out of my back and I've never been sure if that person was real or not. Or how he died, if he was indeed a ghost.

"Good point. I doubt that masseuse died by water," I offer with hopeful optimism.

I hear what sounds like Carmine drinking a glass of wine. "Darling, you have to stop getting your hopes up. I've met many SCANCs, even been to the SCANC convention — which is something you never want to do by the way — and I've never heard of anyone pushing past their specialties."

I still can't give up, feel like reaching Lillye is the reason I got this crazy gift to begin with. But I let it go. For now.

"I'm heading your way on Thursday," and tell Carmine about the hotel job.

"Courtyard is known for being cheap so don't be shy

about asking for a decent amount."

"Okay." I've already agreed to their cheap price because I'm desperate but I don't tell Carmine that.

"Gotta run, sweetheart, dinner's on."

"Wait, what's wrong with the SCANC convention?"

But Carmine's hung up just as TB saunters in.

"What a great guy," he comments on my landlord.

Would love to know how great Reece is, specifically in bed, but I don't tell him that.

"What are you doing here, TB?"

He falls on to the bed and makes himself comfortable, resting his hand behind his head. "They called me back on the job. Turns out they need me for a few more days so I thought…."

"That you could just waltz in here?"

He leans up on one elbow so he can look at me. "Why are you on the floor?"

"I'm looking through some notes. Don't change the subject."

TB leans over the bed and gazes down into Elijah's pile of articles, papers, and whatnots. "New job?"

TB assisted me with a previous haunting, performing research that helped me solve the case. He keeps asking to help out again but thankfully the travel trips have been about travel and not apparitions wanting attention. Not to mention that his last foray into research was probably a fluke. TB never finished college and isn't the brightest light in the chandelier.

I place the lid on the box. "It's pretty complicated."

TB looks like he's been slapped and I wonder if my aggravation with the world is seeping out my mouth.

"I'm not smart enough for it, is that it?"

I don't want to go there tonight. "Why are you here?"

"Is it so bad that I am?"

"We're separated TB. Remember?"

He's closer now, running a lone finger up my arm. "Not for long if I can help it."

I rise and head for the kitchen, wishing I was normal like Carmine and drinking wine, sitting down to dinner with a gorgeous man who also pays the mortgage. What I find in my meager room is a sink chock-full of pots and pans, remnants of something leafy all over the countertop, and empty food boxes lying about. I rub my forehead at the scene before me. The last thing I want to do right now is clean up after my former husband.

Instead, I turn, primed for action.

"This is my house, TB. You can't come in here every time you feel like it. Look at the mess you made." He starts to talk but that train has left the station. "We're separated. That means get your own place when you come to town."

The minute I'm done I regret both my words and my tone. Where is all this anger coming from? Of course, TB would think about staying here. We're still friends, still legally married so I can keep my health benefits, not to mention we can't afford a divorce. I exhale, then attempt a retreat, but I see the damage I've inflicted in the gaze he sends back.

"I got a housing allowance. I can stay somewhere else."

There's a but coming and I know what it is. Why stay in a strange hotel, have nothing to do for hours, when I'm here?

"I thought instead of using the money I'd stay here and give the money to you."

Damn this man. He can make me feel so guilty.

"TB, I didn't mean…."

"Don't worry about it, Vi." He stands and grabs his jacket and heads for the door. "I'll see you around."

"TB," I implore, but I can't help it, want him to leave, want to be left alone digging through this box of possible reasons I'll be able to see Lillye. But, within seconds, he's gone.

I lean back against the wall and sigh while Stinky rubs up against my legs again. He gives me a funny look. No wink this time, something more akin to a reprimand.

"Whose side are you on?"

It's then that I notice the table.

TB has cooked me dinner and displayed fried pork chops and heaping bowls of fresh vegetables — Brussel sprouts, my favorite, among them — next to fresh flowers and lighted candles.

"Damn."

I rush out the door to catch him from driving away, but TB's already halfway down Saint Francis. I stand there feeling a thousand shades of shame, watching a man who loves me hurt by my insensitivity yet again. Behind me I hear Reece cleaning the pool. And staring me straight in the face is my ailing Toyota.

Some days you feel like the world surrounds you, screaming tirades of how worthless you are. Where once I felt hope at seeing Lillye again, my confidence has crashed bigtime. I'm broke, I have no idea how to help the Fontus Springs community, my dreams of being with my landlord are shot, and I sent away the one person who truly cares about me.

I slink back to my potting shed and all that swag brought home from press trips reminds me that I own nothing of value, that I'm patching my broken life with Band-Aides that only I think are cute. In the middle of this mess lies a beautifully set table for two, a bottle of my favorite wine in its center.

I sit down at this lovely feast and text my ex-husband.

"Come back," I write. "I'm sorry. It's my frustration talking. Please come back."

I hope it works. For now, I sit at the delicious meal before me and wait.

Stinky cries out and I look down to find him sprawled out on the box's contents.

"Read that and get back to me," I say to relieve the emptiness that has descended upon the room.

He cries once more but I'm too busy wallowing in guilt to reach over and pet him. Suddenly, Stinky takes his wallowing up a notch, really howls this time, which startles me to the core, like nails on a chalkboard.

"What is it?" I ask, like he's going to answer me in English.

Stinky stands, does the back-arch thing, and walks through the mound of papers now scattered about the floor. But he pauses on a postcard, then pushes the card out of the pile towards me.

The thought that this cat is doing that on purpose runs through my mind, but that's ridiculous. Still, I lean over and pick up the item, a postcard from the turn of the twentieth century boasting of the new resort known as Fontus Springs. I turn over and find nothing on the back, so I flip it back to study the photo. There are several people dressed in suits, long dresses, and hats in front of a modest building sporting a sign that reads, "Medicinal Fontus Springs, Youth Lives Again."

"Gotta get me some of that spring water," I mutter to Stinky, who answers with a cry, only this time more like a normal cat would.

Those thick woods exist in the photo's background and there's a dirt road in front of the establishment. A horse and buggy linger out front of the building, but there's nothing else to provide me with clues.

Just as I'm about to place the card back into the box, my gaze settles on a woman standing at the back of the crowd. There's something about this face that rings a bell, but it's difficult to make out. I reach into my night stand and pull out a magnifying glass, one I found at the local thrift shop and took home because the handle was carved out of mahogany and I thought it an elegant addition to my potting shed.

Plus, it was only two dollars.

I use it to examine the postcard and the face comes into view more clearly. Stinky lets out a howl and shivers rush through my body.

It's Sirona Harmon, the woman who accompanied Elijah to my apartment the day before. The one who tried to pet Stinky. Only this time, Sirona's skin color is decidedly lighter, and she's wearing something out of the Titanic era.

I glance down at my adopted cat and he winks.

CHAPTER FOUR

"How's that cute husband of yours?" Carmine asks me as soon as we sit down.

We're having brunch at the Grand Hyatt of the Dallas Airport, an arrangement I made with my new employer. Courtyard has flown me into town for training before my first assignment, but I managed to have an hour before my ride picks me up, so I could visit with Carmine.

"Things are a bit strained at present."

TB did return that night and we ate the meal he so lovingly prepared, although it had turned cold and neither of us moved to reheat anything. We ate the dinner that I destroyed in silence, then watched TV and headed to bed. TB left early in the morning for his construction job and I worked to finish a magazine piece on fall foliage, dreaming of cool nights that seem so far away. Everything repeated the following day, although a few more words were spoken. TB found the information on Fontus Springs fascinating while I finished up work, and we quietly went our separate ways this morning, TB to work and me to reviewing hotels.

"What did you do?"

Like I said, Carmine knows me so well.

"There's this legend near my home, where the first person you'll see on the rising of a blue moon is the one you'll be in love with forever," I explain. "TB showed up at the festival, looked at me and now he's convinced we'll get back together."

Carmine's eyes light up. "Cool legend. Anyone written about that yet?"

I smile. We travel writers are always looking for that next unexplored story. "Many times, although maybe not for those gay magazines you write for."

The waitress arrives and I hesitate to order much, considering the lack of funds in my checking account, but

Carmine, bless his heart, senses my situation and makes a big fuss over paying. I'm grateful but those screams of worthlessness are at it again.

The waitress pours us both cups of coffee and I raise mine to my lips, inhaling that delicious aroma. "I wonder if it's in the DNA of writers that we love coffee so much."

"Pinot noir is my drink of choice."

Carmine grabs two pink packets and dumps it into his coffee, which makes me cringe. I hate seeing good coffee ruined by saccharin.

"He's a good man, you know?"

I place my coffee back on the table; it's too hot to drink. "I know."

"But what?"

"We got married because I was pregnant."

"I've heard this story."

I lean back in my chair and sigh. "It's not to be, Carmine."

Carmine takes my hand and I know a lecture's coming. I roll my eyes and he gives me that "Don't you roll your eyes at me, young lady" look. He's fifteen years my senior and he's good at it.

"I've got two pets, a dog and a cat," he begins. "The cat takes little effort, comes and offers love here and there, takes care of herself. We have this deep connection, Eva and me. The dog is needy, has to be walked, and pouts if I don't pay attention to him."

"Sounds like someone I know…."

"The dog is loyal and offers unconditional love." Carmine squeezes my hand. "And he would die for me if it came to that. The cat, most likely not."

I know what he's getting at but I choose sarcasm instead. "So, I need to get a dog?"

He looks at me sternly. "Vi, get your intellectual stimulation elsewhere." At this, Carmine drops my hand and swishes his hands in front of him to indicate he's one of that group. "And keep those who love you close at hand."

I know he's right but it reminds me of my other problems,

those who love me but could stay miles away as far as I'm concerned.

"Something's up with my mother," I add. "She refused to give me money unless I move back home and my sister has been unusually horrible."

"You're a big girl, Vi." That fatherly tone returns.

"I'm a freelance writer in a recession, Carmine."

"Like I said, brunch is on me."

I close my eyes and cringe. This is not where I wanted this conversation to go.

"I don't want your money. I want to pay my bills."

"What you really want is your family's approval."

Years ago, there was this ridiculous TV program called *The Gong Show*. My aunt and uncle found old tapes at the library and made me watch it when I visited them in Alabama. There was a panel of judges who watched contestants perform some silly act and if it was too horrible they banged the gong, and the contestant was out of the running.

As soon as Carmine's comment leaves his lips, I hear that gong ring. And, of course, I deny it, then immediately change the subject regarding my family's approval. Carmine, to his credit, lets my family debacle go and listens to me describe my experience with Elijah and the ghosts of Fontus Springs.

"But, you haven't seen any of these ghosts."

The waitress arrives and places a veggie omelet with breakfast potatoes in front of me and I realize I'm extremely hungry. Nothing like a six a.m. flight with only coffee to tide you over.

"I was there Tuesday during the day so no, I didn't see anything."

"Did you feel anything?"

I have a mouthful of eggs so I shake my head.

Carmine doesn't touch his eggs Benedict, thinks about my conundrum while holding his coffee.

"Hate to say this, but it could be like the state guy said, one person saw a ghost and now everyone thinks they have."

I place my fork down and swallow, then lean across the

table.

"Just because you bat for the other side doesn't excuse you from my male scorn when necessary. Margie Branford is scared to death to sleep in her bedroom and she's not making this up."

Carmine holds up both hands. "Sorry. If you believe them, I believe it."

"Hysterical women, my ass."

"I didn't mean to insinuate...."

"If it was a group of men saying these things, no one would question anything."

I feel more than see a hand touch mine. I exhale my anger and look across the table at my good friend, who's not the enemy.

"I'm sorry," Carmine says. "I didn't mean anything by it, but you're right, it was insensitive and chauvinistic."

I feel like someone unplugged me as I was experiencing an energy surge.

"I'm sorry, too," I whisper. "I'm tired of everything these days."

And with those words and the flow of adrenaline leaving my body, the tears begin to fall. I feel more than see that hand squeeze mine again, hear Carmine's words of comfort flow across the table. I quickly regain my composure but I feel like I did after Hurricane Katrina took away everything I owned, like a stick of dynamite resting too close to a fire.

I ruined brunch with my emotional outburst; the conversation seemed strained afterwards or maybe it was me feeling embarrassed, not to mention guilty about not being able to pay my way. We discussed the springs while we finished breakfast, Carmine paid the bill, and we headed for the baggage claim area where my ride would meet me.

"I forgot about Sirona," I tell Carmine as we ride the elevator to the bottom floor. I pull out the postcard of Fontus Springs in the early 1900s and point to the woman lingering behind the crowd.

"What about this woman?"

"She came to my apartment the other day."

Carmine looks at me sideways. "You need to explain that one."

I give him a synopsis of Sirona and Elijah imploring me to clean their town of ghosts, and how Stinky hissed at her when she left. I throw in that Stinky showed me the postcard, waiting for Carmine to call the authorities to take me to the loony bill, but he only grins at this piece of information.

"What? My cat's my intellectual stimulation?"

But all he says is, "Cats are amazing creatures. Don't underestimate them."

I'm not sure what this means.

"What about Sirona? Did I mention that she's African American? In the postcard, she's amazingly pale."

"Maybe her grandmother was white."

I look down at the postcard and shake my head. "The resemblance is striking."

Carmine shakes his head as we exit the elevator and spot a man getting out of a minivan with a sign that reads "Viola Valentine."

"Why didn't you take your husband's name, again?" he asks.

"His last name's Boudreaux."

Carmine looks at me questioningly.

"Viola Boudreaux?" I ask. "Viola Valentine rolls of the tongue. Besides, I had made a name for myself selling stories to local magazines while at LSU, thought it best to keep my original byline."

Carmine kisses me on the cheek, holds my face in his hands, and stares at me hard. "Keep your chin up, *mon amie*. Don't let your family get to you and have faith that all recessions come to an end."

I don't quite believe this but I nod anyway.

"And keep me abreast of this ghost town."

With those final words, my friend and mentor heads toward the parking lot. I look over at the man holding a sign and wave, and I'm off to my new adventure.

Turns out Courtyard Hotels is in Grapevine, Texas, a quaint historic town adjacent to the airport. It's ground zero for the Texas Wine and Grape Growers Association, although you won't find vineyards here, my driver explains. There are several tasting rooms and an urban wine trail to enjoy, and every year the town celebrates GrapeFest, the largest wine festival in the southwest. But, actual grapes are located elsewhere.

"Do you like ghosts?" my driver asks and for a moment I think he's on to me.

"Why?" I ask hesitantly.

He pulls off the main highway and passes what looks like a home from the 1800s with an ancient oak tree and massive barn out back.

"Cross Timbers Winery," my driver explains. "Great wines, and a few ghosts thrown in. Apparently, the former owner of the home, Patti Weatherman, died of pneumonia in the house and she never left. I've also heard there are twelve spirits in the barn, but no one knows who they are."

I don't see anyone looking back so either the daylight has scared them off or no one's died by water. Still, a shiver runs through me. I sense there was a murder by the barn, but that's all I'm getting. This gives me pause, because I never sensed anything at Fontus Springs.

My driver glances back at me with a hopeful smile and seems disappointed that I'm not as excited as he is. If only he knew.

"Guess you don't like ghost stories," he says with a shrug and off we go. I think to explain but I don't bother.

We pull into a lovely Courtyard Hotel situated next to an office building. Ghost lover drops me off at the latter and sends me and my polka dot suitcase, the one I nabbed at Goodwill after Katrina, to Suite B on the third floor. Jacob greets me at the door.

"Viola," he says the wrong way, meaning the instrument and not the Shakespeare heroine, but I let it slide.

We do our obligatory greetings and I follow him down a

55

hallway to a conference room where two other women wait. This is where we'll all learn about our new jobs, Jacob explains, then turns on a video and leaves the room. The film is dreadfully boring, a puff piece about the hotels and their wonderful attributes, and in turn we all twitch in our seats. I'd love to joke to these two about this horrid piece of PR and I sense they feel the same, but like dutiful new employees we all remained fixated on the video, although my eyelids grow heavier by the minute — that six a.m. flight, mind you.

Just before I'm ready to give in to sleep the film ends, Jacob arrives and turns on the lights. The woman to my right did fall asleep but she awakens right before Jacob looks her way. I send her a "Good going, girlfriend" nod and she smiles.

"How about that video?" Jacob announces way too cheerfully. "We had that made last year, right after we reached our one millionth customer. Great things happening here at Courtyard."

We're then given packets that outline the company's amenities, the number of hotels and where they are located (in forty-seven states, Canada and two territories), the rewards program (now in its fourth year and bigger than ever), the company's starred ratings on TripAdvisor — even how many linens are placed on each hotel room's bed (three sheets, a comforter, a bedspread and a throw).

"And for our rewards guests we offer two free bottles of Aquafina water."

The woman next to me rolls her eyes and whispers sarcastically, "Wow."

"Did you have a question?" Jacob asks her.

She immediately rebounds, all smiles. "No, sir."

Jacob then asks us to study our guidebooks after which we will take a multiple-choice test, basically all the elements of a well-tended hotel room and the responsibilities of the staff. Of course, we all pass. After a nice secretary brings us bottles of — you guessed it — Aquafina water and some tasteless muffins, we head over to human resources to fill out paperwork.

"What do you do?" I ask the eye roller as we fill out our W2s.

"You mean what did I do?"

I nod sympathetically.

"Retirement manager at Goldman Sachs."

I look over at the other woman, the one who fell asleep. "Me too. And you?"

"Travel writer."

They both smile at this. "That sounds like a dream job," the first one says.

Yeah, when Wall Street doesn't put your clients out of business, I think, but I say nothing.

By mid-afternoon we're all done with training and paperwork and hungry, so Jacob sends us toward town where there are restaurants. It's a good walk and no one offers us a ride so I'm wondering if Carmine's right about them being cheap. We grab an inexpensive lunch, then split up as we shop the town's boutiques — which is fine with me since the two women talked banking and IRAs the entire lunch. I stop at the Messina Hof Winery tasting room and try out a few vinos, then purchase a lovely port to bring back to my room. The hike back to Courtyard seems longer this time, probably because the early morning flight is catching up to me. I retrieve my bag from the office and check in next door. I turn on the TV and study my huge list of items I am to look for at every hotel I visit but leave the giant packet to later. By eight o'clock and two glasses of port, I fall asleep.

The phone rings at five a.m., the hotel desk clerk waking me for my flight to Memphis. I shower and dress and head down to the lobby for some god-awful coffee, the weak kind where you can almost see the bottom of the cup, with only powdered creamer to assist me. If this is the Courtyard way, it's first on my list of negatives.

The other women arrive and we all head to the airport, but move in different directions once we travel through security. I make it to my gate, but not after stopping at Starbucks and nabbing a café latte. I fall into my seat at the gate, relishing in a decent cup of java this time.

A man in a tight pair of jeans that appear to be ironed and creased — do people do that to jeans? — waltzes by and I can't help but stare and enjoy the view. He's wearing a buttoned-down shirt that's also well ironed and, although I'm usually not attracted to preppy types, this guy's wearing it well. Just as I'm about to fully take in the sight and start imagining things, he opens his mouth.

"My ticket says I'm in a middle seat but I specifically asked for an aisle," he tells the ticket agent in an aggravated voice.

"I'm sorry, sir, but seat assignments are made at the time of the purchase. We don't assign seats."

"I asked for an aisle seat when my company booked this flight. I was told I would have an aisle seat."

"We're a full flight, sir. I doubt there is anything I can do."

The two go round and round, the preppy's voice getting more and more aggravated, and people begin to stare. Finally, the exasperated ticket agent grabs the man's ticket and starts typing away on her keyboard. The man looks around and spots me glaring at him, then winks. I frown, wondering if this is some game he's playing to get his way.

"There's a seat in the emergency aisle," the agent says.

"Hate the emergency aisle. If I'm paying for a flight on your airlines, I don't think it's up to me to save everybody."

The woman looks back at her screen and types away. "There's a seat in priority, but it's an additional forty-five dollars."

The man starts fussing louder and another agent walks over to help. The two try to talk him down, work over the keyboard some more, and I hear the agents acquiescing, giving Mr. Prep Star the priority aisle seat for no extra money. They print out a new boarding pass and hand it over. As the man passes me by, he catches me staring again.

"And that's how it's done," he says smugly.

"Asshole," I think to myself.

It's a quick flight to Memphis and I catch the shuttle to

the hotel, an older property on the south side, a quarter-mile down the street from Graceland. It's too early to check in so I drop off my suitcase and head over to Elvis's old home to enjoy the tacky décor that everyone loves so much.

I tour the house which is surprisingly interesting, do a couple of the extras across the street, museums and exhibits designed to pull more money out of tourists' wallets, then enjoy an Elvis-inspired lunch. When four p.m. rolls around, I walk to my hotel and check in discreetly the way I was told, gather my keys and head to the room.

As I'm turning the corner to the elevators, who should walk in but Asshole himself.

"Well, hey there, girlie," he says when he spots me.

I'm dumbfounded so all I can mutter is "Hey."

"Don't be too nice," he instructs me.

He heads to the hotel counter where he starts complaining about something, but I don't want to stay and find out. I head up to my room and do an immediate search. Was the bed neatly made, the air conditioning cool, and the lights on upon arrival? Is the bathroom neat with adequate towels? Are the carpets clean with no vacuum streaks?

I've been to numerous hotel rooms in my travels so I know what to look for. I make notes of the patched-up water stain in the shower, the lack of a pen and notepad in the desk, and how the mini fridge makes too much noise. All of this will go into a form on the hotel's website, but first I must check out the property. There's a pool here, so I slip on my bathing suit and convince myself the only way to truly find out if the pool is up to snuff is to take a plunge. Besides, I'm sweaty as hell from the walk from Graceland.

Before I'm out the door, my cell phone rings. I recognize the New Orleans number and answer a bit too brusquely. "Hey sis."

"Hey yourself. When can you come home?"

I sigh and hold the phone away from my ear to compose myself. "I'm not moving home. Can we change that tune?"

"Did I say anything about moving?"

"What do you mean, then?"

"How about when are you coming home? I did just say that, didn't I?"

I throw down the towel, thinking this might take a while. "I'm in Memphis on a job."

"I thought you were out of work."

"It's a temporary position reviewing hotels until my magazine work picks up."

"Sounds like fun. Wish I could lounge around hotels for a living."

"I'm not lounging around hotels." I glance at myself in the mirror and cringe.

"Mom wants us together for Sunday dinner."

This is news and it gets my hopes up that Sebastian might finally be heading back to Louisiana. My bratty twin works as a chef and was taken in by colleagues in the restaurant world after Katrina washed away his business. He picked up some impressive work in Atlanta, then got in good with the Delta folks and a few other corporate executives so now he's jet-setting around the country.

"Will Sebastian be there?"

"I think so. Are you coming?"

"I fly in Saturday night. What time is dinner on Sunday?"

"Noon. See ya."

And just like that, Portia hangs up.

"Love you, too," I say to a dial tone.

I grab my towel but the phone rings once more.

"Did you forget to say you love me?"

"You know I do."

It's my faithful dog, and although I should be taking Carmine's advice, I really want to get to that pool. "What's up, TB?"

He hesitates and I realize my tone has derailed him. "I, uh, wanted to see if you got there okay."

I kick myself for being terse. "I'm fine, in the hotel in Memphis."

"Wow, Memphis. Are you going to Beale Street?"

"Maybe." Right now, I can't even get out the door.

"When are you coming back?"

I throw the towel back on the bed and sit down while TB launches into a discourse of his day, the problem he's having on the construction site, and how it looks like it might take longer than necessary to finish the job.

"So, you're saying you need to stay longer at my place?" I ask rubbing my eyes.

"More money for you. Gives me a chance to prove that we belong together."

I try not to moan out loud. I know he's fired up from the blue moon, thinking that fate has a role in our relationship, but we've been separated for two years. If it wasn't for the health insurance and the fact that divorces cost money, I'd be legal by now.

But I bite my tongue and ride along, tell him to stay as long as he likes, accompany me to family dinner on Sunday, and to please feed Stinky for me.

"We're old friends now."

"Great." There's sarcasm there but it flies over TB's head.

By the time TB finishes detailing everything that's happened between yesterday morning and today, he announces that a coworker has arrived and he needs to give him a ride home. I hang up and feel less like a swim but I rally my courage anyway. I reach over to retrieve my towel and spot the massive folder Jacob had given us during training. I flip it open to make sure I know what to do and realize there are pages and pages that need filling out. I need to check out every inch of this property.

"Crap," I mutter, knowing that I have hours of work ahead of me.

I change back into clothes and head to the lobby to grab a bite, lugging the fat folder with me. I figure I will peruse the papers over dinner — something cheap because I must pay for meals myself and get reimbursed later — and plot a course of action. Before I can ask for a table, I spot Asshole in the back of the restaurant, fussing at the waitress who looks like she's about to cry. I immediately turn to leave, but he sees me and calls out.

"Hey Girlie."

I reluctantly turn around and he waves me over. The last thing I want is company with this jerk but I'm not sure how to get out of it. When I reach his table, he motions for me to sit down.

"I've got work to do," I say, holding up the file.

"Lots of work by the look of things."

When he's not yelling at people, the man owns a nice smile. His chocolate brown eyes and cute dimple on his left cheek almost make me forget his bad behavior.

"Yeah, so, nice meeting you."

I turn to leave and he stands, which causes his thick hair to fall seductively over one eye. He pulls out a chair.

"I'll bet I can help you with all that."

I try to smile like I mean it, but his good looks have disarmed me. "Doubtful."

He leans in close and says softly, "There's a trick to reviewing these places. Buy me a drink and I'll show you."

I don't know how he knows why I'm here but I take the seat he's offering.

"Eric J. Faust." He offers his hand and I shake it.

"Viola Valentine."

At this, he chuckles. "Seriously? That's your name?"

I'm not laughing, especially since only yesterday I defended it as something awesome, and I'm about ready to leave when the waitress comes back and asks for my drink order. I'm almost positive she's been crying.

"I'll have another bourbon on the rocks," Eric tells her. "Make it Woodford this time since my friend here is paying. And she'll have the same."

Panic fills me because I don't have much money left in my checking account and my credit card is close to being maxed out but before I can protest, Eric pulls my folder from my hands and looks it over. "Yep, the standard Courtyard bullshit."

"How do you know...?"

He throws the packet on the table. "You don't know who I am, do you?"

"Eric J. Faust."

He gives me a smug look. "I mean within the company."

He can't be a manager at this place. I can't imagine someone so ornery in charge. When I don't answer, he leans in closer.

"You're here to quietly observe and report back to Courtyard, correct?"

I nod.

"Of course, you do. You're a woman." When I frown at this comment, he adds, "No offense but all the angels are women."

"The what?"

That smug smile returns. "They didn't tell you about us, did they?"

The waitress arrives with our drinks and Eric waits until she's finished. "Thanks Doll," he says and sends her a wink that clearly makes her uncomfortable but she says nothing, hurries away.

"She should have smiled. When you work in food and alcohol you have to suck it up."

I've had enough of this guy and I grab my folder. "She didn't smile because you're an asshole."

Eric laughs and places a hand on the folder. "Now, you understand."

I pull at the folder but he's holding tight. "Understand what?"

"You're the angel and I'm the asshole."

I stop my struggle and study him. He's serious. "You're a reviewer."

He leans back in his chair and downs his drink, then signals to the waitress for another. "Now, you got it."

"So, I do it quietly and you do it as a bad customer. Is that it?"

He holds up a finger. "Not a bad customer but one who's

not having his needs met and he's letting the one's responsible know about them."

"In an asshole way."

He smirks at this, as if I'm a child who doesn't understand.

"Did you know they pay us more? The assholes? We're all men, by the way. And guess what? The angels are all women."

Figures, I think to myself, although that tidbit of information rubs me hard.

"And here's some free advice since you're buying drinks. Ask them for more money because they're cheap bastards and they will pay you crap until you do."

"Not free advice if I'm buying."

For the first time, Asshole appears impressed by me. "You've got some mettle. Maybe you'll learn something after all."

I cross my hands in front of me and lean across the table. "And what, exactly, am I supposed to learn from you?"

The waitress places the second drink in front of him and he takes a long sip, all the while staring intently at me as if summing up what I'm capable of.

"First of all, the list is insane. If you walked around this hotel checking out every corner it would take you hours and everyone would be on to you because you'd look like Inspector Hound. Walk around like you're bored, find a few things that need work and mark those on the list. Click okay to all the rest."

Makes sense. "Noted."

"Second, they throw out your forms if you don't write in complete sentences so you can't cut corners."

This insults me a bit. "I'm a writer so no worries there."

He smiles and nods his head in approval, although not for what I imagine. "Let me guess, this is a pay-the-rent job?"

I don't answer so he continues.

"Third, and this is the most important." He downs the rest of his expensive bourbon that has me raking my brain for where the money will come from to pay for. "Don't be too nice. They suspect you're not doing your job if everything's fine. Even if you must exaggerate on how bad something is, like this glass, for instance, which could have been cleaner."

I look at the glass he's holding and don't notice anything unusual. He places it on the table and I attempt a better look but he's already standing.

"Like I said, don't be too nice."

When I don't answer, just stare up at him silently, he sighs and looks heavenward.

"This is where you say, wait, asshole, I never agreed to buy you those drinks so pay up."

I sit there, mouth agape, not sure what to do, when he turns to the waitress. "This is on me. Charge it to my room and include the lady's dinner."

And with that, Eric J. Faust winks and leaves me alone with my thoughts. My first one is, maybe he's right. Time to stop being so nice.

CHAPTER FIVE

Thank goodness for Louisiana swamps I think as we drive across the LaBranche Wetlands west of New Orleans. The sleepy bald cypress and tupelo trees covered in Spanish moss, along with the summer sunlight reflecting off the green shine atop the water, give me something to focus on as TB continues his lengthy tale about some guy named Lanky Thibodeaux who's inept with framing and it's costing them several days' work. This after an hour of explaining the ins and outs of pouring concrete foundations.

"How long are you going to be in Lafayette?" I ask, hoping he doesn't detect the meaning behind my question.

"They're short-handed since most construction is in New Orleans these days. I could make some good money if I hang out in town for a while."

"What about the house?"

When we married, TB's parents gifted us with a home in the Mid-City district of New Orleans, one of those cheaply made houses built after World War II when housing needs were met by quick construction. Katrina did a number on the place, filling it with water from the break in the Seventeenth Street Canal. The linoleum floor buckled along with the plywood walls, and mold covered everything for months. But, that's not why I never want to see the place again.

"The house is coming along nicely." TB brightens because he's hoping against hope that I will return to New Orleans and live with him there. "Want to stop by and see."

"Nope."

I hate to extinguish his expectations but two days on that house's roof, surrounded by water while my government ignored us has ruined the place for me. Wonder why. Plus it's where we spent five years with our darling girl. I managed to save her photos from that bitch's floodwaters so I'm good.

"The kitchen's almost done."

"It's been two years and you've poured everything into that house, TB. You could have bought something new, somewhere else."

TB pouts and I'm reminded of Carmine's simile about the dog. "That's our home, Vi."

I don't say anything, trying to take the high road to those who love me unconditionally, and TB thankfully doesn't pursue it. He goes back to relating his experiences in Lafayette over the past week, this time extoling the virtues of the Cajun plate lunches he enjoyed. I must admit, the smothered fried pork chops at the Creole Lunch House sure sounds good and I make a mental note to visit.

We arrive at my mom's house and I spot Portia's SUV and some cute little sports car that looks vintage.

"Wow, a Karmann Ghia," TB announces.

We grab the bottle of wine I had lying around the apartment and head inside and are greeted with a variety of voices, each one trying to be heard over the other. My family consists of several big personalities, all vying for attention. Speaking your mind — and what you say — in this family means constantly being on your best game. It's exhausting, and most of the time I retreat somewhere quiet with a glass of wine and count the hours before I get to leave.

Sebastian greets me and my heart lifts. I have missed my twin immensely.

"Hey Brat." I wrap him in a tight hug, then lean back and take in his outfit, something nouveau Southern gentleman, a plaid jacket with leather at the elbows and a Polo shirt over jeans. "You look like something out of *Guns & Grits*."

"Funny you should mention that, twin sister."

Guns & Grits started publication the year before and I've been dying to get an assignment with the high-end Southern magazine with a name everyone outside of the South thinks ridiculous. It's a bit high-brow for me, something people dressed like Sebastian is right now would enjoy, but I'm convinced they pay better than my regional mags and I want to tap into that revenue source.

"I'm their new chef," Sebastian tells me proudly.

"What?"

I'm dying to hear more but Portia flits in and asks, "You only brought wine?"

TB, bless his heart, pipes in before I get defensive.

"We weren't sure what to bring so we figured we could pick up whatever you need once we got here."

This disarms Portia so I send my puppy a grateful smile. Still, Portia has the last word, gazing at the cheap wine in TB's hand.

"What did you spend on that? Three bucks?"

"It's all the rage in Breaux Bridge," TB answers without a beat, smiling sweetly, and I picture Carmine's smug face as he says, "I told you so."

"We have all we need, Portia. Go watch those unruly kids of yours," Sebastian inserts.

Portia turns her long sharp nose his way. "So sous chef with the fancy car thinks he's a big shot now, huh?"

The arrow hits its mark, those strikes that siblings inflict so perfectly. Before the storm, the only jobs Sebastian could nab were sous chef positions. Now, because he's a celebrity of sorts in exile, he's risen in the ranks.

"Better than pushing papers in a law firm whose only talents are helping corporations evade taxes and ruin our coastline."

Portia bristles. She's one of Jackson, Weiss and LeBlanc's top lawyers but she rarely goes to court, instead settles for oil companies accused of environmental destruction and the erosion of the Louisiana coast, which disappears more each year, including making New Orleans more susceptible to storms. She and Sebastian argue over preservation of the earth versus rights of businesses every time they get together.

"Well, excuse me for having a real job." Portia makes a point to look at both of us. "Some of us have to make a living and support the family."

She heads to the kitchen in a huff and Sebastian and I laugh in her wake.

"What a drama queen," he says.

The three of us fall on to the couch and catch up, TB and Sebastian talking cars — Sebastian has use of the publisher's Karmann Ghia for the weekend — and he and I sharing news of our careers. I'm pleased for Sebastian's new fame and fortune but miss him terribly. He doesn't seem to miss me as much, unfortunately, and I wonder when I'll see him again.

"Come out to South Carolina," he tells me. "You'd love the Low Country. The publisher has this gorgeous spread near the coast and we go hunting every chance we get."

This doesn't gel with my environmentalist twin. "Hunting? Since when do you go out killing things?"

He looks at me as if I've sprouted wings. "Hunting keeps animal populations in check. I've joined Ducks Unlimited and they're one of the biggest conservationist groups around."

I'm still not convinced. Shooting defenseless animals never appealed to me although I don't begrudge others. Now that I live in Cajun Country, I wouldn't have friends if I took a stand against hunting and fishing. The local newspapers devote whole sections to the outdoors and I have neighbors who walk the streets packing. It's all strange for a city girl like me and I can't believe my liberal brother is falling in step.

"Well, look who's home." My mother walks into the living room wearing an apron and holding a roux spoon. "Glad you could fit me into your busy schedule."

I stand and kiss my mom on her cheek. "Nice to see you, too, Mom."

She looks frail today, and dressed in jeans and a loose-fitting top, unusual for my mother who never leaves the house without being impeccably dressed and made up. Her eyes lack their usual luster as well. I start to inquire but she barks off instructions, we all do some part bringing food to the dining room table, and gather round. Portia's children, who were immersed in some video game in the den, rush in yelling and fighting and my mom looks ready to explode. Sebastian senses her anxiety so he grabs both and shakes them hard until they start laughing. My mom rubs her forehead, still upset by the noise, but I think she realizes the chaos is starting to wane.

"Are you okay, Mom?" I ask.

"Just dandy," she mutters and heads back into the kitchen to retrieve the gravy for the pot roast, the one Portia has slaved over all morning long, says my sister.

"Pot roast is so time-consuming," Sebastian retorts. "You buy the meat, put it in a pan with seasoning and cook it. So kudos to you, Portia."

"Like you would know," she fires back. "Celery slicer."

I can almost picture the hairs on the back of Sebastian's neck at full attention. "Bitch," he whispers so the children won't hear.

"Ingrate slacker," she whispers back.

When my mom returns, Portia's son, Reynaldo, announces to my mom, "Sebastian said a bad word."

"Shut up, Rey," his sister Demetrius says — my sister followed the Shakespeare tradition — and the two begin fighting again.

My mother places the gravy boat on the table too hard, causing its contents to spill, and fusses at Sebastian while Portia admonishes the kids. I look over at TB who smiles, enlarges his eyes as if to say, "Can we leave here fast enough?" Despite the distance between us, I'm thankful for an ally in this familial mess.

After the obligatory hour of dinner, then another hour listening to various family members talk about their lives — no one asks either me or TB how we're doing — we head back to Lafayette, with a quick stop by the house, with me waiting in the car. TB's disappointed I don't come in and peek at the new kitchen but he'll get over it.

Once back on the road, night falls with the sun setting straight ahead, causing us both to squint. As we cross the Mississippi Bridge at Baton Rouge I search the mighty river, thinking about the time I read *Siddhartha* and was blown away at the end when the protagonist finds spiritual enlightenment at the river, noting the interconnectedness of nature. It was something I even discussed with Lillye once.

"Do you realize the water beneath us could be a drop from the river's origins in Minnesota," I tell TB.

I see the wheels turning in his head and wait for an answer, wondering if I'm getting too deep for him, pun intended.

"And it's all the same," TB says quietly. "Individual drops making up the whole river, so what we see here is the same wherever this water is. Like universal consciousness. Individuals connecting to make up the whole of the universe."

I stare at my ex-husband whose idea of intellectual reading is the LSU playbook. "What?"

"Something I read in that box of yours," he says.

"What box?"

"The one you brought back from Lake Lorelei."

"You read all that?"

He shrugs. "Nothing else to do while you were gone. Besides, you know I like helping you with your work."

Elijah had called while we were at my mom's house, leaving a message that his grandmother would be up for a visit this week if I were willing and able. He suggested spending the night, saying he had an extra room, and that Sirona might be able to have us over for dinner. I relay this conversation to TB.

"Can I come?"

I picture TB asking a million questions, many of which are inappropriate — he's prone to do this — but he's been a godsend at times with research. I'm thinking I could drop him off at the library, maybe have him poke around the ruins while I interview grandma.

"If you can get off work."

He frowns. "Not sure, will have to check."

"For now, tell me where you read that bit about consciousness."

TB lights up as he explains the theory behind Masaru

Emoto, a Japanese scientist who experimented with water.

"He took water from a mountain stream and some from a polluted one and froze them both, then studied them under a microscope."

I know the story but it's nice hearing TB talk about something other than construction.

"I think I heard about this guy," I say. "The crystals from the stream were beautiful and the others distorted, right?"

Now TB's getting really excited, and I'm again surprised by his interest.

"Yeah, but it gets better. He did more experiments, this time having people talk to water, write words or place pictures on glasses of water. The ones who said and wrote pleasant things on their glasses had the pretty crystals again. The ones with the angry words and negativity had ugly ones."

"Interesting."

"He believed people could change the molecular structure of water by positive vibrations, which means...." He looks at me, his eyes shining bright, and I don't think I've seen him so fascinated by something so metaphysical. "...that water might be a blueprint for our reality. That's what Emoto said, a 'blueprint for our reality.'"

I ponder this, slurping on my water bottle, thinking about the molecules of what I'm drinking entering my body made up of mostly water in a world that's overwhelmingly water. Not to mention my psychic connection to H2O. How this relates to Lake Lorelie, I haven't yet discerned, but that buzzing has returned so I mull over this new information all the way back to Lafayette.

I'm standing on a ridge above Lake Lorelie with a dramatic drop to the water's edge, amazed at the rolling hills a short distance from flat Lafayette, with below-sea level marshes to Lafayette's south. Elijah had said the lake was here before the state intervened and damned up a nearby stream, but it's hard to imagine this land having more altitude than what's in front of me.

"Beautiful, isn't it?"

An elderly woman known as Miss Bessie to locals, Elijah's grandmother, leans heavily on a cane and approaches to my rear. I attempt to assist but she waves my hand away. "I'm perfectly capable, young lady."

I don't know what to say so I wait patiently while she hobbles to my side. She raises her cane and points it toward the dock at the end of the pathway leading downhill.

"My son built that dock. I used to go fishing there every morning. Would do it still but Elijah won't let me. You slow down a bit and they assume you're ready for the old folk's home."

I can't imagine this frail lady climbing up and down that long staircase, not to mention she's more than slowed down a bit, but I keep quiet.

She glances over at me. "You the ghost lady?"

"Yes ma'am."

"About time someone came up here to help us with this problem." She glances at me sideways; she's a good five inches shorter. "You do know what the problem is, don't you?"

I glance back at the lake, anything to escape those piercing brown eyes. "No ma'am, I'm afraid I don't. I was hoping you would tell me more."

Miss Bessie huffs, turns, and starts back toward the house. "Useless." The word describes me well, I think, and wonder if I'll have to return the money. But grandma turns and waves me over. "Well, come on then. I'll make some coffee."

I wish Elijah were here. He had set up this meeting and met me at Hi Ho's that afternoon but after driving me over to Miss Bessie's, announced that he had some city business to attend to. He dropped me off in the yard leading to his grandmother's house and hurried away, claiming it was an emergency.

I follow the old lady to the house that's a bit worse for wear on the outside but squeaky clean on the inside. In fact, I'm astonished at how neat and clean the home is.

"Didn't think an old lady could keep house?" she asks, giving me that stink eye again.

"No ma'am," I lie. "I'm just impressed. My house is usually never this clean."

"That's because you young people are lazy. Don't have the same work ethic like my generation."

She turns her back to me and pulls out two cups, a mini pitcher of what looks like real cream and a sugar bowl, placing them all on a tray with cloth napkins and little silver spoons. "Get that coffee, will you?"

I search the counter and find a French press next to a bag of hazelnut Starbucks coffee, which smells heavenly. It takes me back a bit.

"Don't think an old lady knows how to make coffee either, do you? Or do you think we backwoods darkies grind it in a pestle and boil it over a fire."

I don't know how to respond. Truth is, I thought only hipsters under thirty, of all colors, used French presses and bought Starbucks by the bag.

She pushes me aside and grabs the French press, places it on the table with the rest of the coffee fixings. "I usually like to grind up the whole beans but Walmart's been out of it since Tuesday."

I want to wait until she sits down, thinking that's the polite response to my elders, but Miss Bessie doesn't comply and gets exasperated with me. "Sit down, ghost girl. You my guest."

I do as I'm told but right now I'm rather frightened of this tiny sprit of a woman. I think she senses it for she pours me a cup and hands it to me along with the cloth napkin and a spoon.

"Thank you, ma'am."

"What do you need to know?" she asks after taking a long, satisfying sip of her Starbucks. I have to admit, this is damn good java, nice and strong with an adequate dollop of cream, just the way I like it.

"Elijah said the ghosts started appearing at Easter. Is that when you saw the mayor coming through the yard?"

I try not to laugh as soon as those words fly out my mouth. If Portia could see me now.

"Easter, right after the sun went down. They come out at dusk, you know?"

I nod. "Is this often?"

"Like clockwork. I take in the clothes off the line, I finish pulling up weeds in my garden — you name it — and when I head into the house as the sun's going down, there they are."

"They?"

"Whomever wants to visit me that day."

This makes me sit up straight. "You've seen more than one in your yard?"

"Half a dozen at last count. Maybe more."

I shake my head trying to make sense of it. "Weird."

"You ever heard of this before?"

"No ma'am."

She looks at me sternly. "You even seen ghosts before?"

"Yes ma'am." I decide to come clean. "To be honest, I only see ghosts that have died by water. I told Elijah this but he asked me to come anyway."

Miss Bessie rubs two fingers over her lips as she studies this. "I knew someone once, had a gift like that. Called it a funny name."

"SCANC?"

She purses her lips like she's tasting something awful. "What? No. That's sounds crazy."

"You don't know the half of it."

Those lips keep moving as Miss Bessie searches her brain, then her eyes light up. "Tea Bags."

"Pardon?"

"Tea Bags. Stands for trauma-induced ability to believe in apparitions, ghosts and specters."

I can't help myself; I laugh this time. This is a new one on me and I'm pretty sure I've heard them all.

"It's not funny," Miss Bessie says sternly.

"Well, ma'am, it is kinda funny and yes, that's me. I was in

Katrina so my trauma relates to water."

"And you'd rather be called a skank?"

I smile. "'Specific communication with apparitions, non-entities, and the comatose.'"

Miss Bessie shakes her head. "They're both rather stupid, if you ask me."

"Yes ma'am." I so agree, but I didn't make this shit up. Finally, we both laugh and take long sips from our coffee.

I look out the window at the placid lake and wonder why this place, why Easter? Miss Bessie reads my mind for she utters, "Who knows?"

I decide to get some history first.

"Matt what's-his-name with the state said they created this lake but Elijah said it was here before the dam."

Miss Bessie sits back in her chair and relaxes, coffee cup still in her gnarly hands. "Oh yes, I grew up on this lake. Even as a child, it was large and deep."

"So, why does the state say they created it as a reservoir?"

Miss Bessie rises and pulls a photo album off a nearby bookshelf and opens it to a page showing what looks like family, shot in the 1930s. There's a Model A truck in the background and the lake is barely visible on the horizon.

"That's my family and you can see the lake in the distance."

"Looks just like it does now," I say.

Miss Bessie nods. "Yes, it does."

"I don't understand."

Miss Bessie turns the album around and runs a loving hand over the photo.

"They screwed up. Folks came in and started looking for oil by the springs and one November night in 1932 the water level dropped. An accident of some kind. The state blamed it on the drought but a lake doesn't half disappear during the night. We woke up and found our boats in the mud, fish flopping everywhere. We knew it was them that did it."

"Them? The state?"

Miss Bessie closes the album and returns it to the

bookshelf. "I ain't saying. Folks get in trouble for saying too much."

"What folks?"

Miss Bessie huffs. "Black folks, of course. Who else is going to get hurt, going to get the blame? If you know what's good for you you'll stay away from that Matt fellow. He knows the truth but it's not safe for some outsider to come here and bring it all up again."

There's something going on and I want to learn more but Miss Bessie looks out the window at the setting sun.

"You ready to see some dead people?"

The sky's turning gorgeous shades of crimson and gold, a myriad of colors reflecting off the lake's waters. I'm entranced by the scene before me but Miss Bessie wakes me from my revelry.

"Come on, Ghost Lady," she says sternly.

I look up to find Miss Bessie standing with her hand on the front door, so I rise and follow her slow steps on to the front porch. We stand at the railing and wait.

"Don't get your hopes up, Miss Bessie," I say. "If these dead people haven't died by water I'm afraid…."

I feel a presence before I see a silhouette of a man in old-fashioned attire appear out of the tree line, walking across the yard as if in a trance. Ripples of heat flow through me and beads of sweat break out on my forehead. A dull ache begins behind my eyes and I rub them to clear my eyesight, afraid I might be hallucinating.

The ghost doesn't acknowledge us, which means he's not an intellectual haunting, and slowly moves toward the lake, passing within a foot of us until he vanishes.

I turn to Miss Bessie with my mouth hanging open. I need to sit down, try to focus on what just happened.

"Wait," Miss Bessie says. "There's more."

As if on cue, four more haunts float across Miss Bessie's back yard and I stand watching this parade in amazement. I hear Miss Bessie call out their names — first, the mayor who died of old age, then the proprietor of the general store who had a heart attack, a girl who fell out of a citrus tree and hit her head, and an African American man Miss Bessie seemed to know personally but refused to say how he died.

Once the sun sets, the parade concludes. All five ghosts simply vanished on the way to the lake. And none, except for possibly the African American, had died by water. I'm so excited about that fact I can barely contain myself. I give Miss Bessie a hug that almost knocks her down.

"Take it easy there, Ghost Lady," she admonishes me, but there's a smile on her face.

"You have no idea what this means to me."

"Hopefully it means you're going to send these people packing."

I hop up and down. "I sure will try."

I can't wait to call TB and tell him the good news, that I can see ghosts who have no connection to water. That I might finally be able to speak to my angel, the love of my life on the other side. I'll call Carmine as well, let him know that his theory on ghost-talking evolution is crap.

"Why you so happy?" Miss Bessie asks.

I feel a kinship to this woman now, so I start to explain how I lost my daughter, Lillye, to leukemia, only to be given the gift of talking to water-logged ghosts, not my spirits of choice. But, Elijah drives up in his truck and parks in front of the porch. When he approaches us, he finds us grinning like schoolgirls. The look on his face, however, doesn't mirror our enthusiasm.

Miss Bessie instantly changes. "What's wrong, Boo?"

"I need to speak with Ms. Valentine, Nana."

Something's definitely wrong but I try to lighten up the situation as I follow Elijah to his truck where we can have some privacy.

"I saw the ghosts." I can't help but gush enthusiastically. "There were five people and I saw every one."

He nods but he's not listening, or at least it's not sinking in.

"Did you hear me? I saw five ghosts. Right here in your

grandmother's front yard."

He runs a hand through his hair. "Vi, I'm afraid we have to discontinue your services."

This stops me cold. "What?"

"The powers that be think it best that we take care of whatever is happening here — if there is something happening here — on our own."

"Of course, something's happening here. Did you not hear what I just said? I saw five...."

"Naturally, we want you to keep the money we already gave you, since you took the time to come up here twice."

"Elijah...."

"But, um, we'll take it from here."

I'm stunned. Flabbergasted. Just when I was getting somewhere after I was the one who doubted I would, the one man who believed in me is firing my ass. I glance over at Miss Bessie who looks as surprised as I am.

"Okay," I say. "I'll be on my way then."

Miss Bessie calls out Elijah's name but he doesn't look her way, gets back into his truck, and drives off. Even his rudeness to both me and his grandmother seems odd.

"I'm sorry," Miss Bessie says. "That's not like him."

I head to the porch to gather my purse that I left on the porch swing and give Miss Bessie one last hug. "Thanks for the coffee."

"Come back anytime," she says, although I doubt I will see this place again.

I head down the porch but remember the postcard. Curiosity getting the best of me, I decide to ask Miss Bessie about the woman in the back of the crowd.

"Miss Bessie, may I ask you something."

"Anything."

I pull the postcard from my purse and hand it to her, pointing to the woman who looks identical to Sirona.

"Do you recognize that woman in the back?"

Miss Bessie pulls a pair of glasses from her apron pocket, places them on her nose, and squints at the photo. She moves back towards the porch light to get a better view and stares harder. I point at the woman again, to make sure she sees who I'm getting at.

Suddenly, Miss Bessie's face pales and her hand begins to shake. Her eyes enlarge and she looks at me in a panic.

"Do you know her?"

She shakes her head, hands me the postcard and starts backing up.

"She's not real," she tells me. "My mother said she's not real."

Before I can inquire further, she rushes through the door and slams it in her wake. I glance back at the postcard with Sirona looking back — or whomever this woman is — and slide it back into my purse.

I leave Miss Bessie's house and Fontus Springs, glad to be rid of this crazy town with ghosts parading about and mysterious people traveling through time, lakes that rise and fall which no one wants to discuss. I drive home to Lafayette, free of the strange mystery that surrounds Lorelie Lake, but I can't think of anything else.

CHAPTER SIX

I call TB as soon as I hit Interstate 49 and tell him about the ghosts, then add that I was fired and Miss Bessie went all crazy on me.

"Why did you get fired?"

"Did you hear what I said? I saw ghosts who have not died by water."

"I know but why did they fire you?"

I grind my teeth and groan. This is why I don't want to stay married to TB. He can be clueless sometimes.

"Don't you get it? I might finally be able to connect with Lillye."

There's silence on the other end, which irritates me further. "Hello?"

"Vi, Carmine said you would only be able to speak to the dead within your specialty."

"Well, Carmine was wrong."

More silence, and now I'm really irritated. "I thought you would be pleased. Do you know what this means."

"I am. I mean, if it's possible I am."

"Of course, it's possible. I saw five people today outside my 'specialty.'" My voice is getting louder and my blood pressure higher, and I know I'm losing control but I can't help myself. I so want this to happen.

"Vi," TB says calmly and softly, "Lillye is gone and you have to come to turns with that."

The standard advice for every grieving parent. I've heard it all from friends and family to the psychiatrist I saw following the storm. Make it through the five stages of grief — denial, anger, bargaining, depression, and acceptance — then learn to live with the loss. I've been through the depths of hell watching my child suffer and die, then Katrina washed away my life. But, I emerged on the other side with this crazy gift. It had to have been bestowed on me for a reason.

"It's a sign, TB. I know it is."

TB sighs and I can almost feel the sadness emanating through the phone. "I don't want you to be disappointed."

I try to breathe but my chest constricts and my heart races. I know he means well and there's logic to what he's saying but I can't let this go. I feel like I've made a breakthrough and I don't want anyone to bring me down.

"I'll talk to you later, TB."

"Vi...."

"See you back at the apartment."

I hang up thinking I did the right thing. He's wrong and I'm breaking new ground but the hum of the car's wheels on the interstate and the darkness surrounding me as I make my way through the rural areas of St. Landry Parish give me pause. What if I'm wrong? Maybe there's something mystical about that lake causing these ghosts to appear, and because it's a water source I'm seeing them like everybody else?

No, I command myself. I'm dedicated to breaking through the confines of my gift inherited from Katrina and I'm going to make this work. But, on the way home, I stop by Blue Moon Bayou and head to the water's edge to see if that girl still lingers there, the one who spoke to me during the rising of the moon. I spot her sitting beneath the bridge, gazing at her reflection in the water. As I quietly approach, I notice there is no reflection staring back.

She senses that I'm near and stands, surprised once again that I can see her.

"Hello."

"Hello," she returns.

We stare at each other for a few moments, not sure how to proceed.

"You can see me?" she finally asks. I nod and she adds, "Of course you can. You're talking to me."

"Has no one talked to you before?"

I move closer and make out her clothes, the same ragged ones from before. If I could date the outfit, I'm guessing 1930s.

She shakes her head. "Just the old ladies who own the mortuary. Kids sometimes." Now she studies me and my outfit. "What are *you*?"

"I'm a ghost whisperer." I laugh at the reference but, of course, my ghostly friend doesn't get it.

"Do you know you're a ghost?" I ask.

She sends me a sly smirk. "Yeah, I know I'm dead."

We stare silently at each other once more until she begins to fade. My heart races. There's so much I need to know.

I shout out, "Who are you?"

She swallows hard, perhaps wondering if she can trust me, but she replies, "Abigail Earhart, like the lady pilot."

I can barely make out Abigail now. Her form fades into a silhouette, like poor television reception in the old days. I feel electricity travel through me standing so close to a vibrating spirit, one about to transform to another realm. There's a buzzing akin to the one I felt at Hi Ho's, like there's a connection being made.

"Wait, how did you die?"

Just before Abigail fades into the night, she raises her arm and points to the bridge where a freight train has begun to cross, its whistle echoing down the bayou.

"The train?" I ask and she nods, then disappears.

I've got my answer. I've finally learned to talk to all spirits, no matter their deathly circumstances. I'll prove TB wrong, I vow, and head back to Lafayette.

TB is standing there when I open the door, waiting, looking as if he's been pacing since our phone call. His bag remains unopened on the floor.

"Vi...," he begins.

I throw my purse and things on to the bed.

"I saw the girl at Blue Moon Bayou. She talked to me and guess what?" I feel so magnanimous. "Her name's Abigail Earhart. She died in a train accident."

TB stares at me with that vacant look, the one that drives me insane, makes me think there are wheels turning in there but it may be weeks before they hit on something significant.

"Did you hear what I said?"

"Vi, don't get angry with me."

"I'm not angry." Am I? "I'm frustrated that you don't get this. As usual."

TB winces like I slapped him and I feel remorse. People — including me — are always accusing my ex of being dense and he's naturally sensitive about it.

"You of all people should understand what this means and how excited I am," I continue. "But, you stand there, like always, looking at me like I've lost my mind."

"I don't think you've lost your mind."

"Really? You and everybody I knew acted like I was doing it all wrong when Lillye died, just because I didn't fall apart like you all did."

"You retreated."

"I dealt."

I am angry. The old hurt and feelings of betrayal come rushing to the surface like the whole thing happened yesterday. The endless crying and talking. People "concerned" that I wasn't doing the same. How would all that outward pain and suffering help me accept the fact that the most precious thing in my life was gone?

I sigh and try to calm the rapid beating of my heart, rub the bridge of my nose to release the tension building there. The psychiatrist I finally saw after years of people begging me to do so called it emotional repression or something to that effect. Talking did help relieve the grief suffocating my soul but in the end, I grew tired of the talk. That's all it is...talk! After a few months, I ended my relationship with Dr. Vincent and moved on.

TB moves forward and touches my arm lovingly and I can't help but wonder if I'm the one who's wrong here.

"I just want to see her again," I whisper, my voice cracking. "I want to talk to her."

TB moves to hug me but I retreat, backing up, and pulling my hair behind my ears.

"Vi, she's right here."

I look up to see him touching the area above his heart, something else everyone kept telling me over the years. "She's always with you," they would say. "You carry her in your heart." Of course, I do, but I want to see my baby girl. I want to talk to her.

I shake my head. "It's not enough."

TB stares at me, hard, and it's unnerving, something that usually doesn't happen with him.

"It's never enough with you, is it?" he whispers.

This takes me aback, but then he always wants more from me that I can deliver.

"If you're talking about me loving you because of that stupid legend on Blue Moon Bayou...."

He surprises me again, steps close to me, and I can feel the tension emanating from his body.

"I'm talking about me loving you, period."

I step back, anything to get away from that disarming look he's sending me and the rigid tone in his voice.

"We're separated, TB. When are you going to get that through your thick skull? Lillye was what kept us together, remember? Nothing else."

I don't mean this, because I think we did love each other once. But, we're different people, both then and now, and I don't see a future between us.

He shakes his head and smiles sadly, then grabs his bag and heads out the door. I don't want him to go, so wanted to discuss my weird day with him and plan a way to speak with Lillye, — after all, he's the only one who truly understands — but too much has been said.

TB pauses at the threshold.

"I made some comments on Fontus Springs, if you're interested. It's on top of the pile in the box."

He pulls an envelope out of his breast pocket and throws it on the bed.

"My hotel bill."

With that final comment, my ex-husband is out the door and out of my life for the time being. I pick up the envelope and find three one hundred dollar bills inside, no doubt his hotel allowance for the week. I fall on to the bed, my energy retreating and my head pounding and I hear a squeak from beneath me. When I turn to look, Stinky emerges with sleepy eyes. I pull my adopted cat on to my lap and hug him tight, which makes my tears fall in torrents.

"How's that Dr. Vincent?" I yell to the heavens. "Enough emotional release for you?"

I'm feeling off balance when morning comes but before I can wallow in my sorrows Jacob emails me with an urgent request. Would I drive over to Biloxi on the Mississippi Gulf Coast and review a hotel there. Still reeling from my anger from the night before, I'm not feeling my usual passive self when it comes to asking for money. I demand extra for the last-minute assignment and Jacob reluctantly gives it to me, plus a small pittance for mileage. That was easy, I surmise, so I add that the reviews require way more time than they insinuated in the training sessions and since he loved my review on the Memphis hotel, I think I should be paid more going forward. To my surprise, he agrees to that as well.

I flip my phone closed, thinking that maybe there's something to being a demanding jerk, after all.

I look through my emails to see if TB had written — he almost always sends an apology after we've fought — but there's nothing there. I know deep down I should be the one writing him but I bristle that he's not reached out and close my laptop and start packing.

The three-hour drive to Biloxi is uneventful, the sky devoid of clouds, and unbearably hot. I left Stinky in my apartment with ample amounts of food and a light on but he was not pleased.

"You'd rather be on the streets hungry?" I ask him and am greeted with a view of his rear end. Sometimes I think that cat really does understand me.

Funny, I think as I pull into the hotel's parking lot, I miss that cat, have gotten used to having him around. I wonder if I can bring him along next time and see how the hotel deals with pets.

I check in with my pink polka dot suitcase and ask the desk clerk about their pet policy. I'm told they don't accept pets but she gives me three names of hotels in the area that do. I make a mental note to include her helpfulness in my review.

My room is on the third floor, I'm told, so I head for the elevators. As the doors open, who's staring back at me but Mr. Eric J. Faust.

"Well, lookie here."

I can't help myself, as much as I despise this man it's good to see a familiar face, especially in the low mood I'm in. "Hey yourself, Asshole."

He laughs and links elbows with me, pulls me in the direction of the beach-side bar. "Let's catch up, Angel," producing my nickname like they do in Cajun Country, where they use Angelle (On-gel) as a given name.

My suitcase bounces along behind me. "I need to drop this off."

"Later."

And in a heartbeat we're sitting in bar stools ordering margaritas and gazing out on the Gulf of Mexico lying placid before us in the sweltering heat.

"What on earth do people see in this place?" Eric asks, looking at the shrimp boats motoring in with their catch. "Hot, humid, and the water's not that pretty. And all there is to do is visit casinos."

The drinks arrive and I throw down a twenty. I'm flush now that TB has shared his hotel allowance and it feels good to finally have money to spend, although how I got it brings me no joy. I push the guilt away and tell Eric the next round's on him.

"Good girl," he answers. "You're getting the picture."

"And the water looks that way because we're close to the Mississippi River. If you get out a ways it's gorgeous."

"But, we're not out a ways."

Biloxi is like a second home to me, a place to escape to when New Orleans summers become unbearably stifling. There's not much of a change in climate here, but a breeze blows in occasionally and there's the water to enjoy. Before the storm battered the Mississippi coast, there were rows and rows of historic homes and massive live oak trees, not to mention great seafood and amusement parks. The city's struggling to rebound after Katrina and I'm sure the recession hasn't helped. I don't want to hear Eric bad-talk my coast but I don't feel up to defending it, either, so I change the subject, making sure the bartender and other staff aren't present.

"So, are we going to be doing these reviews together?"

Eric takes a large gulp from his drink. "Needs more tequila. And probably not. Even though we're both working the Deep South, I was supposed to be paired with those banking girls but I heard they quit."

"Already?"

He smirks. "You didn't think former Goldman Sachs employees would do all this work for so little pay, did you?"

Makes sense. I'm used to traveling, know what to look for, and writing comes second nature. Since I spent time in the newsroom, it's easy for me to turn around copy fast.

"By the way," I tell him, "I asked for a raise and got it."

"All right, Angelle." He raises his glass and we toast. "I knew I'd like you."

I'm still not convinced I like him but he's fun and that goes a long way for me right now. Not to mention he's charming as hell.

"Wait, how did you know they quit? Or were from Goldman Sachs."

He smirks beneath the rim of the glass. "I slept with one of the company secretaries a while back and she gave me the password to the system. I know you worked for the New Orleans Post, lost your job and home in Katrina, and now freelance travel for some silly magazine called *Mais Yeah!*, among others."

"It's a Cajun expression."

"I gathered."

"Why on earth would you want to know all that?"

He shrugs. "I don't really, although I was curious about you." He sends a seductive smile that makes that cute dimple appear. That part of me that's been dormant without the company of men suddenly wakes up. "Mostly, I wanted to know what other people were earning to make sure I wasn't being screwed."

"Well, aren't you the sneaky devil."

Eric smiles behind his glass. "I used to work in banking, too. Goes with the territory. We know how to find things."

The bartender returns to check on us, which I would note in my review as a positive thing, but Eric complains about the lack of tequila.

"They all get one good shot," the bartender explains calmly, but Eric insists they are not up to par and his voice rises, which gives me a chill and I witness the bartender reacting the same way. Sure enough, after a few minutes of complaining, the bartender takes away our drinks and adds another shot of tequila.

"And none of that cheap stuff," Eric yells across the bar and I see the bartender reach for Patron.

"Holy shit." I'm seriously impressed.

"Stick with me, kid. You'll get a whole lot more out of life."

We drink two more margaritas before I head up to my room. I deposit my bag on the luggage rack and glance around at the non-descript furnishings, beige walls with photos of Biloxi landmarks, an equally bland-colored bedspread that matches the comfy chair in the corner. I do the requisite examination, checking out every inch and making notes, then fall into the bed and realize I'm more drunk than I thought I was. The feeling makes me giggle.

I know I've got to get to work so I rise and open the curtains, hoping to open the sliding glass doors and breathe in some fresh Gulf air. Behind the curtains, however, is the wall of the hotel next door, its loud air conditioner blazing.

"Well, crap. That's a bummer."

I grab my notebook and head down the hall, take in the ice and vending machines, move down one floor and check out the fitness room and swimming pool, then the lobby and restaurant on the ground floor. All in all, the place is adequate with a few items to be fixed. I'm still buzzing from the tequila so I take the elevator back to my floor and head to my room for a nap. Who should be waiting by the door is Eric. Before I'm able to inquire, he grabs my hand and walks me down the hallway to the final room on the beachside, flips his key and ushers me inside. There's a gorgeous view of the Gulf, of course, and a basket of fruit with red wine in the center.

"Where'd you get that?"

"I complained about the view of the first room so they moved me here, then threw a fit because the remote didn't work, vowed to write bad reviews on TripAdvisor and complain to corporate, so they brought this up."

I laugh because it all seems so easy. "And I've been working hard the old-fashioned way, go figure."

He sits on the bed and leans back on his elbows, obviously pleased with himself. "It helps to know how to screw up a remote."

I grab some of his grapes and pop them into my mouth, leaning back on the bureau and enjoying a good look at this handsome man before me, his shirt stretched across his chest. He's long and lean and full in all the right places, one in particular I shouldn't be looking at.

I clear my throat. "Did they teach you that at corporate or did you learn how to be a dick all on your own." Shouldn't have used that word.

He straightens so he's right in front of me, our eyes almost level since he's a tall drink of water. That dimple appears along with a twinkle in those brown eyes. "What do you think?"

He slips his arms around my waist and pulls me close and I let him, sliding my own on to his shoulders. I'm not sure I want to do this but then again, why not? I'm feeling empowered by the afternoon, loving the thought of taking life by the horns and creating my own reality, not waiting for something or someone to do it for me.

He starts with my neck, lightly biting my skin and moving over to the breastbone, while he unbuttons my blouse.

"You know, we barely know each other." My voice comes out shaky.

Now that my blouse is undone, he slips his hands up to cover my breasts and I gasp. Pretty loud, too. "I really. Shouldn't. Be. Doing this."

When he fingers my nipples I lose it, lean down and hungrily meet his mouth with mine. I'm starved for sex, I admit it, the drought going on almost two years now and I'm a woman in my prime who shouldn't be without that long. Although, what's a girl to do when her ex doesn't interest her and her fantasy man runs back to his wife?

Eric slips his hands behind me and pulls me on to the bed, shifting as we both fall on the comforter I would give a six out of ten. Make that a five, I think, as my bare back meets the scratchy material. Eric seems to want to take more time than I do so I increase the tempo by ripping off his shirt. A couple of buttons go flying and Eric pauses to notice.

"Wow, I take it you're ready."

I answer him by pulling off my jeans. "You have protection?"

He fakes looking insulted, reaching into his back pocket for his wallet. "Of course. Do I look like a father figure to you?"

These are the kind of men I wouldn't give a second look to, so admire the ones who are great fathers, but I laugh at his comment, so caught up in the seductive moment and those gorgeous brown eyes that I let his hands pull off every last piece of clothing. He pulls me so close my naked body rubs against his jeans and that alone is about to ignite me. I roll with it, though, because I can always do it again. I smile knowing we women have at least one thing going for us that men don't have. And if I work this just right, demand my own satisfaction the way my lover has instructed, I will reach bliss several times this night.

I do climax against him and let out a groan of pleasure. This is his signal to forget foreplay and hop to it so he pulls off his jeans and uses the condom he has hidden in his jeans.

"Hurry up."

I would never be this bold with a strange man, but something about Eric has erased my inhibition. His advice about being assertive, plus all those shots of Patron, have emboldened me like never before. Either that, or I'm hornier than I realize.

Finally, we're together and I wasn't wrong about the size. I bite my lip and thank God for sending me this asshole and let a second round of bliss take me away.

I've inadvertently left a tiny slit in the curtains, and even though my view is of an air conditioning unit and a wall going up five stories, the sun peeks through and nabs me right in the face. I swat at it like it's a fly, then sit up to gauge the time.

"Crap." It's 9:20 and I still have to review breakfast downstairs before it ends at 9:30. I throw on my clothes and brush my teeth at lightning speed, then race down the hallway pulling on my shoes at the same time. A good bit of the buffet bar has been taken away but I implore the clerk for some eggs and to return the dark roast coffee container. I nab some toast and a milk carton and slip some apples and a mini box of cereal into my purse for the ride home.

The clerk returns and announces that they still have bacon and waffles but the chef threw the eggs away. "They don't keep well, you know."

It's all good and I'm about to tell her that, when I think about my day with Eric. I look at my watch and it's 9:28. I do something I would never do, especially since I really don't care if I have eggs or not. I turn my wrist and show her the time.

"You put away breakfast before the deadline. I deserve to

have what you offer here. If not, then what am I paying for?"

She looks taken aback and I instantly feel remorse. She assures me she will find a way to make this work and how do I normally like my eggs? I start to say scrambled is fine but stop myself.

"I love veggie omelets."

I doubt that's part of the buffet but she back-steps into the kitchen, no doubt thinking that if they have to save face by cooking me up something fresh, it might as well be an omelet.

I look around the restaurant and Eric's nowhere to be found. After we made love, he fell asleep, and I regrouped and headed back to my room.

I nabbed his basket of fruit and wine, though.

I smile thinking about both our lovemaking and my theft when the waitress returns, looking penitent.

"The chef says he's very sorry and he has green peppers, onions and cheddar cheese if that works for you."

"Sure."

Now, I'm feeling really pleased with myself. Until I see the waitress enter the kitchen and catch the chef berating her. I know deep in my heart that everything we do in life has consequences, whether it be love or negativity emerging into the world. I see an image of a stone being thrown into a pond by a tiny hand, the waves of its impact with the water moving out in circles, stretching far and wide, reaching distant shores.

"Lillye?" I whisper.

"Talking to yourself?"

Eric stands before me, not a hair out of place, his button-down shirt neatly pressed and perfect. How does he do it?

"Breakfast is over. But since I was here slightly before the deadline and they took away the eggs, they're making me an omelet."

"Great." Eric throws down his newspaper and heads for the kitchen.

"It's past deadline," I say to his back, but he waves me off. When he returns, he doesn't say a word but I know he has an omelet coming as well.

He sits down across from me, grabs my cup of coffee and takes a long swig.

"Hey."

"Payment for the loss of a certain basket."

I feign innocence. "Have no idea what you're taking about."

He grins behind his cup and I realize this guy likes me. I have to admit, this tryst, or whatever I want to call it, has been fun. Just what I needed.

"Where are you headed next?"

He gets that "Oh no, she might be serious" look and I wave him off.

"Dude, I'm not looking for anything here. Believe me, the last thing I need right now is a relationship." I send him a haughty shake of my head. "Besides, I'm not sure I want to do that again."

He leans across the table and that sexy dimple appears making me tingly inside. "Funny, you wanted to do it again last night."

The waitress arrives and her eyes are puffy so whatever delight I received from his flirting disappears instantly. She places two omelets before us and asks if we want more coffee. I start to say "Yes, please" and offer some comforting words but Eric beats me to it, barking, "Of course, we want more coffee."

I feel more than see a tiny head shaking in disgust. Again, I wonder if Lillye's near, now that I can finally see ghosts outside of my realm.

"I'm driving up to Hattiesburg tonight, wherever the hell that is." Eric moves his cup — my cup — over towards the waitress who promptly fills it up from the fresh pot in her hands. I look around the table but there's no cup for me. "Then I drive to Jackson and fly to Branson for the weekend."

Eric asks for a glass of water and the waitress takes off before I have a chance to ask. I head to the buffet and retrieve a cup, once again reminded about the squeaky wheel and all that. By the time I sit back down, the thrill is gone, as B.B. King would say. Eric must have sensed something for he takes my hand and squeezes. "I'm sorry, I didn't realize there wasn't another cup on the table."

It works. For now. "No problem."

We discuss inane subjects over breakfast, then go our separate ways. No kisses, which is fine by me. I head back to my room, finish up the review, and am back on the road to Lafayette by noon. I throw in my retro CD and rock out on the interstate to K.C. and the Sunshine Band. I can't help it. I love funky seventies music. It's one of the rare things TB and I had in common.

The thought of my ex-husband as K.C. sings *I'm Your Boogie Man* brings forth the usual guilt but I'm determined not to let anything get me down today. I just had wild sex and my body sings in gratitude. I even bypass the exit to New Orleans.

"Screw my condescending family who can't bother to call, not to mention lend me money," I shout to no one, and that angry rush feels good.

The cell phone rings and I flip it up with one hand, feeling cocky. "Viola Valentine," I practically sing into the phone.

"Viola, this is Jacob from Courtyard. Where are you?"

I cringe. I know I say it doesn't matter how people say my name but it really chaffs my butt. "Jacob, the name's Vie-o-la, not Vee-o-la like the instrument."

I can't believe I scolded the man who's allowing me to eat this month. Still, would Eric allow it?

"I'm so sorry. I didn't realize."

I'm about to acquiesce and downplay the whole thing — which is what most Southern women would do — but I catch myself. Time to stop acting the polite female and start being a jerk. "I'm north of New Orleans, outside of Hammond."

"Great. I'm so glad I caught you."

Sounds like another job, which would come in handy right now since I have no assignments lined up. But I don't want him to think I'm easy. "Oh yeah? What's up?"

"I need you to do another hotel. Tonight, if you can."

"Does it come with another bonus for being last minute?"

Again, my tone and courage surprises me. I'm sure it's surprising Jacob as well. "Uh, sure. Same as Biloxi."

I smile. Yes, being a jerk does have its perks. "Where's the hotel?"

"Hattiesburg."

My body tingles with anticipation of what lies ahead in the capital of Mississippi, as the signs for Interstate 55 come into view. We make arrangements and I head north into the piney hills, nibbling on grapes from my stolen basket, a goofy smile on my face that won't let go.

CHAPTER SEVEN

I'm not even five minutes into the great state of Mississippi when Portia buzzes me.

"What?" I say into my cell phone a bit too harshly.

"Nice to hear from you, too, sister. When are you coming home?"

"I'm working Portia. What do you want?"

"We need to talk." Heavy sigh. "When are you going to be in town next?"

"If you need to talk to me Portia, there's this wonderful interstate that allows cars to travel west to Lafayette."

Another sigh. "I don't have time for this, Vi."

"Neither do I." I can't believe I'm this assertive. Usually I let my family walk all over me. My blood boils hot and it feels good — sort of.

"I won't give you money and now you're abandoning your family?"

I grit my teeth and count to three to try to cool the fire that's roaring up my chest. "I've been in Lafayette for two years and you just recently graced me with your presence for what, three hours? And for the record, dear sister, I was in town last weekend, remember?"

I hear Portia reprimand the kids in the background, yell something about having to be at work in ten minutes, then sigh again. For a moment, I wonder if something's happened. It's not like her to call me this often.

"Forget it, Vi. Just forget it."

"Fine."

"Fine."

We hang up and that nagging suspicion remains. I reach out to grab the phone again to call her back and inquire what's so important, but my new emotional friend urges me to keep driving, keep thinking about what makes *me* happy.

"Yeah," I say to no one. "It is just fine."

The cell phone rings again and I feel vindicated. I have finally stood up to my family and they are going to speak to me on my terms. But, when I answer, the voice is as meek as I usually act.

"Miss Valentine."

"Sirona?"

"Is this a good time?"

I can't help but laugh. "Not really. I'm on my way to Hattiesburg, Mississippi."

And a good romp in the hay if I'm lucky.

"I need your help." There's a desperation in her voice that hits me to the core. I've heard this emotion in the voices of people with haunted homes or buildings, a mix of fearing the unknown with a lack of control on how to fix it. Only today, I'm not in the mood to be the ghost problem solver.

"Perhaps Elijah hasn't told you but I've been fired."

"I've heard."

"Then why are we having this conversation?"

I swear I can hear the poor woman swallow. Hard. The sound brings my anger fire down a notch. "Because I don't know who else to turn to."

Her words emerge soft and painful, enough to make me re-examine my newfound emotional strength. I want to help, I really do. But Elijah kicked me out of town, Miss Bessie practically slammed the door in my face, and the woman asking for assistance is some mystical being I can't explain. Not to mention the sceptics at the Hi Ho and the state inspector jerk who's hiding something. I relay as much to Sirona, leaving out the part about her appearing in an old photograph.

"Elijah's a good man," she replies. "But he's under pressure and I think they got to him."

"Who got to him?"

There's a long pause and the silence gives me goosebumps.

"Did you look through the box he gave you?" Sirona finally asks, almost in a whisper.

"Most of it." Not enough, I think, and I feel guilty that TB perused the information more than I did.

"The state owns the springs and the dam, most of the lake. They can do what they want with all of it, although I don't blame *them* for what happened."

"What happened?"

Again, silence.

"Sirona, are you saying the state did something they shouldn't have and told Elijah to fire me and stop worrying about whatever is haunting Lorelei Lake? That doesn't make sense. Why would the state care if a small town hires a ghost hunter?"

More empty air.

"Hello?"

"Can we meet in person?" Sirona finally answers. "I'm not comfortable with this modern technology."

Now it's my turn to sigh. What's up with people wanting a piece of me today, on their terms? I must make money, to not worry about others and their ethereal pests, and I need to get laid.

"I'm on the road. And honestly, unless you're paying, I can't do this right now."

Obviously, I can't see her nod but I sense it. "I understand."

The anger once lifting me to enjoyable heights starts blowing out my pores and I deflate. And yet something urges me to stay the course. "Sirona, I'm broke. I have to get paid."

"It's always about money, isn't it?"

My old friend returns. Fast. Like a fuse starting at the base of my spine and racing up to the top of my head.

"Yeah, it *is* about money, especially for those of us who make millions because creative people are so valued in this society." Anger also brings out my other companion, sarcasm. "Or maybe it's because my family demands so much of me but won't give me a dime to help me get through the month."

I shouldn't be getting personal. This woman doesn't care

about my finances, but I'm so angry.

"I'm sorry," Sirona whispers. "I didn't mean you."

I inhale and let it out so hard I practically see stars. "What did you mean?"

"Just that. Call me if you want to talk further. I'll see if I can round up some funds."

Now I feel guilty. I'm not an ugly person, I'm really not. "I'm sorry, Sirona. Been a tough month."

"Yeah." The word emerges quiet and laced with pain and the goosebumps return. "I'll see what I can do."

In a beat, the mysterious woman disappears.

I throw the phone on the seat and scream to the heavens, try to justify why this is not my fault. Who are these people to make demands on me? I yell. Why must I take care of them when I could die at any moment if I have to slam on the brakes? And yet, I feel guilty. Which makes me angry all over again.

By the time I reach Hattiesburg the euphoria I felt this morning has evaporated and I'm in a foul mood. My angel wings have disappeared and I could be nicer to the woman checking me in at the front desk. I have trouble pulling my credit card out of the wallet sleeve — for "incidentals" that I won't be using — and I growl when the sleeve's plastic cuts the skin on my finger.

"Do you have to have this?" I say sucking on my finger to stem the blood. "My company paid online and I'm not going to buy a movie or raid the bar while I'm here."

"It's policy," she says, then gently takes my wallet and removes the card, hands the wallet back. I'm almost positive that move was against policy, but I'm thankful for the gesture. Southern people are like that, and Mississippi is about as Southern as you can get. We enter other people's bubbles all the time with hugs, slaps on the back, and other touchy-feely stuff. Folks up north — and corporate — would probably be horrified but I take note of her name and vow to include a positive assessment of Nettie B. McCarthy.

Until she begins her spiel, listing every aspect of the

Hattiesburg Courtyard Hotel, down to the great biscuits for breakfast and how to turn on the hot tub outside. Then, she asks if I've been to Hattiesburg and begins a long diatribe about the tourist attractions when I admit I've not graced the city limits. She hands me two brochures and a map and, just before I get aggravated, a customer waltzes in and I make my escape.

In the elevator, however, I look down at the tourist information and realize there's a gorgeous old theater, the Lauren Rogers Museum of Art, a historical museum and attractions at the University of Southern Mississippi. This could be good. I might be able to nab a travel story out of this trip.

My room offers a nice view of woods this time and appears to be in good shape. The A/C blows frigid air, which delights the sweat that accumulated on me from the short walk from the parking lot — yes, it's that hot and humid. I do my requisite tour, then plop on the bed, wondering where Eric might be. I never got his digits so I have no way of reaching him.

I check out the brochures again, consider a few places to hit in town, then a nice dinner with the money TB gave me, when I spot a waterpark among the attractions.

"Hell, yeah!"

My travel writer brain kicks in, admonishing me for not exploring downtown or choosing a museum, but I refuse to listen. Throwing my body down a water shoot is just what I need in the mood I'm in.

I pull on my bathing suit, — I refuse to look in the mirror — grab a towel and slip on flip flops and sunglasses, and plant barrettes in my curly hair that's turn wild with the humidity. As I open the door who should be standing in the hallway but the asshole of Biloxi.

"Pool time?"

I push the sunglasses down to get a better look at him. "How did you know I was here?"

He leans against the doorframe like a movie star and his

Polo shirt stretches across his chest. I could easily bypass the water park.

"I have inside knowledge, remember?"

"Jacob called you."

He smiles and that dimple appears. "Yeah, Jacob called. Wow, you're good."

I lean back on the opposite doorframe and grin smugly. "Yes, I am."

Again, I surprise myself, and both the revelation and the action feels good. Maybe I should be the asshole for a while.

"There's a waterpark in town. Wanna go?"

He straightens and frowns. "Water park? Not my scene. I was actually heading to the bar. If you want to join me and include a trip to the pool…it is part of your review, you know?"

There's a twinkle in that eye, which I interpret to mean "Join me and I'll offer lagniappe at the end of the day," so I open the door wider and let Eric in. I pull on jeans and a T-shirt over my bathing suit and grab my purse. Before we make it back to the door, he delivers a long and delicious kiss. Images of waterparks and tours of downtown for travel stories disappear.

We head to the pool, which unfortunately is loaded down with screaming kids and ignoring parents, so we choose the bar instead, load up on a couple of rum drinks, and nab a quieter corner on the patio by the hot tub. I take off the shirt and jeans and lounge in the sticky summer heat, enjoying the sun for a change, even if it's causing me to break out in droplets on every inch of my body. I don't care about being seen in a bathing suit, either. This letting-the-anger-flow thing has given me confidence.

"Funny how we happened to meet up again," Eric says, sipping his rum drink behind those dark sunglasses so I can't gauge his emotions.

"Did you arrange this?"

He shrugs. "Let's just say Jacob needed an angel — although not anytime soon — and I knew of one driving back to New Orleans who could easily detour this way."

I think to correct him that I live in Lafayette now but why bother? To the world Louisiana is New Orleans. I smile instead, one of those coquettish grins that says both thank you and let me show my appreciation later.

Eric leans over to show his gratitude now, and I'm tingling with anticipation of that kiss when three of the noisiest kids discover our oasis and plunge into the spa, squealing about the temperature.

"Yeah, it's hot," Eric admonishes them. "Now, get the hell outta here."

The youngest splits but the other two, both wearing cutoff jeans and T-shirts announcing some school fundraiser, send us defiant looks and start splashing. The water flies but misses us by an inch but my jeans and shirt lying at the end of my lounge chair are soaked. The kid with the funky haircut sends us a sly smile, proud of his actions, and I want to reach over and slap that grin away.

Eric sits up, primed for action, but thankfully Nettie arrives and tells the hoodlums that the spa is for adults only. They begin to argue so Eric stands and gives them both what I'd call the "daddy look."

"Did you hear what this lady said," he tells the boys, raising his voice to add, "Get the hell outta here."

The boys take off and I can see them relaying the information to their parents, who send us the evil eye. Nettie notices the interchange and appears nervous, rubs her hands on the front of her skirt. I sense she's embarrassed he came to her rescue, partly because he used foul language to customers.

"Thank you," she says shyly to Eric. "Usually the kids stay out of the hot tub."

"Doubtful. Sounds more like they run the place."

It's difficult to find anyone to police a hotel pool so my vote is for Nettie as all-around counter woman of the year, but I know Eric's doing his job. I remain quiet even though Nettie appears as if she's been slapped. I think to come to her defense to soften the blows of Eric the Asshole. Until she opens her mouth.

Nettie turns on the Southern charm, explaining in her adorable Mississippi accent how the work staff must take turns manning the pool and sometimes it falls to the desk staff, but she had a line of conventioneers coming through and just now saw the situation....

Eric holds up a hand. "Obviously, it's not working so maybe you need to...."

Nettie launches into another explanation, this one dealing with staff hours and how summertime they get locals wanting staycations so they check into the hotel for the use of the pool and tend to space out and let the kids go wild.

At this point, and in the mood that's been my ugly friend all day, I've had enough of listening to this sorority girl from Ole Miss chat on about her job. I say, and in a not-so-Southern-polite voice, "Okay, okay, we get the picture. Can you stop talking and just keep these brats away from us. Please?"

Nettie stops talking, thank you Jesus, and nods nervously and turns to leave, her head bowed all the way back to the counter and a few straggling conventioneers.

"Thank you, sweetheart. I thought that diatribe would never end."

I send Eric a smile but my heart plummets somewhere near my belly button. I'm not the asshole. What has gotten into me today?

Eric distracts me, however, leaning over and whispering in my ear, "Why don't we forgo the pool and enjoy these drinks upstairs."

Yes, I think, wild sex with this man is what I need, pour my frustrations and agitation in something resulting in pleasure, something that's been missing in my life for quite some time. I let him take my hand as he rises, forgetting that swim, my bitchy sister, and my clinging ex-husband back in Lafayette. Forget the creepy ghost town of central Louisiana where residents can't make up their minds if they need me or not.

As I pass Nettie at the counter, her countenance now one of an unsmiling busy person, she doesn't look up. I long to apologize, explain the bad month I've been having, explain how I received this gift of speaking to the dead but my daughter's not on the list, but I keep walking, following Eric up to Room 315 and another afternoon of carnal bliss.

The phone wakes me from a deep, rum-infused sleep and I slap the side table trying to shut it up. The phone goes flying, hits the wall and turns silent, which jolts me more awake than the alarm. I stumble out of bed, getting tangled in the sheets and hit the floor, my cheek skidding across the carpet. I turn on my back and howl a few expletives while feeling the floor to my left until it hits the dang phone. Before I gaze at my link to the outside world, I close my eyes and beg God, "Oh please, not the cell phone."

In my hangover state, feet still tangled in sheets on the bed about a foot higher than my head, my cheek burning from the carpet contact, I swear God is laughing his tootsie off. Either that or uttering, "Serves you right."

I flip it open to find the time staring me in the face, no harm done. I close my eyes again and thank God this time. Looking through the phone's history, I spot messages from TB, my aunt Mimi in Alabama, and Elijah, the last one making me wonder if Sirona had called him and pleaded my case. First things, first. I slide my butt closer to the bed and reach up to free my feet. I sit up, ready to face the day, when my head explodes and I want only to crawl back into those delicious sheets that only hotels can deliver.

Why did I drink so much for the second night in a row? I went to LSU, studied drinking, so I know not to mix alcohol and imbibe as much as I did. Eric and I had taken our rum drinks to the room and disposed of clothes and common thinking. Once that performance was out of the way, we donned bathrobes we found in the closet and called room service for another round of rum. When the staff appeared at our door, there was a bottle of cabernet, a cheese plate and a note from Nettie apologizing for both the kids in the pool and her actions.

Oh, and the two rum cocktails we ordered. All gratis.

"Told you being a jerk pays off," Eric said, reading the card. "Although this is one cheap ass bottle of wine."

We slurped the cocktails first and watched porn — which I absolutely despise but Eric thought it'd be funny, — then drank every last drop of that cheap ass bottle of cab during which we tangled our whole bodies in his sheets doing the nasty. And, of course, I stole away close to midnight because Eric likes to sleep alone.

"So, do I," I told him with a laugh, "hate to snuggle with drunk assholes," but something about his dismissal pinched a nerve. That and the fact that he had a dozen condoms in his suitcase.

I stand, knowing it's time to shower, dress and finish my review, but my head forces me back on the bed. I cradle my cranium in my hands and wonder when I got so stupid. Yes, I wanted sex with this man and the unabashed drinking was fun, but I took this job to pay bills and I should have toured the town for travel writing fodder. *Mais Yeah!* magazine will be calling soon for a travel idea and I have none.

I flip open the phone and realize I have two hours until checkout so I let out a groan that would have attracted a moose and head to the showers. Hangover or not, I have work to do.

I clean up fast, am even faster when it comes to packing. My sister writes dissertations faster than packing, sweating over every last piece of clothing, but I can throw things together in a heartbeat. I grin doing it now, rolling my clothes built for travel, many flimsy shirts that go well over black, a pair of jeans and a pair of shorts, my bathing suit I nabbed at Dillard's during their awesome sixty-five percent off sale and an extra pair of shoes. Add my ditty bag containing everything from emergency Band-Aids and a wine opener to those little shampoos and moisturizers I bring home from hotels. As I zip up my suitcase that still has room to spare, I mutter, "Take that, Portia."

I suddenly think of Carmine insisting I want my family's approval, but I push that thought away. I grab my notebook and head to breakfast, this time ten minutes before deadline and they're still serving those biscuits Nettie raved about. Since I'm an Angel, and need to remember that, I hang in the back of the restaurant inhaling my coffee and reading the local newspaper, while outside a summer thunderstorm shakes the building with its lightning and thunder display.

Nettie pops in, all smiles and bubbles, asking another staff member for more coffee and thanking her profusely when said woman fills her cup. She glances my way and the smile disappears. I wave, hoping that she might saunter over and I can apologize. Instead, Nettie frowns, turns to the staff woman, points out a dirty table and walks away. The sweet smile of the woman who waited on her disappears as well.

Stones in a pond, I think.

On days like today Lillye loved the thunderstorms, couldn't wait until the lightning died down so she could run outside and play in the puddles. I bought her these adorable plastic waders with Hello Kitty on the side. Of course, they were on sale, a size too large and a bit too big for her tiny feet. I felt guilty watching her play in those oversized waders that I skimped on which turned out to be her favorite shoes. But she didn't care. That's the beauty of children; they don't see the imperfections of the world. She would don those big boots and head out to the waterlogged yard and jump so hard in those puddles she would be covered in mud, including dirty inside those giant waders. And all the while she would laugh, arms outstretched to the world.

I take a sip of coffee and it lodges in my throat. I swallow hard but that gulp of coffee goes down hard.

"Watch, Mommy," I remember Lillye instructing me as she planted both feet into a puddle, then jumped backwards. "See the wavy lines?"

I explained how one stone in a pond would create waves

that traveled all the way to the edges of the water and Lillye watched fascinated. She gave up destroying the puddles, instead throwing pebbles into the water to watch the waves float away.

"It's all connected," she told me once, although I never knew what she meant. Staring into my coffee cup, watching how the thunder rocking the outside world creates waves in my caffeine, I know now.

I throw down a twenty, not worrying about my receipt for reimbursement, and I head to the lobby. Nettie's at the counter and she's not happy to see me. I reach over and take her hand like a Southerner because that's what we touchy-feely people do.

"I'm really sorry. I was tired, in a bad mood and it was so hot. I didn't mean to take it out on you."

Nettie's countenance shifts. Also, like a Southerner, she begins that female dance, saying things like "No worries" and "It's all good," but I insist I was being a brat and that I shouldn't have said what I said and please accept my apology. Finally, she acquiesces and we're now best friends. We both have moist eyes and if there wasn't a counter between us we'd hug. If only the world leaders would emulate Southern women.

Before she gets too comfortable and starts talking my ear off again, I ask to check out and excuse myself to visit the ladies room while she's doing the paperwork. Actually, I'm touring the rest of the downstairs, indeed checking out the bathroom but also the business center, the laundry, the meeting room, and the state of the pool area now empty of screaming kids due to the rain.

When I come back fifteen minutes later, Nettie doesn't inquire. We're women, and it's not unusual for us to linger in restrooms. I grab my bill and thank Nettie once more. She comes around the counter and gives me a hug. Now, *she's* apologizing. Southern women really are insufferable, but like I said, we should rule the world.

On the way to the car, my polka dot suitcase bopping

along behind me, I realize I never asked about Eric. He mentioned exchanging cell phone numbers for "business purposes" but I had balked. I didn't want TB looking through my messages and finding a strange man among them. A man I had wanton sex with on two occasions.

Besides, I'm not good with goodbyes. At least that's what I tell myself.

Once I drive around the hotel and make notes on landscaping, upkeep and the overflowing trash receptacles out back, I head to the interstate and back to my Lafayette potting shed. I thought about taking in a few Hattiesburg attractions, even had my bathing suit on the top of my suitcase in the off chance I visited that water park, but my head still aches, I need more caffeine, and I'm pooped from the lack of two night's sleep.

Before I hit the Louisiana border, TB rings.

"Hey," I answer.

"Where are you?"

I rub the bridge of my nose. "On my way back to Lafayette."

"I've been waiting for you since yesterday."

I should have told TB I detoured to Hattiesburg for another review, but why? I mean, we're not really married.

"I got another assignment. Why are you waiting for me?"

"I didn't know what to do with your cat."

"Stinky? He's not my cat. I just feed him."

"Then why is he living in your house?"

Stinky never spends more than a meal, a nap, sometimes an overnight with me. If TB had used the apartment, Stinky would have, no doubt, taken off for his daily adventures. I explain to TB as much but he insists the cat never left my apartment.

"He never went outside?"

"Never. I kinda liked it. We watched major league baseball together."

I start to say, "He's yours if you want him" but something stills my tongue. I'm getting attached to that cat, would be sad to see him go, but he's still not mine.

"He's the neighborhood cat," I tell TB. "I just feed him sometimes."

"Well, I got him a litter box and one of those water things that rejuvenates itself. Oh, and a few toys. He loves this feather thing on a string."

"No wonder he won't leave."

TB pauses, then whispers, "There's something weird about him."

I don't know why I have goosebumps running up my arms; we're discussing a stray cat. But TB's tone has given me the shivers.

"Why do you say that?" I ask.

TB laughs nervously. "It's nothing. Never mind."

I want to inquire more but I'm reminded of Sirona's phone call yesterday. "TB, did you look through that whole box of stuff from Fontus Springs?"

"Funny you should mention that."

The goosebumps return. "Why?"

"I had spread the pages out on the floor and was looking through them, trying to see if anything connected. All of a sudden, Stinky waltzes over and lands on this one particular document."

Now, I really shiver. Hard.

"Was it an old postcard?" TB pauses again and I know he's busy thinking. "Hello?"

"What? Postcard?"

I close my eyes and count to ten, shouldn't be aggravated with this man for all the help he's given me but conversations routinely take twice as long as they should. I remind myself my head hurts and I hate talking on the phone — years of working the newsroom — and patience is a virtue. Then, in an instant, I see a stone thrown in a pond.

"Lillye?"

This time, the pause on the other end is TB, no doubt worried about my sanity. "Vi? Are you okay?"

I shake off the premonition, but I'm reminded to be nice

to the man who fathered the best thing in my life, who's watching my cat and happily assisting with this investigation. To finally let go of this anger that's been gripping my heart of late.

But how do I explain my last outburst?

"I'm fine, was just thinking of something. Did the cat sit on a postcard?"

"Vi, I'm worried about you."

The sincere love coming through the phone nearly breaks my heart. TB's my best friend and yet I keep pushing him away, finding fault when there isn't any. I think back on the last two days and how heady running with the Asshole made me feel. I don't want to be angry, especially at TB, but I want to stay on top, not visit that dark place where the world insists I'll never see Lillye again.

"I'm fine," I say a bit too harshly, then soften. "Just tell me what the cat sat on."

"Fine." TB sighs. "It was a document about water quality."

You know those moments when the planets align and you can almost hear angels singing? This wasn't quite as good as that but close.

"What did it say?"

"Uh, let me go get it."

While I hear TB shuffling papers, my mind races. The state owns that property and the state tests the water. Could something similar to the accident of the 1930s have happened and someone's covering it up? Could it be why Elijah freaked on me? Of course, how this all connects to ghosts is beyond me, but my gut tells me the water quality leads to something important.

"Got it," TB announces when he's back on the line. "Looks like they did testing in early June after someone complained. The letter is to Elijah, and it pretty much says there is nothing wrong with the lake.

"But here's what's interesting," he continues. "This state document is attached to a copy of the letter Elijah wrote them on March 25. He mentions the guy who complained, a Frederick Hilderbrand. This guy apparently lives next to the springs and swears the water's tainted, in addition — and get this Vi — unusual things happening at night."

"Elijah's letter would have been a little past Easter, when people first started seeing the ghosts."

"Do you think it's related?"

I glance at my car's clock. It's 11:30 and I can make Baton Rouge in an hour or two.

"TB, are you busy?"

"I was waiting for you to arrive so I could head back home. My job here ended yesterday."

"Wanna meet me at the Louisiana Department of Water Quality?"

CHAPTER EIGHT

I pull into the parking lot of the Capital Complex in downtown Baton Rouge and find TB snoozing in his pickup, head tilted back, mouth wide open. I tap hard on the window which would rattle most people. TB slowly opens his eyes, leans forward and looks around as if in a fog. Which describes my ex-husband to a T.

When he spots me, he rolls down the window — his pickup's as old as my Toyota but it's mostly because TB thinks buying new cars is a waste of money — and studies me hard.

"What happened to your face?"

I touch my cheek, find that spot rough and sensitive where I was intimate with the hotel carpet.

"Does it look bad?" I ask TB, wondering how the hell I missed this.

"Looks like you've been slapped."

"Just God reminding me not to drink so much."

Shouldn't have admitted that.

"What?"

"Never mind. Are you ready?"

We head to the Louisiana Department of Water Quality, an austere building that's new to the Baton Rouge government scene but created to match the older, Huey P. Long-era buildings lying in the state capitol's shadow. The art deco lobby even contains a Works Progress Administration-inspired mural, like the ones designed by local artists in the 1930s after FDR initiated the program. Baton Rouge contains several original murals in the old government buildings and a few at LSU, some leaning toward the left with images many equated with socialistic ideas popular in the Great Depression. This one, however, screams tourism marketing with happy people visiting Jackson Square, a smiling child reaching for a bead at Mardi Gras, a yuppie white couple on a swamp tour. While TB admires the mural's landmarks from around the state, I greet the lobby receptionist. She sends us to the second floor where records are kept, and I jolt TB from the picture.

"Don't say anything," I instruct him. "Let me do the talking."

Even though the building's relatively new, the records department reeks of that mustiness you find in old libraries and archives. I approach the desk and pull out my wallet.

"I'm with the New Orleans Post," I say as I show the woman behind the desk my now expired press card. "I need to research water quality tests done after Katrina."

The woman glances at my card, but I slip it back into my wallet quickly so she doesn't get a good look.

"You need to sign in," she tells me, pushing a questionnaire in my direction. "Most of those records are on the computer. I'll show you where to look and set you up."

I fill out the questionnaire, wondering if I should make up a name and address. If this woman asks for my press card again, I'll be caught in the lie so I use my name and TB's New Orleans address. I don't know why I'm being paranoid but the fear in Sirona's voice has me wondering if something illegal has happened in Fontus Springs.

"You really need to know my car type and license number?" I ask the mousey woman. I mean, really, how much does the government need to know?

"It's a demographic thing. Plus, only Louisiana residents can access the records."

That's not true, but I let it go. I hand the information over and the woman studies my answers, which ratchets my paranoia up a notch. I search my brain for the public records act in regards to the media should I have to start making demands as a working journalist. Basically, governmental records are available for public use, so says the State Legislature, but there are some stipulations, such as giving them so many days to produce. There have been incidences where government agencies have not responded accordingly and media outlets have had to take them to court. I have no media outlet behind me, so I'm on my own here.

Marie — I now see the woman's name from her lanyard — leads us to a dark corner where there's two computers amidst boxes of documents. I'm used to doing research in caves like these, but TB glances around surprised, his eyes blinking to adjust to the darkness. Marie plugs in a password that I log into my brain and opens a search page.

"What's the parish you want to research?" she asks.

Again, I'm afraid to give out too much information so I blurt out Orleans and Saint Bernard parishes, since I'm supposed to be doing Katrina research. Marie brings up those sections, explains how to search the records and leaves us to it. TB plops into the chair next to mine.

"Why is it so dark in here?"

Because government doesn't like to make anything easy, I want to say. "It's because of the computers. They need to keep it cool in here for them, plus it's easier to see the screens." That much is true.

I lean across TB and bring his computer to life, then type in the password I saw Marie use. The home page appears and I type in Rapides Parish.

"Switch places with me."

Instead of rising, TB rolls his chair around to my computer and I do the same to his.

"Look up water quality tests for 2006 in Saint Bernard Parish," I tell him. "There should be plenty considering the entire parish flooded after the hurricane. Print out one or two for a cover. I'll be looking up Fontus Springs over here."

Bless his heart, he gets it. Even looks happy to be performing this covert research.

"This is exciting," he says as he starts perusing web pages, and I almost want to kiss him.

Almost.

I plug in March 2008 into my computer to see if anything unusual happened after Easter, which was March 23, but nothing comes up. I try April, May and June, but again nothing. When I search July, the form that TB found thanks to Stinky emerges on the screen, repeating the same water quality results.

I lean back in my chair. "Nothing. Just the same form that was in the box." TB says nothing so I assume he hasn't heard me. "There's nothing here."

TB turns his monitor so I can see what's on his screen. It's a page marked "Private" and the header is Rapides Parish, underneath which is Bayou State Transport Co. and a listing of tests and dates. I instantly spot April 4, 2008.

"How did you find that?"

TB grins confidently. "I did a search, figured they must have had some private companies paying them to test the water as well. Although I'm surprised that this hasn't gone public."

Those stubborn goosebumps return. "Why?"

He clicks on the link and pages of technical terms greet us, most of which I can't understand. But at the bottom are numbers and chemical names and it all becomes clear.

"Print this out," I tell TB. "Quick before Marie comes back."

He does as he's told and sure enough, as if us mentioning her name has attracted her back to our dark enclave, Marie appears. I've managed to get out of my research and pull the sheets from the printer, the last page appearing into my greedy hands before Marie has reached us, but I'm worried TB still has that page up on his computer. I look over nervously and find Solitaire on his screen.

"Y'all need assistance?"

"We were just finishing up," I tell Marie, sliding the sheets into my folder. "Thank you so much. Found exactly what I needed."

She frowns glancing at TB. "Looks like he found something else."

I shrug. "Can't take him anywhere."

Before the conversation can continue, I grab TB by the sleeve and pull him up.

"Darn," he says, sending Marie a seductive smile, "almost got that one."

We head toward the door, Marie following behind, a goofy smile on her face. TB, with his boyish good looks, does that to people.

"Thanks for everything," I say over my shoulder.

I saunter out of the office and toward the elevator as confidently as I can muster, TB and I not saying a word. I can feel his grin at my side at our expertise in rooting out evil and I smile as well. Without even thinking, I reach down and take his hand and he squeezes mine when I do.

"We make a good team," he whispers.

I think back on the last two days and that rush I felt being naughty with Eric. But this feels good too, like spring sunshine on your face after months of cold. Remembering Eric, however, makes me pull my hand away and my smile disappears. TB glances down at me but I refuse to look his way.

Just then the elevator door opens and who should emerge but Matt Wilson, the jerk from the Hi Ho. My heart races but he doesn't appear to recognize me. TB and I slip past him and enter the elevator, TB pushing the lobby button.

"Want to grab something to eat, Vi?"

I say nothing, praying that the elevator doors will shut soon, but it's one of those elevators that takes its dang sweet time. Just as the doors slowly close, a hand jolts in between to stop them.

"Viola Valentine?" Matt says when the doors open again. "The ghost hunter?"

He says it with the same snide way he greeted me in Fontus Springs. I want so badly to slap that grin off his face, but say instead with an inquisitive frown, "Matt something or another?"

He gets straight to the point. "What are you doing here?"

"Oh, right. You work here. What is it you do again? Clerk?"

He's not buying it but I have what I need so screw him.

He starts to say something, but TB pushes the lobby button again. "Sorry, we have a meeting to get to." And with my ex-husband's last comment, the doors close and Matt's frown disappears.

I let out a deep exhale.

"What was that about?" TB asks.

"I'll tell you over dinner."

We quietly exit the building and don't say a word as we head down Third Street, turn on to Florida Boulevard and enter Poor Boy Lloyd's, a restaurant that's popular with locals although I never eat a poboy outside of New Orleans. Call me a snob, but the bread's not the same. It's slightly after three, when the establishment closes, but several of the entrees and sides are still out so we convince the woman behind the counter to serve us. We take our plates and iced tea to a quiet corner — hell, no one's here — and now both of us are exhaling loudly.

"Who was that guy?" TB finally asks.

"I met him in Fontus Springs. He's with the department and he came to our meeting to explain how there's nothing wrong with the water."

TB digs into his crawfish étouffée, the dish I wouldn't touch because Louisiana crawfish are out of season now and no imported Chinese crawfish will touch these lips — yes, I'm a food snob. Instead, I enjoy the eggplant Parmesan which is quite tasty despite being under a heating lamp for hours.

"Man, I didn't realize how hungry I was. Didn't have much for breakfast."

TB studies me and I feel naked under his gaze. "Hungover?"

I avert my eyes but I'm pretty sure he's on to me. Instead, I change the subject. "Matt insisted the water quality was fine, talked about the study they did, and acted like everyone was crazy for seeing ghosts. Even said it was a bunch of hysterical women doing the seeing."

"Is it only women that see these ghosts?"

Now that I think about it, there were few men in town spotting wisps of the departed, but again, that could mean that women are more sensitive to the paranormal or men are refusing to admit as much. There was that young worker at the auto repair shop and a one Frederick Hilderbrand. I pull the sheets out of my folder and study the results. There's no mention of Hilderbrand, but the test date is ten days past Easter, right after the time he would have complained.

"This is a test conducted privately for Bayou State Transport on April 4 of this year and the reason, it says, is because of 'unusual smells' coming from the lake. They mention two people complaining, and I'm assuming one of them is Hilderbrand."

"Why a transport company?" TB asks.

"They might lease the property from the state and use the land to store materials. Miss Bessie mentioned something about oil when I visited her."

Thinking of my elderly friend with enough gusto to run her own oil company, I'm thinking she might have been the second complainer.

TB leans across the table to study the report. "The numbers aren't good, are they?"

I get to the last page and spot technical terms I will Google later, but I know that the water quality is suffering. There's mention of chemicals such as benzene, toluene, ethylbenzene and xylenes. Benzene I know is a carcinogen. Bioremediation, dispersants, and in some cases burns are required, the report says, to solve these "contaminant issues," and water berms should be placed on the lake outside of the springs area to "contain contaminant area."

"Wow," TB says. "What do you think caused all this?"

I scan the document to find the culprit but there are pages and pages of this report. "I don't know. Could be oil, gas or any type of chemical made in Louisiana. I'll have to read this thoroughly when I get home and see."

"Better yet," TB adds, "the big question is why did this

spill or whatever it was cause ghosts to appear?"

I smirk. "If it's not all about hysterical women, of course."

TB places his fork down and stares out the window to the Mississippi River rolling by. He's unusually quiet.

"What is it?"

He looks back at me. "Do know that there are legends behind Fontus Springs and Lorelei Lake?"

I shrug, thinking again I should have read more of the box's information. "Every place has a legend."

TB crosses his hands as he leans his elbows on the table. "Not like this."

Now, I'm leaning forward. "Like what?" I whisper.

TB glances around the room but again, no one's here except for the server and a chef cleaning up in the kitchen. "Fontus in Roman religion was a god of the springs. They used to honor him in October with a festival and put garlands on the town's fountains and wellheads. It all hails back, I think, to something called the Mith-rayovac mysteries."

"Mithraic mysteries," I correct him.

"Yeah, whatever. Anyway, there's this scene where Fontus, or whatever they called him, struck a rock and water came pouring out. Water was a big thing to those people. Meant regeneration, not to mention that wells and springs were necessary for life."

My husband's ink-brown eyes light up as he's talking and it reminds me of how good-looking he is, an innocent nicely-formed face beneath beautiful blond locks. He really is a cutie, would be perfect as the star of a Lifetime movie, the kind set out west where some cowboy has a baby but doesn't know it until he moseys back to town and reunites with the heroine, pushing up his ten-gallon hat as he glances seductively down on her from his horse.

I shake my head of the image but for a moment, it's like old times. We're enjoying a meal, laughing or discussing some interesting subject while playing footsies under the table, arranging a love date later with our eyes. Lillye would watch us from her high chair and smile.

"Did you hear me?" TB asks.

Did I mention I'm also ADHD as hell?

I clear my throat. "Yes, Fontus. God of the spring."

"There's more. He was the son of Jacob, I believe."

"Janus. And the festival was called Fontinalia." TB turns his head like a puppy, so I come clean. "I read through some of the box. Plus, I love mythology."

"Then you know about the naiads."

The goosebumps return and I shiver. "There was something about naiads in that box?"

TB resumes eating but nods, then utters between bites, "Elijah must have researched them because his writing was all over it."

Naiads go back further, to Greek mythology, a female nymph if you will who loves water. I studied them in fourth grade for a play, was fascinated. I used to wish one would appear every time we visited Lake Pontchartrain in New Orleans, envisioning her a Carnival Queen with Mardi Gras beads around her neck and a tiara in her hair, rising from the waters to invite me to join her in her adventures under the sea.

I shake my head again. I had such an imagination as a child. Then again, back when I was young I also talked to the dead until social and family pressure made me force them away.

"What did Elijah's research say?" I ask to get back on track.

"The naiads are spirits, minor but beautiful goddesses that inhabit springs and other bodies of fresh water. Pegaiai were the type that preferred springs but I have no idea how to pronounce that. They also were protectors of girls, making sure they were safe into adulthood."

Now, it's my turn to study the Mississippi moving like a mighty ship toward the Gulf of Mexico. Would the Mississippi have naiads? It's a body of fresh water. But, would beautiful goddesses hang out in such a polluted river moving ships and agriculture runoff toward the ever-growing dead zone of the Gulf.

"Vi?"

I'm veering again, think about a goddess living among that beaver on top of the Hi Ho and those crazy signs on the side of the road, saying "Hey, y'all" as people enter the bait shop.

"So, saying there are naiads in the world, would they hang out in Lorelei Lake?"

I'm smiling as I say this, but TB stops eating and gazes at me with a puzzled expression. "Say what?"

"These are *Greek* goddesses, right?"

"Yeah, but if they live in Greece, they might as well as live here."

The hunky cowboy scene disappears and I'm back to thinking my husband is clueless. "TB, there's no such thing as a naiad."

TB, on the other hand, is sober as a priest on Sunday morning. "There's no such thing as ghosts, either."

Touché, I think, but I offer a patronizing smile as he mops up his lunch with French bread, finishing it off with one bite that's followed by the rest of his tea. The server who was kind enough to let us in is now at our side, anxious to remove our plates and be done with us.

TB throws a twenty and a ten on to the table. "Does that cover it?"

"Yes, thanks," the server says, suddenly becoming more hospitable. "Can I get you anything else? Dessert? Teas to go."

I'm about to politely decline when TB smiles his boyish grin, leans back in his chair. "Why that would be really sweet of you."

The girl blushes and heads off to the counter.

"Aren't you mister charming."

TB shrugs. "I'm just a nice guy being nice." He picks up my hand, rubs his thumb along the inside of my palm. "I wish you would appreciate me."

"I do appreciate you. Very much."

I'm just not in love with you.

We gather our servings of bread pudding and iced tea within Styrofoam containers — God, I hate those, see them bopping all over Louisiana's wetlands — and head back to the cars. We reach TB's pickup first and I hand him his share of the bounty. He stares at the containers in his hands, then looks at me with a painful gaze. I brace myself, waiting for his endless declaration of love, something I'm not able to return.

"Vi," TB finally says, "who were you drinking with last night?"

This is not what I'm expecting and I find myself speechless. I never thought TB would catch on and question me so I don't have a proper lie to volley back. I bite my lower lip and look down at my sandals.

"Just someone I met at the hotel. A colleague."

TB sighs and looks heavenward, that painful look still glistening in his eyes. "You must think I'm an idiot."

Again, this takes me aback. "Not at all. Why do you say that?"

He looks at me then, a sad smile playing. "I know when you're hiding something. You slept with him, didn't you?"

"I've never lied to you, TB. I've never been unfaithful." I add, "When we were together."

"But, you are now."

I bite my lip again and watch a mother and her daughter cross the street. "Why do you say that?"

"Because you never look me in the eye when you're not being truthful."

I look back and realize he's right. I'm avoiding his eyes because I don't want to witness his pain. I know my husband still loves me but it's not going to happen so how do I explain Eric and watch his reaction?

"And you always bite your lip."

Half of my lip is inside my mouth, so I let it go and exhale. "He doesn't mean anything. Just a guy I met who works with me."

TB turns and places the container on the hood of his car, then pulls his keys from his pants pocket. He doesn't look back.

"It's okay Vi."

I can't stand leaving things this way, can't bear the pain emerging through his voice. I grab his shoulder and urge him to turn but he opens the door and slides inside.

"You forgot your food." I pull the items from the hood and hand them to him one at a time. Just before he closes the door, I pull a Matt Wilson and stick my hand in between. "Please don't leave like this."

He doesn't say anything, just gives me a defeated look, so I let him close the door. He starts the engine, but pauses, hands planted on the wheel as he gazes off toward the tall state capitol that Huey Long built. Finally, he rolls down the window, extending an arm.

"Let me know what happens with the case. I'm curious how this all turns out."

I touch his elbow. "Honestly, it meant nothing."

"Good-bye Vi."

And with those final words, my ex-husband who's been nothing but awesome to me from the moment we met in world history class at LSU drives off into the night, heading to the interstate and our former home in New Orleans. I watch his pickup head down North Street until the brake lights are no longer visible, feeling as low as a snake's belly in a wagon's rut.

I pull out my own keys and look for my Toyota, half a block away. Just before I reach it, I'm approached by a capital policeman.

"Is that your Corolla?"

He's looking at my car so I assume he's talking to me.

"Yeah, that's it."

"I hope you're not going far. Someone busted your window."

The sidewalk side of my car looks fine so I walk around to the driver's side window and find it shattered with tiny pieces of glass all over my front seat.

"What happened?" I ask the cop.

"I don't know, I wasn't on duty then. But one of the people in the coffee shop over there said she thought someone drove by and threw a rock at it."

I open the door and search the seat but there's only glass about. The sun's still on the horizon but the nearby building has cast a dark shadow on my car's interior. I reach my left hand down to the floor and pat the floorboards and sure enough, there's an object large and hard enough to do the damage. I curl my fingers around the coarse object, straighten and show the policeman what I've found.

"Wow, do you have any enemies?"

I start to dispute, imagine this incident as a random crime, when Matt Wilson's face comes to mind. That and the fact that I'm holding an old water meter in my hands.

CHAPTER NINE

My window replacement I was assured would be forty-five minutes at best has turned into a long morning and my anger buddy has returned full force. Not only is the money I made reviewing three hotels going to Boudreaux's Auto Shop but the man in charge speaks to me like a child. I'm standing at the counter to inquire once again how long this will take now that noon is approaching but Boudreaux won't glance my way. He's busy filling out a form and for the life of me I'm stumped why people don't get how one little "I'll be right with you" will calm me faster than a shot of bourbon. He doesn't look up and my chest gets tighter and tighter and I'm ready to reach through this window and stab Boudreaux with the pen he's using.

Finally, I've had enough.

"Am I invisible or do you just like treating women this horribly?"

Boudreaux looks at me — finally — and acts like I'm crazy. "Excuse me?"

"I'm standing here at this counter and you can't give me the time of day?"

I hear my voice rising but I don't care. I think back on what Eric taught me, that only the squeaking wheel gets the grease, although as a writer I really hate clichés.

Boudreaux looks back at his paper. "I'm working on a client's car at the moment."

I'm not going down with this. No sir.

"And I'm a client who you said would have a car within an hour. Again, am I invisible? Because if I am, or that form is more important than my business, I am happy to bring my service elsewhere."

A woman behind me applauds and says, "You tell him sister," and Boudreaux becomes almost flustered. Almost. He sighs and puts down the clipboard.

"What is your name again?"

This sends me over the edge. I can feel myself falling into the abyss like Thelma and Louise.

"Just give me the keys," I say, holding out my hand. "I'm done with this horrible customer service and I'm done waiting. Oh, and I'm a local journalist so you can best believe I'll be spreading this around."

This spurs Boudreaux into action. He opens the door and walks into the lobby, looking me in the eye this time.

"I'm sorry. We've been very busy this morning. Give me your name and I'll check on it ASAP."

I shake my head incredulously. "How do you not know my name? I've been here for hours, constantly asking about my Toyota."

His eyes light up and there's a semblance of a kind smile emerging. "The broken window. It's being worked on right now."

"I've heard that numerous times already, been here since daybreak."

He holds his hands up to placate me — that or he's afraid I'm going to hit him. "I had to order the window from the dealership and it took a while to get here."

"More like you guys took your time retrieving it from the dealership."

Again, I've derailed the man, placing me on top of the situation. Damn, this feels good.

He sighs, knowing he's defeated. "I'll go check on the progress. How about we knock off fifty dollars for the inconvenience."

I narrow my eyes and think why not keep going? "I think a hundred might do it."

Boudreaux says nothing but nods, then hurries off to the garage.

"Wow, that was impressive," the lobby woman with the Metallica T-shirt says.

If I was in my right mind, I might take a bow. I'm thrilled that I got my way, made this jerk notice me and correct a situation where I, the customer, was right. I mean, when does that ever happen? But as the anger slips away and my adrenaline balances out, I feel sick. Is this who I really am?

No, I command myself, I'm not backing down, not returning to easy-going Vi who takes what people hand out.

"Hell yeah!" I tell the woman, who smiles and goes back to watching Donald Trump being his own jerk on *The Apprentice*.

I exhale way too loudly and plop into the hard plastic chair that's attached to the wall as if we might steal it away. As if. I'm incredibly tired, didn't sleep much the night before and hauled myself over here first thing in the morning because I was told to by the person answering the phone. Little good it did since even though I was first in the door, other people have come and gone since. Maybe it wasn't their fault. Maybe they really had to wait on the dealership and I'm just too damn tired.

It was a long drive home from Baton Rouge the night before. By the time I reached Lafayette I was royally pissed. My face suffered wind burns from driving the interstate without a window, even though I puttered along at the minimum speed of forty miles per hour, which turned a forty-five-minute drive into two excruciating hours. My carpet burn turned raw from the experience, making it hurt to cuss, which I did anyway. And I swore I swallowed a large bug crossing the Atchafalaya Basin swamp.

Once I reached home I grabbed my bag from the car and stumbled into my potting shed, throwing everything on to the floor in disgust and thinking of nothing but a hot shower. Then I remembered the pool.

I'm not supposed to use the pool unless Reece is staying at the house across town he shares with his wife and two kids. He never asked me to abstain from swimming when he was separated but now that the kids and wifey visit our property on numerous occasions, I'm assuming the potting shed girlfriend should remain off limits.

"I'm not his girlfriend," I muttered on my way to the pool,

catching Reece and family through the main house's bay windows. They were enjoying a meal together in the back gallery, the only room he managed to finish before getting back with his wife. The four of them glow in the moonlight, all smiles and perfection, and I tried to grit my teeth but the wind burn winched and I followed up with a few expletives.

I started entering the pool slowly, quietly walking down the steps, but the water felt so amazing and my body ached from leaning two hours to avoid the interstate wind. Besides, who cares if the Cormier family hears me, I thought, so I dove in and starting swimming, letting the sound of my splashes echo throughout the yard.

My frustration and anger spent, I let myself sink to the bottom of the pool and looked up at the yard lights filtering through. The cool water enveloped me like a mother and for a moment all anger dissipated and a sense of calm invaded my soul. I had forgotten how peaceful and spiritual water could be when the world goes away.

Until Reece showed his head.

I grunted, and bubbles came flying out my mouth as I headed to the surface. My landlord had interrupted my solace and my anger returned.

"I know, I shouldn't be here," I said too harshly when I hit the surface.

He looked taken aback. "I wasn't here to tell you to get out of the pool."

I headed toward the steps, trying to absorb the feel of the water one last time. "But you want me to leave before your family spots me."

"Vi, I'm not here to…."

"No worries, Reece. I'm gone."

I left the pool's comfort and grabbed my towel. He took my arm, halting my drying progress.

"Vi, I just came out to say hello."

Thinking back on it now, I don't know why I doubted him. I pulled away, mumbling something about interrupting his family time.

"I came out here to invite you to join us," he said, looking injured. "We picked up some boiled shrimp and have more than enough."

I gazed at the happy family gathered around the table and did something I would never do otherwise. I declined impolitely. My Deep South grandmother must have been turning in her grave.

"Thanks, but no thanks," I said with a harsh tone, and I wince now thinking how rude I had been.

The cell phone saves me from complete self-degradation. I look down and see it's my Aunt Mimi, who called yesterday and I forgot to call back. The guilt returns.

"Hey Aunt Mimi."

"Hey darling." Her Alabama accent rolls off sweet and cheerful, even though she's now running an assisted living facility in Branson.

Growing up in New Orleans no one in my family had the drawl. New Orleans accents — not the kind you hear in those ridiculous Hollywood movies — lean more toward Brooklyn but slower and with lots of y'alls. Most people never believe me when I explain this but it's true. One theory is that both New Orleans and New York had huge groups of Sicilians immigrating in the first half of the twentieth century.

My mother studied Shakespeare at the finest schools, first UCLA, then Yale, and a Ph.D. from Oxford, so whatever Southern accent she may have had as a youth, she conquered early on. Now, she sounds almost English. Mimi's also Bohemian while my mother requires suits, high heels, and briefcases.

Oh, and Mimi's psychic. Apparently, it runs in the family. According to my aunt, my grandmother was quite the Bama soothsayer. I inherited my share of this DNA, one reason I'm now a SCANC.

"Mimi, I'm sorry I haven't called back. I was on the road and I had a mishap with my car's window."

"Oh no, honey, is everything alright?"

I look over toward the garage and see a man in overalls

wiping my new window clean. "It will be."

"I'm calling about your mom."

That nagging feeling I had when Portia called the day before returns. "Why?"

"It's nothing, I'm sure. She hasn't been returning my calls."

My mother loves talking on the phone so this worries me. "Have you talked to Portia?"

"Yes, and she said your mother is fine but that I should come visit soon."

"That's so like Portia. The woman must have everyone come to her."

Mimi pauses and I wonder if that tone that's been leaking out my mouth lately has made an appearance.

"Portia asking me to come visit has me worried, nonetheless. I'm thinking something's up with Deliah."

Anger and guilt. It's a constant waltz with me these days. "Yeah, maybe so."

"Portia invited me over for the Fourth of July weekend so I'll check in on her. And that way I get to see you, too."

"That would be awesome, Mimi."

Another pause. "Are you okay, sweetpea?"

Question of the new century. I got asked that a lot when Lillye died, then after Katrina when I lost nearly everything. And you know I'm not exaggerating. Lake Pontchartrain waters filled our house and remained standing until officials fixed levee holes and pumped that stagnant mess out so even if some things were salvageable, I wanted none of it.

The death of a child and the nation's worst natural disaster. I used to laugh when people asked me how I was. I mean, really?

"I'm fine," I lie. As always.

Mimi isn't buying it. As always.

"We're going to talk when I get to town, okay?"

The concern in her voice, so loving and sweet, brings emotions racing to the surface. I'm ready to bawl uncontrollably right there in the lobby but Metallica Woman is watching and Boudreaux emerges with my car keys. I have a reputation to uphold.

I swallow hard, assure Mimi I'll be there with bells on and silently retrieve my keys and pay my bill while Boudreaux grunts swiping my debit card. By the time I get in the car and roll up my new window, the tears fall. I gaze heavenward and wonder who the hell I am anymore.

Thankfully, the cell phone rings and breaks my pity fest.

"Isn't this a surprise," I say to Elijah.

"Uh, hi, Ms. Valentine."

I wonder if Sirona intervened, but then I'm reminded of my espionage the day before.

"Did Matt the Brat call you?"

"I'm sorry?"

"Matt Wilson, the man with a strong pitching arm."

Silence follows and I'm wondering what Elijah's motives are. Will he avoid the subject which might show guilt on Matt's part or warn me about investigating further?

"Can we meet?"

This isn't what I'm expecting, but now that I have blown my hotel review money on a car window, I'm not eager to keep meeting with folks who aren't paying my bills. "You fired me, remember?"

"I know, Ms. Valentine, and I'm sorry about that. I can explain."

I let out a long sigh. Suddenly, I'm so very tired.

"Elijah, I couldn't help myself yesterday, got wind of something and because I'm a journalist with an insatiable curiosity, I just had to know. But it got me a broken car window, something I can't afford right now, so I'm done. This weird thing going on in your town and the fact that the state is polluting your water is your business from now on." Then, with an afterthought, because I really am curious, I add, "...unless you want to start paying me again."

"Ms. Valentine, do you know the Diamond Grill in downtown Alexandria?"

"Yes."

This isn't what I'm expecting but I agree. The landmark jewelry store in the central Louisiana town has been renovated and turned into a fine dining restaurant and I've been dying to see it.

"Can you meet me there in an hour and a half?"

Elijah's whispering now so my curiosity doubles. I shouldn't agree — considering — but I can't help myself. Plus, I'm starving.

"Fine, but you pay."

"Of course."

"And I'm ordering wine with dinner and two desserts to follow."

I can sense him smiling. "Anything you want."

"Now I know you're crazy."

I believe the smile remains but I hear him exhale a heavy sigh. "More than you know."

We quickly wrap things up and I head toward Interstate 49 for the trip to Alexandria, this time thankfully without the wind in my hair. It's too early for NPR's *All Things Considered* and the radio stations are playing the same five pop songs so I give TB a call. He doesn't pick up so I know he's still mad at me, but I leave a message.

"Hey." I've such a way with words, but he's hurt and I honestly don't know what to say. "I have something to tell you." Oh lord, now he's going to think there's more to the affair which really wasn't an affair considering. "I mean, something happened after you left Baton Rouge."

I stare at the eighteen-wheeler in front of me, wondering once again why men put outlines of big-busted women on their tire flaps. It's up there with those deer head decals that if you look at them funny resemble people dancing.

I shake my ADHD head and command myself to focus.

"Someone broke my car window last night. I found the top of a water meter inside the car so you can guess who. Anyway, Elijah just called me and wants to meet in Alexandria so I'm on my way there. If you don't hear from me in a week, call the FBI."

I'm trying to be funny, but I must admit, I'm a bit scared. Maybe it's a trap and I'll emerge from this meeting with a broken kneecap. I wish TB was here.

"I'm really sorry about last night," I continue and those damn tears return. "And I swear TB, that guy meant nothing to me. I was lonely, he was around, there was liquor involved...."

Those stupid women on the tire flaps begin to blur so I wipe my hand across my eyes. "Anyway, call me."

Screw my composure, I think, and allow myself a good long cry until Bunkie, where I force myself to man up. That's another thing I've never understood. Manhood has degrees? You can see why I'm a journalist, my brain never stops inquiring.

By the time I reach the Diamond Grill in downtown Alexandria, my emotions are in check. It's one-thirty and the place is deserted, all except for Elijah looking forlorn in a dark back corner. He waves and I head his way, but not without taking in the elegant art nouveau/art deco architecture that stretches up two stories to the ceiling. The building used to house C.A. Schnack's Jewelry Store, which moved to the spot in 1931. Straight ahead a curving staircase leads to a balcony where I spot an equally elegant bar. A grand piano sits to the rear of the dining room and a man dressed in a nice suit and tie plays *Memory* from *Cats* and he sends me a wink as I walk past.

"Little good that'll do ya," I think, wondering if he's aiming for a tip.

I reach Elijah's table and check to see if there's a quick getaway in sight. Then I choose the chair on the side where I have a good view of the restaurant and no one can sneak up behind me, a trick journalists share with mobsters.

Elijah rises and pulls out my chair, the perfect gentleman. "Thank you for coming."

I throw my purse in the opposite seat, pulling my napkin into my lap as I sit down. "You may have second thoughts when you see the bill."

Elijah grins but he's avoiding my gaze. "I'm really sorry about what happened."

I place both elbows on the table and look at him sternly. "Just what did happen?"

Elijah glances around the restaurant but there's only Mr. Mistoffelees at the piano. He leans in close and looks at me for the first time. "It's a long story, which is why I asked you here."

Those damn goosebumps are crawling up my spine and I shake them off before they reach my neck. "How about you start at the beginning, then."

The waitress arrives and Elijah wastes no time ordering. There are two lunch specials today and both sound enticing so he orders one of each with a stuffed mushroom appetizer, then asks for a wine list.

"I was kidding about the wine," I quickly say, before the waitress leaves us. "Unsweetened iced tea for me."

We say nothing until the waitress is out of earshot and Piano Man starts a medley from *West Side Story*. Elijah's avoiding my eyes again. "Is it true someone threw something through your car window?"

"More like a water meter found its way in."

Elijah exhales and takes a long drink from his glass. "I take it you know why."

He nods. "Matt called me this morning, although he left out the part about the window. It's all my fault. I shouldn't have gotten you involved in this but Sirona insisted we bring in help."

"Involved in what exactly?"

Elijah finally makes himself comfortable but he keeps his voice low. "As you might remember, Fontus Springs is surrounded by piney woods and rolling hills. It's not good for farming so until trains were brought to central Louisiana and people started logging, hardly anyone lived there."

He takes another long drink of his water. I want to interrupt and tell him that I read his box of information, but I want to hear him explain. "All but a family of Germans," he continues. "And with them came the legend."

I sit up and lean forward. "What legend?"

"Along the Rhine River in Germany people used to hear a woman singing. The story goes that a woman named Lorelie who was jilted by her lover threw herself in the river in despair and now she haunts the place, singing on the rocks or something to that effect. Lots of people have written about this siren, including composers Franz Liszt and Shostakovich."

"So, let me guess," I interject. "These Germans who stumbled upon Lorelie Lake in Louisiana think a siren lives there?"

Elijah takes another long sip and I notice his glass is empty. The waitress is suddenly at our table refilling our glasses and an assistant arrives with the mushrooms.

"Those entrees will be up soon," she says as I instantly dig into the stuffed fungi. "Would you all like some bread?"

I agree at the same time Elijah declines. We laugh, then he instructs the waitress to bring some.

"Sorry, been a long time since breakfast," I say. "Now, what were you saying?"

The interruption helps Elijah get back on track. He resumes the story with more confidence.

"The lake murmurs, like in the stories, so the Germans thought the name appropriate. They also named Fontus Springs after the Greek god of wells."

"Yeah, I heard that one."

"And you probably also know, since you're a travel writer, that Germans love springs. They're all over that part of Europe. So, the Hilderbrand family that settled at Lorelie Lake took really good care of Fontus."

I pause in my mushroom devouring. "Wait, is this the same family as Frederick Hilderbrand, the man who complained about the smell?"

Elijah nods as Judy — it's on her name tag — delivers bread and three types of whipped butter. Hallelujah! I dive in, but keep inquiring. "Does Fred still own the property and lease it to the state?"

That freaky look returns to Elijah's face and he checks out the restaurant once more, then leans in close.

"The Hilderbrands didn't have children, so it ended up being sold at auction to a businessman from Alexandria who took interest in the springs as a tourist attraction. There was a Hilderbrand brother who was supposedly on the deed but he was working laying rails out west at the time so the property was sold without his consent and approval. One reason why Old Man Frederick hates state government so much. He's tried time and again to prove ownership, has a copy of the deed with his grandfather's name on it, but the case never goes anywhere. If you want to get an earful, ask him about lawyers."

"What happened between the Alexandria businessman and the state taking over?"

The entrees arrive, so we both lean back and decide that I want the catfish and Elijah prefers the meatballs and spaghetti. Judy refills our glasses and tries to strike up small-talk conversation but I'm ready to get back to the details.

After she leaves, Elijah continues, while I almost inhale the fish. I think to apologize for my un-ladylike actions — Southern women were brought up to be dainty, don't you know — but I'm not that girl these days. Now that I think about it, why should I be?

"The guy who bought the springs, Jessie Parker, was a good man and his heart was in the right place," Elijah says. "He constructed the hotel, restaurant and pumped the spring water into a pool. People came and it brought business to the area, which I suppose was a good thing."

"Suppose?" I mumble between bites.

"A lot of development happened in those early days, some good, some not so good."

I let Elijah take a bite while I ponder this information. I had read in Elijah's box of information that the springs were a hit in the 1920s but fell into neglect by the Great Depression. I think back on my visit to the Branfords and

Margie saying something about a tortured woman waking her up the Monday after Easter.

"The man who owned the springs...."

"Jessie Parker, the Alexandria businessman...."

"He had a heart attack one night and some slimy cousin named Brock Parker took over the property," Elijah continues. "The springs then turned into a speakeasy of sorts. Bootlegging, prostitution. Some people said the mob used it as a hideout when the Feds got too close. Then, when the Depression hit, things got really bad. Desperate people will do anything for a buck and they usually did in Fontus. And Brock got rich."

"Your grandma said something about the lake disappearing one night."

Elijah's fork is halfway to his mouth, but he stops mid-air. "She told you that?"

I nod, then Elijah places his fork down and does a scan of the restaurant one more time. Piano Man is gone and the staff appears hunkered down in the kitchen.

"Brock leased part of the land to an oil company that came in and started drilling on the back property."

"She said that everyone woke up one morning and half the lake was gone."

Elijah takes another gulp of his water and I see that it's almost drained again.

"Something happened one night. Some kind of accident. Old Man Frederick has a few ideas but no one else will speak of it. I'm surprised my grandma told you. The only people around that night were black folks and when my granddad was run out of town, they all shut up."

Now, it's my turn to take a drink. "Your grandfather?"

Elijah sends me a sad smile. "Why do you think I sound the way I do? My grandfather started talking about what happened at the lake that night so they forced him out. He ended up in Chicago where he married and my dad was born. I came back because I wanted to know my grandmother and ended up becoming the librarian, then the mayor of Fontus

Springs." He smirks. "Ironic, isn't it?"

"But your name is Fontenot and Miss Bessie's is Jefferson. Was she originally a Fontenot?"

For the first time since I sat down, Elijah looks me dead in the eyes and his smile is one of triumph. "They know how to spot your car in all of downtown Baton Rouge, but they have yet to make that connection. My grandmother married twice."

Judy arrives and we both jump; we hadn't seen her coming.

"I'm sorry," she immediately says. "I was just checkin' to see if y'all needed anything."

"What's for dessert?" Elijah asks.

I raise my hand. "That's okay. I've had enough."

Elijah ignores me. "Bring us some of your awesome bread pudding and one of those chocolate lava cakes. Oh, and two coffees."

"You got it," Judy says happily and I wonder if she's adding up that ever-growing tip in her head.

"Whatever you don't eat, you can take home," Elijah tells me.

Ordinarily, that Southern woman thing again, I would object and lie that I couldn't possibly eat all that, but I'm too busy thinking about the return of the prodigal son and a lake vanishing overnight.

"This is all too good," I say, hoping Elijah doesn't catch the excitement in my voice. "So, what do we do now? It must be connected. The accident, the cover-up and what's going on now."

"Maybe. I don't know if the state's involved or not but Matt definitely is."

"How did the state get the property?"

Elijah explains over coffee and dessert — yes, I ate a good bit of each without hesitation — that when World War II rolled around and the Louisiana Maneuvers started, Brock Parker disappeared when military men used the hot springs and insisted on everything being on the up and up.

"There were camps all over Central Louisiana," Elijah

says. "Hundreds of thousands of men being trained here so the military was strict about those things. According to Old Man Frederick...."

I hold up a hand. "Why do you keep calling him that?"

Elijah laughs. "Wait until you meet him. Anyway, he claims that one of Brock's heirs saw promise in the site and updated the hotel, built a new pool. It did well for a while but the attraction of hot springs diminished over time and when they built the interstate away from the lake, it fell into disarray again."

"That's when the state came in?"

"They thought the springs might drive tourism, since they had built the dam next door and the 'reservoir'" — Elijah uses his fingers to indicate quotes — "would complement it and people would love the double attraction. Once again, it failed to bring in people so they capped the well and the old hotel and restaurant was deserted. The last I heard they tore down one of the buildings because it was condemned."

I put down my coffee cup. I've had two and am starting to feel the buzz and I'd hate to have to pee at the truck stop halfway between here and home.

"So why is the springs smelling bad, why is the water polluted, and why are there ghosts running around town?"

Judy arrives with the check and Elijah pays. I offer to assist but he waves me off. "Are you kidding?" he asks.

He remains silent until he walks me to my car. We pause at my Toyota and once again check the street, which is deserted except for a lone pickup truck.

"The state built the dam to cover up the accident. It gave them an excuse for what happened, more than likely friends in government helping out a company that made a mistake. But the land where the accident happened, just beyond the springs, always stayed in the Parker family."

"But I thought...."

"Follow the money."

I smile because it's the line in *All the President's Men* I loved the most, a film about Watergate that inspired me to go to journalism school.

"Old Man Frederick will help, but you didn't hear that from me."

"What about Sirona."

Elijah looks at his feet. "Possibly."

"What does that mean?"

He meets my eyes and sighs. "She's not a reliable source."

Now, it's my turn to sigh. "Elijah, I can't help you without getting paid. Honestly, I'm broke."

He reaches into his breast pocket and pulls out an envelope. I glance inside and see several hundred dollar bills and gasp. "What?"

Elijah searches the street one more time, then leans in close. "We're desperate Ms. Valentine. So much so that the folks of Fontus Springs raided their savings after the City Council pulled the funds."

"I didn't mean for you all to pay this much."

"Please, you've got to help us."

It's spoken with so much passion and fear that I simply nod.

"Follow the money," Elijah says before leaving me. "And drive a different car."

CHAPTER TEN

After my meeting with Elijah I visit the Rapides Parish Courthouse and do a title search on Fontus Springs. The paper trail shows a Louis Frederick selling the property to Jessie Parker, then Brock Parker inheriting the springs after Jessie's death. After that, the property falls to Brock Parker's heirs, a collective group, when Brock Parker passes away.

Here and there papers are missing. On one deed, pages three and four are absent. I think to inquire but don't want anyone asking for my name.

Two things I know for sure: the title trail is one heck of a mess and the state of Louisiana doesn't own an inch of this land.

I pop into the Alexandria main library and head toward the Louisiana section, looking up information on the Lorelei dam project, which began in 1933. Miss Bessie had said the accident occurred one fall night in 1932, although she also claimed the state blamed it on a drought. I then researched weather patterns for that year, and although the country experienced drought in several areas, Louisiana wasn't one of them.

"Do you need some help, darling?" the nice librarian asks me.

On a lark, I request information on Lorelei Lake and Fontus Springs, hoping no one's around to hear me and break another window. Or worse. The librarian pulls out several folders and hands them to me.

"You want the ghost ones, too?"

I'm about to head to a quiet corner but I stop cold — so does my heart. "Ghosts?"

She smiles and heads back to the file cabinets. "I'll get you that one, too."

I stand there like an idiot, mouth hanging open, thinking I need to go straight to the history folder and focus. Every town in Louisiana has ghosts, I command myself, and this may be another folder full of myths and teenage pranks. But I wait patiently like a schoolgirl, palms up while she places a folder there marked "Lorelei legends and ghost tales."

I find a nice, quiet corner in the back where I have a good view of the door and there's no one around. I gulp hard and open the folder, finding a series of articles written since the turn of the century. Apparently, ghosts have haunted Fontus Springs for years. Residents had reported eerie activities when the resort was functioning, mostly staff members recalling strange incidents and refusing to work there again. Another article details the unusual lake noises, repeating what Elijah had told me at lunch. "What the...?" I speak out loud, reading about how residents heard singing at night coming from the lake.

There's way too much to read in one sitting and, being a weekday, the library announces it's closing soon. I make copies of everything and head toward the interstate. I'm at a traffic light and the signs point in two directions, north and south. I could head back to Lafayette and digest everything I've found at the library or sneak back toward Fontus Springs and do a little snooping.

Against my better judgment, I head north.

The sun's beginning to dip in the west when I hit the turnoff to Fontus Springs and the glare blasts me in the face. I slip on my sunglasses, as much for a disguise as for comfort. I glance down every road I pass, constantly checking my rearview mirror and letting every car go first when I hit the stop signs. Before my lunch with Elijah I might have thought I was being overly paranoid, even with a broken window. But his last comment about driving a different car — which I'm not doing — has my heart thumping in my chest.

I come to the four-way stop outside of town and in front of me are three dump trucks hauling something beneath tarps. The man waves to me to go first and I'm assuming they are part of a caravan. I wave back, and he doesn't move, so I wave again, this time more dramatically and hold up my cell phone as if I'm on a call. Finally, the first truck turns toward town and the rest follow. I give them a few minutes headway, then follow.

"You're going to get yourself killed," I mutter to myself but I trail them anyway.

The three trucks slow down at the gravel road Elijah took me by during my first visit. I slow to give them time to turn without noticing me in their rearview mirror and slowly move ahead. There's a large cloud of dust on the deserted road to my right so I've lost sight of the trucks, but I pull off the road beneath a strand of trees and check one of the old maps Elijah had included in his box. Sure enough, the road leads to the springs but there's another road a few hundred feet away that parallels the property, so I drive on.

The parallel road listed on the map is nothing but a dirt trail with no trespassing signs and potholes the size of my head. I pause, wondering if I will need to replace more than my brakes after this gig — not to mention another window — but I drive down anyway. It feels like no one has traveled this way in decades as my car rolls over dips and bumps so on one hand, that bodes well for me not getting shot, but on the other hand, who knows who lives back here which means I might be killed anyway. I check my cell phone and sure enough, no service. I gulp hard and keep going.

I gaze through the thick woods to my right to try and spot the trucks but all I manage to see is that dust cloud they spewed behind. I spot something significant through the trees — a building perhaps? — so I slow the car and lean toward the passenger window to get a better look. I lean over, squint through the thick underbrush and notice something white and tall. I'm thinking the corner of a concrete block building, so I lean further over to get a better look.

That's when I hear a man yell. It startles me so much I slam on the brakes and nearly fall to the floorboards. There, in front of my hood, is a grizzly looking man in camouflage clothing with a shotgun aimed right at my face. I raise my hands as he approaches and I understand why Elijah gave the man his name. Old Man Frederick looks like he was rode hard and put up wet, as my Aunt Mimi likes to say, with a face completely devoid of smoothness and wild, white hair peeking out everywhere from beneath a ragged John Deere cap.

"Get out of your car," he demands.

I do as I'm told, my hands still raised high. "Are you Mister Hilderbrand?"

"If you're from Hobart Industries you'd best get that car in reverse fast before I shoot your ass."

I shake my head. "I'm Viola Valentine. Elijah Fontenot hired me."

Old Man Frederick grunts and his eyes narrow but that gun never moves.

"I'm trying to find out what's going on at the springs," I continue. "You can call Elijah. He'll vouch for me."

He says nothing, keeps staring behind that shotgun.

"Please put down the gun," I mutter.

"Hired you for what?"

I swallow, because I have no idea how he will take what I'm going to say next. "The ghosts."

Amazingly, Old Man Frederick lowers his shotgun, but that suspecting gaze never falters. "And just how are you going to do that, young lady?"

I shrug. "No idea."

He steps closer and takes me in from head to foot, even walks around and checks me out from every angle, perhaps to see if I have a pistol tucked in my waist. And yes, my hands are still reaching for the heavens.

His shoulders relax and the gun points downward, then Old Man Frederick starts walking down the road. "Come on, then," he says to me without looking around.

I lower my hands, run to the car and retrieve my keys and purse, and lock up, then follow like an obedient puppy. We travel about one hundred feet and turn left into a dense thicket, almost crawling through several bushes before I spot the house. There's a lovely clearing before the home, with flowers, blooming crape myrtle trees, and a vegetable garden off to the side. The home itself is in immaculate condition, a soft brown Craftsman cottage from the 1920s with a broad porch in front and one of those cute rounded doors with a circular window in the center. It's off the ground, built that way to provide good air circulation, and I spot a few chickens underneath.

"Expecting a double wide?" Old Man Frederick asks.

"No, sir."

I really need to stop calling him that, even if it's only in my head, as I follow him into the house which is filled with antique furnishings, what looks like original artwork, and lots and lots of plants, all neatly trimmed and flourishing. Photos, articles and books are piled everywhere, and I get the impression Frederick loves both gardening and history.

"Sit down," he orders me as he heads to the kitchen, so I follow and sit at the small kitchen table off to the right. "Coffee?"

"Yes, sir. Thank you."

"I hope you're not expecting some of that fancy stuff Bessie serves. Around here it's plain ole Community Coffee dark roast."

I was raised on Community, a Louisiana coffee company out of Baton Rouge, but with added chicory that's popular among New Orleanians. I've learned not to mention that in Cajun Country, where dark roast reigns. Cajuns get testy about the habits of New Orleans residents, living in the more popular Louisiana city to the east. No chicory in Cajun coffee, thank you, and there dang well better not be any tomatoes in their gumbo.

Being that we're above the what we call in Louisiana the French line, I doubt Frederick cares.

"Community sounds wonderful," I offer.

While Fred makes coffee, I decide to be bold and get answers.

"Why is your house so secluded back here?" I look out the back window and spot a gorgeous view of the lake and add,

"Oh my goodness. That's beautiful."

Fred turns and his look is as inhospitable as it was at the car. "I don't need to show off anything. I'm not like you young people who have to prove to the world you got something."

"I wasn't saying...."

"This land has been in my family for generations and it's staying that way. And I don't need anybody telling me how beautiful my view of the lake is."

My brain bypasses the insult and focuses on his first comment. "I thought that Jessie Parker bought the Hilderbrand land."

Fred slams the coffee cups down hard on the counter and it's amazing that they haven't shattered. "Don't mention that name or his sorry son in this house."

I'm so stunned by his reaction that all I can say is "Yes, sir."

Neither of us speaks while the coffee maker gurgles and Fred puts sugar, cream and those indestructible cups on the table. Finally, when the coffee's brewed, he brings the pot over and sits down, fills both cups.

"My dad took him to court when he pulled this land out from under us," Fred begins and I can only assume he's talking about Jesse Parker. "They transferred the land when my father was out west working on the railroad. When he got back, the springs was gone, but he managed to wrestle back this here property." His face distorts, making all those wrinkles double in intensity. "Nice of them, huh? Allow us to live on our own land. Of course, we had to buy it from him."

I sip my coffee in silence, thinking of how this man spent his life watching his family's once beautiful resort being turned into a crime-filled business, then falling into disrepair. Now, god only knows what's going on inside those woods. I gaze into that weather-worn face and imagine every wrinkle born of frustration and despair.

"Does Bayou State Transport own the property?" I finally ask. "I did a title search at the Rapides Parish Courthouse but there's lots of information missing and I couldn't find anything about the company on the Internet."

Fred gives me that suspicious look again. "I thought you were here about the ghosts."

"I am."

I feel a tickle on my leg and look down to find a fat and happy calico.

"That's Tootsie."

"Hey Tootsie."

I reach down and give the feline a scratch to the back of her neck. Old Man Frederick can't be that bad if he owns a cat named Tootsie, so I relax and decide to come clean. I explain how I spent a few years working the cops beat in Saint Bernard Parish until Katrina took my newspaper job and home away. Even though I'm in the ghost business now, in addition to travel writing, my journalism curiosity caused me to investigate the Department of Water Quality when I heard Fred had made a formal complaint around Easter. I tell him what TB and I found in the department archives, thanks to my press card, and how my car window was broken shortly afterwards. I mention the lunch with Elijah and my visit with Miss Bessie, but I have a feeling he knew about the latter.

"Miss Bessie knows more than she's letting on," Fred says. "But then she has a right to be wary."

"Because of her son having to leave town?" Fred's suspicious look returns, so I quickly add, "Elijah told me."

Fred takes a long drink from his coffee, then sits back in his chair. "Did he tell you about Sirona?"

I'm getting sick of these goosebumps. This round gives me the hard shivers and I shake it off with a frown.

"You cold?"

I ignore his question and get to the point. "What about Sirona?"

Fred picks up the pot and refills our cups. I'm thinking again of that nasty truck stop on the way back to Lafayette but I don't want to be rude so I let him pour me another.

"You'll have to ask her yourself."

"And the ghosts? Have you seen them too?"

Fred smirks and his almost smile nearly makes me spit my coffee. "Of course, I've seen them. Everyone has seen them."

"Everyone? Men, too?"

"The ones man enough to admit it."

"Since Easter?"

"Since Easter and that awful smell coming from the springs."

"Do you have any idea why these ghosts are here all of a sudden?"

Fred leans forward and looks me dead in the face. "Ask Sirona."

He rises abruptly and gathers up our cups — mine still half full — and heads to the kitchen. I realize that's the end of the conversation so I change the subject once again.

"Do you think it's Hobart or whomever — Bayou State Transport maybe — dumping stuff back there? As far as I know, the state doesn't own that property."

"Who said anything about the state?" Fred asks at the sink, not turning around.

"Until today, I thought they owned the property."

Those cups clatter in the sink and I once again wonder how they don't break. "That's what Matt Wilson wants us to believe." Fred turns and shakes a finger at me. "Don't believe a word that lying skunk says."

I shake my head. "Don't worry, I don't. And if I ever see him again, I may return that water meter. To his head."

Fred wipes his hands on a dish towel, then heads toward the back door. "I have to feed my goats. You can find yourself out."

I'm still scared of this man with his brusque tone, so I do as I'm told and not even consider he's being rude as hell. Just as I'm about to head off the front porch, he calls to me from the side of the house.

"Come back at night. Put a handkerchief on your car's antenna."

"Why?"

He grabs up a sack of what looks like feed and gives me one of those "Are you stupid?" looks. "So I don't shoot you."

"No, I mean why at night? I've already seen the ghosts at Miss Bessie's house."

Fred spits and throws the bag over his shoulder. I'm amazed at the agility of this man who must be at least eighty years old. "There's more than ghosts haunting this lake."

I wonder if he means those dumping next door, but Fred turns his attention to four goats who come running. I tell his back that I'll return after the Fourth of July weekend and start for my car.

"Oh, and Miss Valentine," he calls after me. "Drive a different car."

I make it past the dreaded truck stop but I'm outside of Blue Moon Bayou when those cups of coffee come calling. I pull off at the welcome center and pee in the public restrooms which, thank you Jesus, smell nice and have ample toilet paper. On the way back to my car I detour to the bayou. Almost immediately, Abigail Earhart is there, giving me the once-over. I can feel her staring at me before I turn and check.

"You again?" Abigail asks.

"I need answers," I reply.

She shrugs, like teenagers love to do. "Answers for what?"

There's so many things I want to know but what exactly are the questions? There's no manual for this kind of thing.

I deflect. "Do you know where you are?"

There's that shrug again. "Yeah."

I wonder if she's thinking Blue Moon Bayou and not the ever-after but she grins at me and adds, "I told you, I know I'm dead."

I can't explain how weird that is hearing a person, standing clear as day in front of me, admitting they're no longer living. It's as if uttering to a friend, "Pass the salt for the margaritas. Oh, and by the way, I'm dead."

"The train?" I offer.

"Yeah, jumped the rails and ran off the bayou bridge."

What's equally strange is that this girl takes it all in stride. It's like she's comfortable in her deceased skin.

I decide to get to the point before Abigail fades away. "Can you talk to people on the other side? You know, heaven, if there is such a place?"

She's chewing on a blade of grass, which seems so human. I can't help but wonder if the grass is dead, too. "Some. Mostly I don't talk to them, just see them pass on to the light."

"When they die?"

Shrug. "I guess. One minute they're here, next minute there's this light and they disappear."

"And that's that? You can reach them?"

Abigail spits like Old Man Frederick did only an hour before and looks away. "My mom prays a lot from the other side. I hear her sometimes, not really, just feel it kinda like."

"And you don't answer?"

She spits harder. "Heck no. She gave me up. Why would I want to talk to her?"

I raise my hands to appease her because I've clearly hit a nerve. "Sorry. I didn't know."

The shrug returns and she turns to leave. "Whatever."

"Wait," I call out but she's already heading down the bank, disappearing into the water before fading away. I watch her go, my heart aching because I have to know why I'm witnessing this young girl from the 1930s and not my precious baby.

"Talking to yourself?"

Annie Breaux peers down from the bayou bridge, her arms full of groceries, a baguette peering out from the top.

"Just myself," I lie. "The only person who will listen these days."

She pauses in her stroll from Hebert's Grocery, debating on whether to get home and relieve herself of the grocery bags or come down the bank to say hello. She decides the latter and I walk up the incline so we meet halfway, me taking one of her bags and giving her a half hug since we both now have groceries between us.

"You okay?"

"Of course." I give her a smile worthy of Meryl Streep.

She doesn't buy it. "Who were you talking to, really? And remember, I run a haunted bed and breakfast."

Now it's my turn to shrug, feeling every bit as self-conscious as the teenager I've been courting.

Annie places a bag on one hip. "You know I don't see ghosts or anything, but my aunts do. They talk to the people haunting our B&B all the time."

"So, you've said." I interviewed Annie for a travel feature and she had explained how their establishment was popular with ghost hunters, but I instead focused the article on the building's former incarnation — it was once a mortuary run by long-standing members of the community — and not on those who refuse to check out. Annie's B&B has fallen on hard times and I was hoping the travel feature would bring her some business, sans ghosts.

"My aunts claim there's a girl who hangs out down here," Annie continues, nodding toward the bayou. "A runaway. You didn't happen to see her, did you? She's thin, wears overalls. But not someone who's living."

I decide to come clean. I like Annie. Trust her. When I had interviewed her she had offered me some of her incredible baked goods she uses to spoil her guests. We talked forever, and I opened up about life, TB, and the loss of Lillye.

"I did see someone to that description."

Annie shifts the bag to the other hip. "Want some iced tea? I'm getting ready to make a pot of gumbo. I know it's still sweltering outside but I've got a serious *envie* for a shrimp gumbo."

The last thing I need is more caffeine but after a day that started with aggravating Boudreaux and ended up with more questions to be answered about Lorelei Lake, sitting down with a friend sounds good. I still haven't heard from TB, and for the first time in a long while I dread going home to an empty potting shed.

I follow her to the Mortuary B&B, an ugly, sterile building on the outside that probably scares most tourists away, if the ghosts haven't done so already. The old mortuary sign still graces the front, although Annie and her aunts, two elderly sisters who own the place, added the "B&B" part on to the sign's bottom.

The inside is quite another story. When Annie took over management of the old place to assist her aunts, she transformed the interior with warm blues and yellows and filled the place with soft, comfortable furnishings. The mortuary sitting room became the library, where guests may relax in oversized chairs and enjoy a number of Louisiana books, view movies filmed in the Bayou State or cozy up to the fireplace on the few days it's actually cold in Louisiana.

The upstairs bedrooms are equally inviting. It took years of her working a bartending job at night and scouring thrift shops for antiques until Annie could restore the bed and breakfast to her liking and start attracting guests. This, all the while raising her daughter on her own. She's a success story and one I was proud to write about.

We step into the hallway and turn on the lights.

"No guests?"

Annie laughs. "I had one of those couples who spook easily. They weren't here ten minutes and I was explaining that they might hear an odd thing or two when they bolted out the door."

According to Annie, the place is home to three apparitions: a grumpy old man whom everyone avoided in life (I'm thinking he will be good company for Old Man Frederick when he passes), a young girl who died from polio who routinely skips through the property because in death her legs work fine, and a beautiful woman locals claim died of a broken heart. She's popular with the male visitors.

I never saw a ghost when I interviewed Annie but then they all died by natural means. My heart skips thinking I may see one now, if it's true I've evolved in my SCANCy abilities.

We head to the kitchen where Annie unloads the grocery bags and pulls out a couple of pots for the gumbo. We chitchat until the iced tea's brewed, filled with the appropriate amount of sugar, and iced.

"So, you never see the ghosts that live here?" I ask her as she pours me a glass and I take a sip.

"Nope. I'm the normal one in the family."

I spray my tea over her red metallic table from the 1950s.

"Oh, I didn't mean it that way." She rises and grabs a paper towel to wipe up my mess while I apologize profusely. "It's just that my mom, bless her heart, lives in Lala Land, which is why she's in the assisted living complex down the street, and my aunts routinely talk to the dead, so I'm the logical one with no paranormal abilities."

I do the Meryl Streep smile again because Annie doesn't know about my SCANCy talents.

"Seriously, I think it's cool," she adds and I sense she thinks she offended me. "I just meant I'm the normal one in the family." She uses quote marks with her fingers when she says "normal" as if to indicate it's society's label, not hers.

"I get it," I say and wave her off. "I'm not the normal one in my family so it caught me funny." I'm surprised I admitted as much.

"You see ghosts?"

Again, I'm hungry for a friend, so I explain how I saw apparitions as a child but repressed the talent until Katrina forced the paranormal door open again. She laughs when I discuss SCANC, but turns solemn when I mention the water ghosts who won't leave me alone.

"But I'm evolving," I finish. "I believe I can see ghosts who have not died by water so I'm hoping to finally be able to talk to my sweet baby."

"So, you don't think bayou girl was a water death?"

"Her name is Abigail Earhart and she told me she died in a train accident."

Annie frowns, then gets up and heads to the library, pulling out an old book from the shelf. When she returns to the kitchen, she opens it to a section on Blue Moon Bayou and a photo showing the train derailment of 1934. According to the caption, several people on the train were killed in the accident, including a young runaway that had come to the area via the Orphan Train.

"They sent orphans from New York to Louisiana to work on farms," Annie explains.

"It was the Orphan Train that derailed?"

Annie frowns and looks at the photo again. "I'm not sure. I always heard that train went to Opelousas," mentioning the town twenty minutes north of Lafayette. "They even have an Orphan Train Museum up there."

This excites me to no end, because it means Earhart was probably on that train when it left the tracks and she haunts the bayou because that's where she died, not because of the water. I share this with Annie but she's hesitant to agree with me.

"I don't know, Vi. I'm not sure it's the same train that transported orphans. I've never heard of them coming here. At least not by train."

"It has to be. It all makes sense."

She looks down at the photo in front of her and frowns. "There are freight cars in this picture."

I glance at my watch and rise. "It's getting late. I better go."

Annie grabs my hand. "Vi, I'm not saying it's not true, just offering some facts."

"Facts?" I say a little too loudly. "We're talking about ghosts here."

She looks taken aback and I feel bad for my abruptness. But how does someone understand the pain I carry when they haven't lost a child? Any chance I have of reaching Lillye is a chance I'm going to take.

"You don't want to stay for gumbo?" she asks sweetly. "I have bottled roux so it won't take me long."

"Thanks, but I really need to go."

We walk to the door in silence and I know I should

apologize for my rudeness but the words won't come. Instead, I tell her I'll research the accident and see if I can find anything about the young girl. I'm still convinced this means I can reach all ghosts now. Why else would I be seeing Earhart and the host of apparitions at Lorelie Lake?

When I return home that night, with that pile of papers I snagged at the Alexandria library, who should be waiting by my back door but TB, traitor Stinky lying in his lap.

"What are you doing here?" I ask, then unlock the front door and let both inside.

"I was worried about you." TB lets the cat down who does a beeline to his food and water, but TB lingers by the door.

"I'm fine. That jerk by the elevator tried to scare me off by busting my car window, but he's got something coming if he thinks I'm letting this case alone."

TB crosses his arms about his chest and looks away.

"What are you doing here?" I repeat. "Really."

He looks back at me with such pain in those rich brown eyes I want to crawl into a hole for being so insensitive. I could have at least acted glad to see him, given him a hug.

"I've got another job here," TB says, "but don't worry, I'm getting a hotel. I just came over to make sure you were all right since you called in tears a few hours ago."

I look down at my feet, ashamed that I had reached out to a man who cares, then dusted him off when things got better. Truth be told, I was happy to see him waiting on my doorstep, couldn't wait to share my lunch meeting with Elijah and all that I had found at the courthouse and library. Not to mention my meeting with Bayou Girl and what I found out from Annie.

I'm about to tell him so when TB utters, "See ya, Vi," and waltzes out of my apartment.

CHAPTER ELEVEN

It was before sunrise the first time I drove into New Orleans after the storm. TB and I had this insane idea there would be lines of cars on the interstate waiting to return. We were right about the crowds, but off on the time. We had no problem getting into Orleans Parish before sunrise — the lines came later — but we couldn't see a thing due to the city being completely without power and lights.

With flashlights in hand, and handkerchiefs to fight off the stench, we did what we needed to do, gathered up anything salvageable from the house which was pretty much nothing, viewed the damage, and took photos for our insurance company who would spend almost a year getting around to cutting us a check. TB insisted on rebuilding but I wanted nothing of the place, a house gifted by his parents they had previously hoped to flip. TB tried over the years to make it livable but it was always one thing or another. I don't know if it was the weird neighbors, crappy yard with its giant holes that prevented Lillye from playing there, or the fact that no renovation could redeem that ugly house, but once we found Lillye's photos high in a closet, carefully wrapped in plastic and saved from that bitch Katrina, I found refuge in the car until TB was done. That horrid day, I cried all the way to Baton Rouge, determined never to return.

Once I got control of my emotions and halfway back to Lafayette, I asked TB for a divorce.

I think about that horrid morning in 2005 and TB's reaction as I drive into New Orleans now, passing the trees at the 310 interchange still leaning as if Katrina's winds blew in that morning. There's a large swath of wetlands cypress that's never coming back, I notice, stripped of branches and leaves and standing sentinel like telephone poles. The only redeeming sight this morning is the Motel 6 at Williams Boulevard and Interstate 10, which has been rebuilt after half of its façade was ripped apart and left flapping in the breeze for visitors to witness, shoot photos of, and show to the world.

I hate coming home. I wish that wasn't the case because New Orleans remains one of the world's most incredible cities. It's not just the thousands of people who have drowned here from Katrina and other disasters, but the endless memories and few of them good. I'm the ordinary child of an overachieving, extroverted family. I got pregnant in college and married a man with a name that couples as a disease. I reported on murder victims and school board meetings for the second-best newspaper in the city, and ended up on my roof for two days; reporters weren't allowed to evacuate.

And then there's Lillye. I spot Metairie Cemetery in my right peripheral vision but I can't bear to turn and look. Even after all these years, the pain constricts my chest, holds it hostage like a madman, and it's difficult to breathe. I pause at Metairie Road, then turn left and let out a large sigh.

"I'm sorry, sweetheart," I whisper. "I can't bear to visit you there."

I'm waiting for a sound, a whisper back, anything to let me know she hears me. But the only sounds are cars whizzing past, hip hop on a neighboring car's radio, and the honk of the impatient person behind me, for I've slowed down, waiting for my eyes to clear. The man pulls in the lane next to me and rushes past, screams an obscenity as he does.

So much for answers.

I did get one this week, in the form of a telephone call from the Louisiana Orphan Train Museum in Opelousas. I grind my teeth remembering how a sweet older lady named Celeste called to inform me that yes, an Abigail Earhart arrived in Louisiana in 1928, given up by her widowed mother somewhere near New York City because the mother couldn't care for the child while she worked. Abigail had disembarked in Opelousas and was given to a family that lived outside Blue Moon Bayou.

"So, she arrived on the train in Opelousas, then took another train to Blue Moon Bayou?" I had asked the volunteer who was nice enough to look this up.

"No, ma'am," Celeste replied. "Once they arrived in Opelousas, the families picked them up, usually by horse and buggy or car."

"But, what if this particular girl took a train south?"

"No, ma'am," Celeste repeated, and if I hadn't learned to respect my elders I would have pointed out that she was older than I and the ma'am business was headed in the wrong direction. "Your Abigail was one of the last to arrive. They stopped sending children on the Orphan Train shortly after that."

"But, the train south...."

"I have it here in my notes." I heard shuffling sounds as Celeste searched for the right paper. "Abigail Earhart arrived that summer and the Pinckley family picked her up seven hours later at the Opelousas train station."

So, this lovely family left the poor girl waiting, I surmised. Still, I can't let it go that Abigail is speaking to me because of the train accident.

"There was a train derailment in Blue Moon, and I think Abigail might have been on that train."

"Oh no," Celeste says in that tone that old people get when you're wrong, which rubbed me raw then and does so now just thinking about it. "She went home with the Pinckley family that day. She ran away twice, both times east towards New Orleans, and the Pinckleys almost sent her back to the New York Sisters. It's all in the files."

One thing's for sure, my research showed that the train crossing Blue Moon Bayou back in 1934, which hit a rogue animal and derailed, was heading west.

"Do you think Abigail might have jumped on this train, deciding to go west that night, and not towards New Orleans?" I had asked Celeste.

"Honey, she wasn't on the train. They found her body in the bayou, next to the canoe she stole from the Pinckleys. She was running away again, and in the same fashion. Usually, she paddled the bayou into Lafayette and then jumped a train to New Orleans. On the night of her death, she must have been hit by something coming off the train derailment and drowned in the bayou."

"Or she was on that train and was killed in the derailment."

I had shouted that last part and the kind volunteer admonished me and quickly hung up. I felt bad for being so rude but she didn't know what she was talking about. That suffocating pain I felt during the phone call changes to anger once again. It's all so confusing and so wrong.

This time, I yell at the dick speeding past, "Up yours, jerk!"

I get on to Canal and head toward the lakefront and a series of New Orleans neighborhoods that popped up in the nineteen-thirties and forties when wetlands around Lake Pontchartrain were turned into subdivisions and dredged lake mud used as filler. And yes, we know, we shouldn't have done that considering this area of the city flooded extensively. Funny how the world loves to point fingers after a disaster.

Lake Vista, however, differs from the larger Lakeview District Area in that it was a planned community, a "superblock" design popular in the early twentieth century aimed at emphasizing pedestrian sidewalks — what a concept! My mother's World War II-era house, for instance, faces the interior sidewalks and not the street.

Ironically, most of Lake Vista didn't flood like the rest of the lakefront, even though it's closest to Lake Pontchartrain than most houses. The lake seawall and the higher elevation of the man-made land saved the historic subdivision. My mother's one of the lucky few, but don't ever tell her that. A tree damaged the game room of the house, and even though she had the roof repaired quickly and moved back in, she had to endure driving "miles" into Jefferson Parish for groceries and other basic needs. Like ten miles, max.

One thing I've learned from surviving disasters, everyone

has a story and once one gets started — particularly if there's alcohol involved — a competition arises as to who suffered the most. I've known people who have lost loved ones, not to mention my two-day vacation on the rooftop, but talk to my mother and you'd swear she had it worst.

I pull up to my childhood house and notice Portia and Aunt Mimi are already here. I enter through the back door — remember the front faces the pedestrian thoroughfare — and announce my presence. There's no response.

I head to the kitchen where three adult women gaggle like geese, all holding wine glasses and ignoring the small child running circles beneath their feet. Aunt Mimi spots me first, places her glass down and pulls me into a tight hug. She smells of old-fashioned roses, like always, and her embrace is tight and comforting. I could settle right here and never leave.

She pulls back and takes me in. "Are you eating?"

"A bit too much if you ask me," my mother says, glass still perched high in her hand. "She goes on those press trips where they feed them constantly."

I ignore my mom and smile at Aunt Mimi. "I'm a writer and the food's free. I mean, come on."

I want to add that I'm starving, having skipped breakfast (there's nothing in the fridge and I was too cheap to stop on the way) but I don't want to hear more about my weight. I glance over at Portia, who's definitely a bit wide in the middle, and nod hello.

"It's about time you got here," she says.

So, I'm fat and I'm late. Nice to see you, too, family.

Aunt Mimi seems to sense my feelings for she asks me if I want something to drink and how about a deviled egg. Gawd love her, as we say in New Orleans.

"I'd love a beer and a deviled egg," I say and smile.

"You can get it yourself," Portia adds.

Now, I'm labeled lazy.

I send Portia a scathing look and am about to retort when Sebastian waltzes in and pokes me from behind. "Hey brat."

"Hey yourself."

I miss my twin so much it hurts. The fact that he doesn't miss me as much tears my heart to shreds. I don't know when he drifted off and left me behind but it's been years since we confided in each other or had a real sibling talk. I'm hoping today might change that.

Aunt Mimi hands me an egg, sprinkled on top with paprika. I'm so hungry I pop the whole thing in my mouth which makes Mimi laugh. "You *are* hungry."

"Yes ma'am," I mutter.

She then pops open a beer, pours it into a chilled glass, hands it to me, and we clink drinks. I add, "It's so good to see you."

And I mean that with all my heart. My aunt stands among this collection of perfection in faded Levi's and a peasant top, several hemp bracelets and honest-to-god clip-on earrings that look like blue sunbursts; she was too frightened to have her ears pierced. Top it off with a blue streak running through her gray hair and I'd laugh if it weren't impolite.

"If you lived in New Orleans you'd see Mimi more often," my mother says.

I shake my head digesting this information. "Uh, Lafayette is closer to Branson than New Orleans."

"Don't be rude," Portia says. "Mimi flies in."

I hate it when Portia acts the smartie, especially when she's right. I glance over at Sebastian but he's busy tickling Demi and while my mother stirs something smelling delicious on the stove she strikes up a new conversation with Portia about the lack of beef variety in New Orleans grocery stores. Once again, either I'm in the wrong with this group or I'm out of the loop. I can't decide if I want to cry or grind my teeth.

Aunt Mimi comes to the rescue and pulls me into the living room where Reynaldo is playing some baby video game with talking turtles.

"Turn that down, honey, so Vi and I can talk."

Reynaldo groans but he does as he's told and Aunt Mimi and I settle on the couch.

"What's going on?" she says.

I pull my hand through my hair. "What isn't?"

"Start with one thing."

I take a long sip from my beer, wishing I had another deviled egg. "The recession, for one. I'm broke, magazines aren't buying and my car is on its last leg, if cars had legs."

"Well, this downturn won't last forever and I have some money if you need it...."

I close my eyes because the last person I want to mooch on is Aunt Mimi, or make her feel like she should offer. "It's okay, Aunt Mimi. Things are picking up. I got a new job reviewing hotels so that should bring in a few dollars."

"Seriously, honey, I can help. I have savings."

I should shut up and agree, allow her to take the pressure off, but more than my family driving me nuts with their attitude is the feeling that I'm the pauper of the group, not to mention that I have to pay it back and I'm not sure I can.

I smile and shake it off, like it's no big deal. "No worries, Mimi. This week I got a job helping people in central Louisiana tackle a ghost problem. They paid me in advance so things are looking up."

"What's the job."

Mimi is the only family member who knows about my SCANC abilities. Right after I discovered I could see ghosts who have died by water, and learned from Carmine why, I found out that Mimi was also psychic and a descendent in a long line of Alabama mediums. She helped me through that disastrous first month when everything came down on a press trip to Arkansas.

"There's this place called Fontus Springs that's besieged with ghosts," I explain. "They don't know why but since Easter a host of them starting coming out around sunset. Old residents of the town, like a former mayor and a Confederate soldier."

Mimi leans back on the couch and frowns, studying this phenomenon. "That's odd."

"I'll say. But here's the interesting part. I saw them. All of them. As in people who did *not* die by water."

She appears not to have heard that last part. "There's a lot of them?"

"I must have seen five at least. They walked past like zombies. Definitely not intellectual hauntings, but there was this other apparition closer to home...."

"How long did the vision last?"

I exhale. "I don't know, just a few seconds. I was standing in a resident's yard and they appeared out of the woods, walked across her lawn and disappeared."

"Was this near the springs?"

I sigh. "Yes."

"That might be why you're seeing them."

I shrug. "Everyone's seeing them."

"That might be it, too."

I sigh way too heavily this time and Mimi places a soft hand on my forearm. "What is it?"

I want to tell her I'm evolving, but I sense she will disagree. Still, I can't believe this is happening for no reason. "I think I can finally see those who have not died by water."

Mimi doesn't remove her hand. Instead, she squeezes my arm. "Darling, I told you that's unlikely."

I rise from the couch abruptly and it startles Mimi and, to my surprise, the comatose two-year-old at the video console. I should take note of this and calm down, but my blood is already racing to my head.

"Why can't anyone believe that I'm evolving? Why is it so difficult for anyone to think that I might have the capabilities to see beyond my talent?"

Mimi reaches for me but I step backwards.

"I may be the dumb one in this family but perhaps I'm good at this. Maybe I can break out of my SCANCness."

Aunt Mimi rises and places both hands on my shoulders and it's then I can feel my heart beating rapidly. For a moment, I'm not even sure what happened.

"Sit down, sweetheart," she whispers soothingly.

I do as I'm told but I can still feel the thumping in my chest, as if someone took over my body and raised my blood pressure with a wrench. I want to apologize. I *should* apologize. But I'm too busy focusing on how I'm seeing these people, know I can finally reach Lillye, and no one will believe me.

"What else happened?" she asks, slipping an arm around my shoulders and hugging me tight.

"There's a girl who hangs out at this bayou near my house," I begin, this time softly. "She said she died in a train derailment."

I explain how I met Abigail Earhart, our conversations by the bayou, and how she mentioned the train twice. I relay what Annie told me about the Orphan Train and the photo she had of the derailment, leaving out the information Celeste related over the phone. All the while, Mimi slips her arm free of my shoulders, leans back on the couch, and now it's her turn to run fingers through her hair.

"You see, I think I'm developing my talents," I finish.

Mimi sends me a look and I can't decipher if it's understanding or sympathy. "Be careful, Vi. I want this to be true but you do realize both of these incidents are near water."

I sit up straight. "Yeah, I'm aware of that but I've been reading a lot about water mythology and science and it might be because water is a great conduit for energy. There's this Japanese guy named Masaru Emoto who believes that human consciousness can change the molecules of water. What if my desires and hopes of being with Lillye have stretched my abilities?"

Mimi takes a long drink from her wine glass and ponders this. "Perhaps."

I then go into a long discourse about Emoto's experiments and how people thinking of different things produced unique molecules in the water. It occurs to me during this long discourse that TB introduced me to this guy, left me a copy of Emoto's *The Hidden Messages in Water* on my desk after he had spent the night in the potting shed. I pause in my explanation, realizing that I should have invited my ex-husband to this lunch. Mimi would have loved to have seen TB, and vice versa, and I'm grossly insensitive for omitting him.

"Well, he's the one who won't return my phone calls."

Mimi pauses in her drinking and looks at me. "What?"

Damn, I said that out loud. "Nothing."

Now, she's looking at me with concern and I wonder — for not the first time, let me tell you — if I'm finally losing it. I'm expecting that the next thing out of Mimi's mouth is for me to reconnect with the psychologist.

"You might want to call that Orphan Train Museum in Opelousas," she says instead, thank goodness. "Ask them if the train in Blue Moon Bayou was one of theirs."

I wince. "I did."

"And?"

"It wasn't an Orphan Train but Abigail ran away a lot and she did that night."

"Was she on the train or on the bayou?"

I stand and begin pacing, ignoring her last question. "Why else would I see this girl, if I'm not evolving?"

Mimi places her glass on to the coffee table, grabs my hand to stop my pacing and looks me dead in the eyes. This must be the stare she gives her nursing home residents when they haven't taken their meds.

"Vi, you're a journalist. You live on facts. Get the facts and try to figure this out logically."

I offer up a snide grin. "Logically about ghosts?"

"Believe it or not, sweetie, there is logic to the magic side of the universe. Didn't Mr. Emoto discover that?"

I'm about to retort when Portia appears. "Lunch is ready, but we could use some help, Vi. Or are you going to lounge around all day?"

I place my glass of beer too hard on the coffee table and Reynaldo jumps again. "Sorry, Portia. I forgot I'm the fat lazy one."

I head to the kitchen where I nab whatever dish is sitting out and haul it to the dining room. It's quiet behind me, no doubt because I rarely talk back to any of these crazy people. My mom is already in the dining room putting out a platter of roast beef that smells heavenly and she sends me a worried glance. I plop my dish down a bit too hard and tomato gravy spills out the side on to grandma Valentine's lace tablecloth.

"Great, now I'm the fat lazy one who's also a klutz."

I don't wait for a rebuttal, head back to the kitchen for a dishtowel and cleaner, passing Mimi and Portia picking up their own dishes to bring to the table. Out of the corner of my eye, I see Portia raising her eyebrows to my mom, which makes me grind my teeth.

By the time I clean the stain from the tablecloth, all the food had been brought in, and we all sit down with one empty seat at the table's head. I start to inquire who we're saving the place setting for when my oblivious twin — who never helped do anything to set the table, I might add, no doubt because of the anatomy piece between his leg — starts rattling on about his great job in the wilds of South Carolina. He bagged a boar this week, he tells us, who almost ripped up his leg, he got that close.

"Why would you want to hunt something that could kill you?" I ask.

"Why not?"

"Hunting is stupid." I reach for the butter beans and ham. "Go to the grocery store, for god's sakes."

"The boars are taking over the woods, Vi. We keep the numbers in check by hunting."

"Right. That's what people say about deer."

"And you disagree?"

I pause with my ham piece on a fork. "All I know is there used to be deer on the side of the interstate when I drove back and forth to Lafayette." I turn and give Portia a look. "Yes, I travel repeatedly to New Orleans to visit you all, in case you missed that."

She gives me the evil eye.

"And now, I hardly see them." I shove that ham into my mouth and do notice the irony of the action.

Sebastian shrugs. "I don't know anything about the stupid deer, Vi. I'm just explaining about the boar I took down last week."

"'Took down,'" I repeat. "That's lovely."

"We ate the damn thing."

My mother raises a hand to create peace between us but Portia will have none of that. "You like what's on your plate, Vi?" she asks me with a smirk. "The pig that was raised inhumanely and killed with a ton of other animals in a horrible stockyard?"

I look down at my plate full of meat. One of these days, I have vowed, I was going to turn to vegetarianism but I never had the courage to do so in a state where practically every dish has some animal in it. Still, I hate when she's right. Against my better judgment and proper etiquette, and despite that it makes me ill to do so thinking of said stockyard, I smile smugly at Portia and shove the ham slice into my mouth and groan with pleasure.

"What is the matter with you?" my mother asks, clearly shocked at my actions.

"What's the matter with me? Why can't I walk into this house and have a decent conversation with you people?"

"You people?" I hear Sebastian say, but my mother retorts, "I think the person with the problem right now is you, Vi."

I throw my fork down, which clangs against my plate loudly and I cringe. I can't even be defiant right.

"I'm the problem?" I ask anyway. "I'm not here five minutes and you all have pointed out every fault I could possibly have."

"Maybe if you got here on time," Portia inserts, "we wouldn't label you late. As for being fat and lazy...."

"Portia," Mimi admonishes her, but I interrupt by saying, "I did drive in from Lafayette and had to go through Baton Rouge, you know, that town that absorbed all those Katrina evacuees and now has a tremendous traffic problem."

Portia squints her eyes at me. "Yeah, I think mom knows

all about that since she has to commute there twice a day."

I glance at mom, waiting for her to take the bait and launch into a diatribe of how horrible it is to drive the seventy miles to the capital city to teach ingrates basic English, but she says nothing. Now, that I notice it, she looks pale.

"Mom, are you okay?" I ask.

"No, she's not okay," Portia says. "And if you came into town more often...."

I'm so done with this argument. I close my eyes and can hear my teeth grinding against each other.

"I'm a little busy, Portia," I say when I look back at my aggravating sister. "I'm working my ass off trying to stay alive because I am my own business, I don't have a husband who brings home six figures, and there's a recession on."

She leans across the table prepared for a fight. "You think you're the only one suffering."

I smile sarcastically. "Oh, of course Portia. How silly of me. I forgot you lost everything in Katrina, got stuck on your roof for two days, had to move into a three hundred square foot apartment. Oh," I say as I throw down my napkin, "you lost your job and benefits, started a business from scratch, and had to stay married to a man you don't love anymore just for the health insurance."

"Vi," I hear my aunt say with concern, and know she wants me to stop but I'm on a roll.

"How about the fact that I can't pay half my bills this month thanks to Wall Street? Or that my car out back has faulty brakes, not to mention miles from traveling back and forth from New Orleans all the time even though you think I never visit."

"Vi," my aunt repeats, harder this time.

"And I guess you lost a child, too, after spending years watching her suffer through chemotherapy."

Now, Portia throws down her napkin. "Jesus, Gawd, Vi, how long are you going to beat that horse?"

I can't believe my sister uttered those words. I vaguely hear my mother admonish her and instruct her to apologize but Portia's busy defending her statement, claiming how they all cater to me because of what happened and it was years ago and I need to move on. I'm stunned, devastated, and I can't breathe. I feel Aunt Mimi's warm hand on my forearm but if I don't get out of here fast I will unravel on the spot.

"Sweetheart," Aunt Mimi whispers in my ear, but I rise and move my arm away, trying desperately to find some air. I stumble backwards, my chair tipping over, and turn. It's then I realize that TB has been standing in the doorway to the kitchen, listening to every word I just said.

"Oh shit," I whisper, but I still can't breathe so I push past him and head through the house, running out the front door and leaving it open in my wake. I dash through the neighborhood, climbing the lake levee that separates the homes from Lakeshore Drive. I pause at the top, gazing out to the glistening waters of Lake Pontchartrain, an enormous body of water that destroyed my hometown only two years before but now sits peacefully, smiling at me.

I fall onto the grass, thinking about how Lillye loved visiting the lakefront. Every time we visited Nana's house — my mom refused to be called grandma — we would walk out here, roll down the lake side of the levee, cross Lakeshore Drive and sit on the seawall, watching the sailboats fly past and search for jumping fish.

Until she got sick, that is. Even then, there was that one day after a visit to Ochsner Hospital, the day our doctor said to prepare ourselves for the worse since the latest round of therapy had failed. TB and I were driving to my mother's for Sunday dinner, much like today, when TB started crying and couldn't stop. Poor Lillye, pale and weak in the back seat, asked why daddy was upset; she always thought of others. I pulled into a parking spot by the lake's edge and retrieved her from her car seat, then the two of us sat on the seawall, watching the waves, her limp in my arms and me holding her tight as if I could physically keep her on this earthly plane.

"Is daddy okay?" she had said.

"He's fine," I lied, knowing that neither TB or I would

ever be the same. "He's just sad because you don't feel good."

"Let's get him some ice cream."

I smiled, fighting back my own tears because it's what we always did for Lillye after a cancer treatment. "I think Nana has some."

Lillye raised her head slightly to gaze out over the lake. Her body was half the size it should have been, so tiny and frail, yet she acted as if nothing was wrong.

"I love water," she had said, and I remember seeing a turtle raise its nose above the water while dragonflies flitted past. I spotted our reflection in the waves as they beat against the concrete steps of the seawall, our feet dangling over the edge. Such a beautiful moment underlined by enormous sadness.

"Yes, it's nice sweetheart."

"No, I mean I really love the water." She grabbed my chin in an effort to make me intently look at the lake. "It's in one place but it's everywhere."

I close my eyes at the memory and begin to sob, my chest raking with the pain. I want to believe she's with me now, want to believe like everyone else that Lillye exists in my heart forever. I do know that to be true, but I want to feel that child pressed against my bosom, hear her voice, smell the top of her head one more time.

Silently, I ask for her. Beg her within my mind to come forward, to ease my constant pain, to assure me that life on the other side is comforting and peaceful. Instead, two strong arms encircle me from behind, hug me close. I spot TB's legs stretched out on either side of my body and I lean back into his embrace.

"I'm sorry. I didn't mean...."

"Shhh," he says and I continue sobbing while he kisses the side of my head. We remain like this for what seems like an eternity, me crying until my emotions are spent. When I finally get control, I wipe the tears and snot with the hem of my shirt.

"That's lovely," TB says, and we both laugh. It's then that I turn around and notice that he's been crying, too.

"I'm sorry," I repeat, like that will repair the damage I have done to this sweet man, this excellent father, and the person who gave me the most joyous of gifts.

He hugs me once more and I place my head upon his chest, swing my legs over one of his and nestle there like Lillye had nestled into me that day so long ago.

"I don't know what's the matter with me anymore," I tell him. "I'm so angry."

"I know, Babe."

"I didn't mean what I said."

"It's okay."

He's not believing me, mainly because it's true. Or at least I have convinced myself of that fact. I close my eyes, hating that I yelled to my family that I no longer loved my husband, and that the one person who understands my pain heard me say it.

"We married too young," TB says, stroking my hair. "And then we had this beautiful person who got taken away."

I sit up and pull back enough to look him in the eyes. "We were too young. We barely knew each other when I got pregnant. I just feel like I have to...."

"...sow some wild oats, see what else the world has to offer."

My normally clueless husband nails it, but I hate to admit as such, to myself or to TB.

"Honestly, all I know is I want to keep traveling," I tell him. "It's what I love to do. And talk to Lillye, but I guess that's a pipe dream." I swallow hard because I'm beginning to think that Carmine, Mimi, Annie and TB are right. I'm a water SCANC and Lillye remains off limits.

The tears threaten again so TB pulls the hair from my face and rubs his thumb over my cheek. He smiles but it's a sad one. "She's always with us, Vi. You just have to believe that."

I nod, and TB pulls me back into his embrace. We both look toward Lake Pontchartrain and somewhere in the deep recesses of my mind, I swear I can feel Lillye smile.

CHAPTER TWELVE

TB and I stay on the levee until the sun slips near the horizon and Mimi arrives, carrying three wine glasses and a bottle of cabernet.

"Are we allowed to do this in public?" she asks, joining us on the grass.

"Are you kidding?" I reply. "It's New Orleans."

She hands us each a glass. "In that case, I should have brought the weed."

TB laughs, thinking she's kidding, and takes the bottle from beneath Mimi's arm and starts pouring us each a glass. "What's going on back at the house?"

Mini settles back on her elbows and stares at the water. "Sebastian went out with friends, Portia and the kids went home after Demi started a temper tantrum, and your mom is watching *Masterpiece Theatre*."

I sigh, take a long drink from my wine and watch the sunset paint colors on the tips of waves. "Great, that's two people I don't have to face."

"You need to talk to your mother."

I glance at Mimi who has that take-your-medicine look again, so I nod. "I will."

"You really do, Vi." Now it's TB talking.

"I will."

They give each other a look and I realize they both know something I don't. "What's going on?"

Mimi sits up and places her glass on the ground between her legs. "She got fired from her job at the community college."

"What?"

I look at TB and he nods. "Some of her students thought she was drinking on the job so they complained."

I'm stunned. My mother takes her career seriously. Too seriously if you ask me. "Mom would never do that."

Mimi rubs her palms across her knees. "Of course not."

I look at TB but he looks out at the water.

"What aren't you all telling me?"

"I found out when Portia called to ask me to dinner," TB says with a shrug.

"Found out what?"

"Deliah wanted to tell you herself," Mimi adds.

I shake my head, tired of this roundabout conversation. "Come on guys, tell me what?"

Mimi takes my hand. "She found out she has Parkinson's. Went to a neurologist in Baton Rouge but decided to get a second opinion from her doctor at Ochsner's. He confirmed it."

"It's why they thought she was drunk," TB says. "She was slurring her words and stumbled a few times."

My mind is racing trying to make sense of this. I know that Michael J. Fox has this disease but he's still alive and kicking, although not acting much anymore. Other than that, I'm confused. "Is it life threatening?"

"Oh no, honey. She could live a very long life."

I exhale the breath I was holding. "So, why the big drama? I mean, if it's not a big deal...."

"It's a big deal, Vi," TB says. "I looked it up. It's a degenerative neurological disorder and she'll have to take medicines for life. Everybody's different. Some do well on treatment, some don't. It's a crap shoot and we'll have to see."

"They offered her the job back when she had her lawyer call and explain, but I think your mom is ready to find something better," Mimi adds. "But, she may have to give up her career, eventually."

My heart sinks. My mother's career is her life.

We sit on the levee drinking our wine and discussing the matter until the light becomes bleak. We head back to the house and TB hugs me before hopping into his pickup truck to go home.

"I'll be in Lafayette Tuesday on a job," he tells me through the car window. "But I can stay at a hotel."

"Don't be silly," I say. "You're always welcome and the extra key is under the begonia by the front door. Besides, Stinky loves you."

"It's the filet mignon I serve him." He waves to Mimi who waves back from the door and then drives off.

"Did my simple-minded husband just crack a good joke?" I ask Mimi.

She smiles that grin she gets when she's hearing someone wonderful on the other side. "He's a sweetie, that one. Give it some time."

We enter the house and I hear Gillian Anderson explaining what's coming up on *Masterpiece* the following week. Mimi hands me the bottle and glasses and heads to the guest room.

"What does that mean, give it some time?" I ask her back and she waves me off without turning around.

I reluctantly join mom on the couch, placing my wine stash on to the coffee table, hoping she doesn't tear into me right away. She doesn't say anything, watches the announcement of upcoming episodes of a Jane Austen movie.

"It's a rerun," my mom finally says. "Saw those last spring."

"Good adaptations?"

My mom shrugs. Austen isn't her thing. "If you like sappy Victorian love stories."

"Actually, I love sappy Victorian love stories."

My mom shakes her head. "Are you sure you're not Mimi's child?"

I laugh, because I sure as hell could be. "Are you trying to tell me something, Mom? Kinda weird, though, because I do have a twin and I'm positive he's yours."

She smiles and my anxiety lowers. Maybe she's not as pissed off as I think. I take her hand. "I'm sorry, Mom. I didn't mean to blow up at Portia."

"Didn't you, though?"

I look up and she's smiling again. I smile back hesitantly and add, "Okay, yes, I did."

"She's a pain in the neck sometimes."

"Most of the time."

"Doesn't excuse your outburst at dinner, though."

"Yes, ma'am."

We both look at the television where someone holding a Jane Austen DVD is asking for money. "It's part of the grieving process, you know."

I was about to start asking about my mom's diagnosis when she derails me. "What is?"

"Anger." She looks at me and pushes a stray hair behind my ear like she did when I was a kid. "I was so angry after your father left. Then when Katrina blew in and took away my job, made me go teach at that horrid community college, I could have bit everyone's head off. But it's a stage you have to go through, just like everything else."

"Stage?"

She frowns. "I'm surprised your therapist never told you that. The stages of grief. Anger is number two."

I look back at the rows of phones ringing on TV while someone brags about the power of public television. I heard all about the stages but Lillye's passing was years ago. "I'm past all that, Mom."

She laughs, which startles me again. "Hardly." "You're supposed to grieve for a year and a day or something to that effect. It's been years."

My mom turns on the couch so she's facing me. "Vi, everyone grieves differently and in their own time. And there's no getting over losing our precious Lillye Beatrice. Surely you know that by now."

I nod and stare at my feet.

"Besides, Katrina came along and now you have to grieve the loss of your life, your home, your hometown. And believe me, Katrina has made a mess of us all."

I need wine, I think, so I lean over and retrieve my glass and fill it up. "So, what's next? Slitting my wrists?"

"Denial is first," my mom says quietly. "Then anger. After that you try to bargain with God and when he doesn't grant you your wish, depression sets in. Finally, you come to acceptance."

I look over at my mom and realize, for the first time, that she went through every one of those stages when dad left. I remember because I felt abandoned by them both. He for leaving us and she for throwing herself into work and being so weird and unresponsive when she got home. And what has my mom been going through lately? A storm that took away her life, her town, her job, and now a disease that's threatening to do the same.

"I'm sorry, Mom," I repeat, and this time I'm talking about her. "I'm sorry about the job and the disease...."

"Don't go all sappy on me, romance lover. I won't have it. I have this thing and I will deal with it. But," and with that comment she looks me dead in the eyes, "it would be nice if you came home more often."

She says it with such force, I can only nod.

"Don't let Portia be the only one who helps me out." Then, with an exasperated look, adds, "Please."

I can't help but laugh because I know what she means. I get it now, and that feeling of being needed warms my soul. Mom laughs too, and I know the topic of her Parkinson's is now closed. She looks back to the TV set, but I reach over and squeeze her hand and she squeezes back. We watch the telethon numbly until we realize what it is we're watching, then switch over to *The Wire* on HBO.

"Has an Eric Faust checked in?" I ask the front desk clerk when I receive my hotel room key.

Unlike sweet Mississippi, this big-city gal's not talkative at all. She looks through her computer and sure enough, I'm paired up with Eric again. The clerk gives me his room number, and I make my way to mine to drop off the suitcase and check out the place, then head over to his. He's not expecting me so I wonder if I'll find him in bed with another woman. I tell myself that it wouldn't matter if he is, but I'm lying. I'm still not sure I like this guy, but I have questions and I wouldn't say no to a drink.

I got another hotel assignment, this time for a swank place in the heart of downtown Houston. Jacob called at the crack of dawn on Independence Day, and if he hadn't sounded so desperate, I would have turned down the gig. Now, that I'm here and viewing the exciting new things happening in America's fourth largest city, I'm thinking this could be my chance to nab some travel writing story ideas.

At the moment, however, I'm exhausted from the eight-hour drive from New Orleans — two hours more than necessary due to road construction through Beaumont — and even though it's mid-afternoon, I'm primed for a cocktail. I would also love to share my last review with Eric and watch his pride at me for taking charge in Baton Rouge and at the car repair shop, even though I feel like crap after the blowout at home.

I knock on the door when I hear movement inside the room. Eric opens the door in ironed perfection, but his hair is mussed so I peer around him for a female body.

"What are you doing here?"

Not the greeting I was hoping for, and I understand now how TB felt the night I greeted him that way on the threshold of my potting shed. I also catch that wariness in Eric's gaze, the one men get running into women they hope to never see again. Honestly, I wouldn't mind this relationship being a two-night stand but his reaction annoys me. I turn my head one way and then the other in the hopes of relieving the tension building there and waltz into the room like I own the place.

"The hedge fund girls must have left a big hole." I glance around and find the place empty. "Jacob asked me to swing over and review the place. Gave me a nice bonus, too."

Eric closes the door and his countenance doesn't change. "How did you know my room number?"

"The front desk, of course."

Eric pulls his hands through his hair. He's not happy to see me and I'm not sure why. "We're not supposed to know each other, remember? You shouldn't have done that. They might catch on."

This takes the wind out of my sails. "I didn't think about that."

"Yeah, you didn't."

It's not that big of a thing, I reason, but then I need this job, this money. "I'm sure it will be okay. How would they know?"

Eric hasn't smiled yet, and now he's frowning, and I wonder if I really screwed up as much as all that. "Stick to the rules, okay Angelle."

I'm tired of following rules, doing what people expect of me. One of the reasons why I was attracted to this man. Not to mention that he taught me to break Courtyard protocol.

"Why are you being such a dick?"

He grabs his suitcase and throws it on the bed, doesn't look at me while he unzips the case and starts taking out his perfectly folded clothes. "I don't like surprises."

I've never been assertive with men, always caved in when they acted like this. Apologized. Acquiesced. Remember that Southern female book of rules?

Not today. "I don't like surprises either," I say to him and move toward the door.

He grabs my arm inches from leaving. "Now, don't be like that. You made a mistake and I'll forgive you."

I turn and smile sweetly. "Oh gee, thanks."

"I'm not into relationships. I thought you got that."

I shake my head, because as much as finding him with another woman would have shaken up my afternoon, I want no part of this man. "Who said I was? I'm married, asshole."

I pull my arm free and leave, slamming the door in my wake. I head down the hallway to my room that I notice has another horrible view. In fact, my room's one step lower than Eric's, less attractive, less furniture, and a much smaller bathroom, another reminder that angels linger lower on the totem pole. I start to feel aggravated but then a tiny voice in the deep caves of my brain reminds me that I should be grateful for the job and for that heavenly bed before me. I pop back into my tiny bathroom and notice there's a tub.

"Thank you, Lillye, or whomever is slapping me upside my head," I say to the air. "Tonight, that tub and I are communing."

I change into my bathing suit and head out, pausing at the Tiki bar to order a rum and Coke, then head for the pool, which is inside and away from the humid swelter, thank the heavens. After I dive in and take in a few laps, I plop on a lounge chair and open my laptop to start inserting information on the bar area, the bartender's service, and the cleanliness of the pool. Too much chlorine, not enough rum. There are towels lying about and the construction dust has left a fine film on half of the lounge chairs, so I note that as well.

"Working hard?"

I look up to find Eric staring down on me, of course a drink in his hand.

"What do you want?" I ask, while getting back to my typing.

I sense him sitting on the lounge chair next to me, then relaxing back while he turns a towel into a pillow. "Are you really married?"

Seriously? I look up and find him grinning which, against my better judgment, forces me to smile too. "You're a piece of work, you know that?"

He holds up his free hand and shrugs. "You get what you get."

Yes, you do, I think, and return to my typing.

"So, what's the story with you and your husband?"

I think back on the two of us on the levee, watching the sun set while sharing mutual pain. "We're separated, but still married for the health insurance."

Eric sits up and throws his legs over the side of the lounge chair. "I think you need to change places, be the asshole for a while. You're made of stronger stuff than I gave you credit for."

He means it as a compliment, but the comment pierces my heart like an arrow. "I'm not like you," I say with as much conviction as I can muster because despite the power that comes with being a jerk demanding action, it's not who I am. Or at least, it's not who I want to be.

I turn to look at Eric who's sitting by a pool in a starched, ironed shirt and khaki pants with a distinct crease down the middle. His hair hangs loose about his forehead and those brown eyes twinkle with mischief but I'm not attracted to this man. I can't imagine what I saw in him.

"I came to your room because I wanted some advice."

"More lessons in assholeness?"

"More like money laundering, tax fraud, illegal transfer of property."

He sits up straighter. "Wow, what are you planning on doing?"

"I was a hard news reporter in a previous life and now I'm investigating some weird going-ons in a town in the middle of Louisiana."

Eric's interested, but he signals the bartender for another round, thankfully including me. As much as I need to get this work done, the rum softens my edges.

"What do you need to know?" he asks when he turns back.

"You said you worked for a bank and was good at finding out information about people."

Eric smiles and his eyes narrow. "Good memory, Lois Lane."

"I'm trying to find out who owns a piece of property."

"Did you do a title search at the county courthouse?"

"Parish courthouse. This is Louisiana."

He rolls his eyes. "Whatever. Did you?"

I hand the papers I had copied and point out the missing pages, explain that most of Brock Parker's heirs appear to have moved out of state — although someone must be paying the property taxes to keep it in the family— and how Bayou State Transport doesn't appear to be in existence anymore, if they ever were.

"Can you buy property with a fake company?"

He studies the deeds and rubs the faint stubble appearing on his cheek. "Maybe in Louisiana."

"Seriously?"

"Not legally, no."

I look over at the paper in his hands. "I can't find anything about this company."

"It might be a subsidiary of a larger corporation. Or they may be out of business since this is quite a few years ago."

"How do I find that out?"

He hands me back the paper. "Better Business Bureau. Search the state's database of registered businesses. Websites."

I shake my head. "Did all that. Nothing."

Eric shrugs. "Maybe they're not in Louisiana."

I never thought of that. "Still, wouldn't something come up on Google?"

The bartender arrives with our drinks and Eric complains about its weakness and use of canned fruit juices, which the bartender reputes, of course. Eric signs the bill and moves to leave.

"Where you going?" I ask.

"There's a cute blond at the bar." He pauses and sends me a questioning grin. "Unless...."

I shake my head. "Sorry, asshole, that train left the station."

Just then a woman and her two kids emerge into the pool area and the mom blanches at my remark. Eric laughs, places a hand at his chest as if he's been injured, and heads over to where a blonde with impossibly long legs sits waiting. The mother's still giving me the evil eye so I grab my laptop and head back to my room.

I love hotel rooms. Even though I consider myself an environmentalist and recycle my trash, drive one mile per hour below the speed limit and conserve energy in my home, when I'm on the road I ratchet up the A/C and lie on those comfy beds in my underwear. It's payback for those sacrifices and one I deserve for living in the sweltering Deep South.

I spread out the papers I copied the day before and try to connect the dots of Fontus Springs. Ghost reports began when the resort was in full swing in the 1920s, but they intensified during the 1930s, particularly, I note, around 1932-33. When the military cleaned up the place and soldiers used the property, the ghost sightings ceased and so did the newspapers accounts.

The lake murmurs were another issue altogether. An article bragging of the health benefits of Fontus Springs mentions the Lorelie legend in a box off to the side, how late at night when the moon is full a woman's singing could be heard. Sounds hokey to me but those early Germans didn't name the lake for no reason. Still, could there be a logical explanation? Wind through the pines or something to that effect?

The historical articles paint a different story, touting the springs as a top attraction with modern facilities until lack of tourism led to its ruin. There's the ebb and flow success story that Elijah imparted, until the 1980s when Brock Parker throws in the towel and closes up shop. After that, nothing. No mention of a sale, no mention of Bayou State Transport, water quality issues, or the state of Louisiana.

I draw out a timeline and include the ghost sightings, call TB in the hopes of sharing this information. The call goes to voicemail.

"You won't believe what I've found," I tell him, explaining the ghost stories and how, to my knowledge, the state doesn't own Fontus Springs. As I'm rattling on, the voicemail buzzes and the call ends.

I fling my phone on to the bed and sigh. I'm dying to discuss this with someone but don't dare call Elijah at his work. Yes, I'm getting paranoid but I have a right to be. Instead, I call the next best thing. Sirona doesn't answer and it goes straight to voice mail, which I find weird, but I leave a message.

"You asked about meeting so let's meet," I say. "I'm in Houston right now but I'll be home soon. Call me."

I check the time and realize it's close to six-thirty so I shower and put on something nice. Time for dinner, then I'll check out every inch of the hotel. I'm giving Jacob the finest review of his career with this one. Tomorrow, I head back to Lafayette and hand in my resignation to Courtyard. It's time to get my travel writing career back on track.

My hotel faces the new downtown park called Discovery Green, a twelve-acre space that opened earlier this year and includes gardens, splash pads, event stages and a restaurant overlooking it all. I climb to the second floor of the restaurant and enjoy a hint of a breeze beneath oak trees. Because I'm starved for the outdoors after weeks of air conditioned solitude, I decide to sweat on the patio and watch the people walk by below.

"Good evening," my twenty-something waiter with a man bun says as he hands me a menu. "Our drink special tonight is the Space City Cosmo and it's half off until eight."

He also mentions beer and wine on tap but I immediately order the cocktail along with the chips and salsa appetizer. Then I lean back in my chair, put on my sunglasses and enjoy the evening.

My body has no problem relaxing but my brain remains in first gear. I keep thinking about Fontus Springs and its unfortunate history, about Bayou State Transport which doesn't exist as far as my internet research goes. What caused Lorelei Lake to suddenly drop by half? And, of course, there's the ghosts. Why there, why the 1930s, why now?

I nibble on my chips and slurp down the cosmos a little too fast but it's cool and refreshing and drops of sweat are traveling down my back and behind my knees. I dream about cabin life in the Smoky Mountains or a seaside retreat in Maine, wonder if I could find a summer job somewhere far from the steamy Gulf States, when I spot it. There, peering at me across the Houston cityscape, is a giant neon sign atop one of the downtown buildings. In bright red letters it reads Hobart Industries.

I bolt up, because I know this name. But where? It's wasn't in the title search, nor the library documents and articles. Still, I've heard this name before.

"Another Cosmo?" the waiter asks me.

I look up and shake my head, but I grab his hand, which startles him.

"I'm sorry," I say, immediately releasing him. "But what is Hobart Industries?"

The waiter frowns and looks in the direction of the building. "It's an oil and gas company."

Figures. After all, it's Houston.

"I know that name. But I can't remember where."

The waiter looks around as to if to see who may be listening, then leans in close. "Probably because they're one of the largest polluters in the country, but you didn't hear that from me."

I ask for the check and he drops it on the table, while picking up my used cocktail glass and plates. I throw down cash and add a nice percentage for a tip, then grab my things. I'm about to head out and finish my tour of the hotel but questions still need answering.

I pause and exhale. Mimi always said those on the other side would come to my aid if I needed them, so I close my eyes behind my sunglasses and try to breathe gently. In and out. In and out. Do you know how hard it is to calm one's mind when you suffer from ADHD? Still, I focus on the breath, in and out, in and out.

After a while, the jumble inside my head disappears. I think of the gentle breeze stirring the oak trees around me, hear the families laughing in the splash pad a few hundred feet away. I'm reminded of the relaxing effects of the cocktails I've been imbibing and smile. Life is good.

Suddenly, Old Man Frederick is standing before me, that shotgun pointed at my face.

"If you're from Hobart Industries," he shouts at me, "you'd best get that car in reverse fast before I shoot your ass."

I open my eyes and sit up straight. "Of course."

I abandon my review of the Houston Courtyard Hotel and head to one of the most familiar places I know. The local library.

CHAPTER THIRTEEN

Like the Alexandria Library, the Central Houston Library downtown has a folder on Hobart Industries, but it's mainly business articles and stock reports. The librarian comes back with another folder titled Hobart Court Cases and my waiter was right, these guys have been dumping oilfield waste on properties where owners have taken them to court for lease violations. I should say allegedly because most of the cases are still in process, according to my internet search, and no court has yet proven them guilty.

Regardless of what may or may not be true of their misdoings, Hobart Industries is a multi-national corporation with friends in high places. The folder contains photos of CEOs and presidents, members of Congress and a few guys in Arabic dress.

I ask the librarian for anything on Bayou State Transport but she has none. And, because I depend on libraries so much and appreciate everything they do, I commend her on keeping such awesome files. Like most librarians, she sends back a small grin and comments that it's her job. I know better. These people are next to gods in my book.

It's eight-thirty when I head back to the hotel and I'm thinking about that bathtub, grateful that I remembered to bring my bath salts with me. I pass the Discovery Green restaurant and spot my waiter having a cigarette by the back door.

"Taking a walk?" he asks me.

"Visit to the library." I pause, thinking back on our earlier conversation. "Hey, what did you mean by Hobart being such a polluter."

He shrugs. "Just that."

I'm thinking maybe he's read the same articles I have copied tonight, the ones sticking out of my purse, but I ask anyway. "Do you know something most people don't know?"

He exhales smoke and looks at me with suspicion. "Why?"

"I'm helping out a friend who lost some property in central Louisiana." Not exactly the truth, but Old Man Frederick will benefit from me sending those ghosts packing. "He mentioned Hobart Industries to me once, which is why I asked you when I spotted their building. The library doesn't have much on the company, but it did mention pollution cases in Texas and Oklahoma."

Man Bun extinguishes his cigarette by stepping on it and twisting his foot, then exhales the last of the nicotine out the side of his mouth so the waves of smoke skirt up the side of the building like a sultry snake. He glances around like he did upstairs and leans in close. "My sister works there. Hobart's a piece of work."

This makes my journalistic juices flow. "And your sister says they're dumping illegally?"

He laughs. "Dumping illegally, working past lease deadlines, paying off people to keep things quiet. You name it but you didn't hear that from me."

Now, I lean in close. "There's this rural piece of property in Louisiana and I think someone's dumping on it because the water's polluted and there's been awful smells. When my friend complains, the state says everything's fine."

"Like I said, paying off people."

That makes sense. Why else would Matt Wilson throw a water meter into my car unless he's personally involved. I digest this information and Man Bun takes out his cell phone, flips it open and calls someone, asks if they would be willing to talk to me.

"How long are you here?" he asks me.

"Until tomorrow."

He makes some arrangement and then flips the phone closed. "My sister said she can meet with you at seven-thirty tomorrow, before the office officially opens. She said she doesn't know if she can help and you can't use her name."

I'm so excited, I can only nod and say, "Of course."

"Seriously." My waiter friend's eyes become dark and

menacing. "You can't include us at all."

I nod again. I shouldn't admit this but I feel it's called for. "I'm a former journalist, been displaced by Katrina and am now writing travel stories. But I never expose my sources. Never."

Telling people you write for the media can go two ways. They run screaming from your side or they trust you and know you will do what's right. Man Bun is the latter, thankfully, and he hands me a napkin with his sister's first name on it and a number to call at the front desk, should I have any trouble. I thank him profusely and we part ways.

I'm up early so I can check out breakfast downstairs, see how well the night shift cleaned the lobby and a host of other reviewer duties. The coffee passes muster — the most important thing to this journalist — and the breakfast spread is larger than I expected, all good marks. I'm trying to stay focused but all I can think about is my meeting with the waiter's sister.

Seven rolls around, so I finish off my cup of Joe and head out, wearing the most professional thing I brought, basically my knit black pants and a simple top. It'll have to do. Just as I'm heading out the door, who should waltz in but Eric, looking prime in his coifed outfit and hair damp from a shower.

"Where you heading off to in such a hurry, Angelle? Time to join me for a coffee?"

I look around and notice there's several people in the café and the waitress looks around and smiles. "Gosh, I thought we weren't supposed to talk to one another." I lean in close and whisper, "They might catch on."

I don't wait for an answer, head out the door. It's early morning in Houston but the heat and humidity hit me like running into a glass door. I'm not halfway to Hobart and my body's clammy from the sweat. I vow to find me a job in a cool place next August, someplace like Greenland.

The Hobart building stretches up before me as an

imposing giant, towering about thirty floors above the flat Houston skyline. The lobby's bare except for a lone security guard in the center. I swallow and enter, all smiles, hoping to make my way to the elevators where Man Bun's sister works on the tenth floor.

The security guard doesn't buy it, stops me right away. "Can I help you?"

"I'm here to see Lindsey." Crap, I don't know her last name.

"Lindsey who?"

I shrug. "She works in finance, said to meet her in her office for seven-thirty."

His brow furrows and he starts to retort, so I quickly pull out my phone. "Let me call her."

I punch in the numbers Man Bun gave me and a tiny voice answers, "Lindsey McDaniel."

"Hey Lindsey." I smile at the guard. "Viola Valentine in the lobby. Mr.," I look at his name tag, "Wallace needs to verify something."

"You're the friend of Toby's?"

"Yes." I hope that's her brother's name.

She asks to speak to the guard and I pass over the phone. After a brief back and forth, Wallace points to the elevators and I'm through. As I enter the elevator car I realize I gave out my real name.

"Not a good move, Vi," I say to my reflection as the doors close.

Lindsey waits for me in the hallway, we say a few hi, how are yous, and then I follow her into an office that's devoid of people.

"Everyone gets in around eight," she tells me.

Her personal office feels more like a closet and we squeeze in and I take the small seat across from her desk, which contains only a computer and two piles of files.

"Sorry about the tight fit," she says. "I'm only the person who pays the bills, plus I don't have the right anatomy."

There's bitterness here and I can so relate. "The media can

be like that, too. Mostly men at the top and difficult to move up." I look around the tiny office and notice there's a nice window overlooking downtown Houston. "But I never had my own office, not to mention a window, so you've got that going for you."

"I guess," Lindsey looks at me a bit impatiently. "What can I help you with?"

I glance back at the slightly opened door, just to be sure, even though no one's around. "I have a friend who lives in central Louisiana and there's been some funny activity happening on the property next door. He believes Hobart is involved."

Lindsey turns back to her computer. "What's the county?"

"Parish. And it's Rapides." I start to spell out Rapides because it's pronounced rap-eeds, the French name for the rapids in the Red River, but Lindsey's ahead of me, shaking her head. "We don't own anything there."

My heart sinks because I knew this would lead to something. "How about Lorelei Lake? Fontus Springs?"

I spell those out but nothing comes up.

"Sorry."

I don't know what to say because I had been so hopeful only moments before. I sit, searching my brain in case I missed something, hoping this woman doesn't get too impatient and throw me out.

"Hobart does a lot of business with third parties," she finally says. "Maybe it's owned by someone else and we just do business with them."

You know in those cartoons when the characters get a good idea and a lightbulb goes off on top of their head? I can almost feel the heat of the bulb burning my scalp.

"How about Bayou State Transport?" I ask.

Lindsey looks at me cautiously. "Matt Wilson's company?"

The breath I've been holding comes out in a rush. Holy Mother of Pearl. "Seriously?"

She frowns. "You know him?"

I smirk. "Only met him twice and both times were not

good. He, or someone he paid, threw a water meter at my car when I checked up on the water quality of the nearby lake."

Lindsey leans back in her chair and smiles for the first time this morning. "Sounds like him. He's a piece of work."

I lean forward, excited that dots are finally being connected. "How do you know him?"

Lindsey leans to the right and checks out the still empty office, then gets up and closes the door.

"He comes in once a month, plays golf with the guys in transportation. He's always asking me out, even though I've told him I have a boyfriend. Not that that matters, I would never date that jerk. He's one of those always-starring-at-your-breasts kinda guy."

"Transportation?"

"Yeah." She sits back down and starts typing. "Hobart uses his property for storage or something like that. His company picks up the product; I don't know the details. We pay him once a month, which he gets in an envelope when he arrives for his golf game." She stops typing and I hear the printer coming to life in some corner of the room. Lindsey leans across the desk and whispers, "It's a bit under the table."

I lean forward, too. "Under the table?"

Now, she's really whispering, "I write his checks out by hand, per my boss's instructions. Understand?"

This is all so good, feel my heart skipping along inside my chest while Lindsey hands me a spreadsheet of payments made to Bayou State Transport of Oklahoma.

"Oklahoma. No wonder I couldn't find them."

"You didn't get that from me and you can't use that in print. For deep background only."

I glance down at the enormous figures on the sheet, thinking what a wonderful story this would be, plus the fact that Lindsey knows the journalism lingo, must have loved *All the President's Men* as much as Elijah and I did. "Absolutely."

I hear a knocking on the desk and look up to find Lindsey giving me a hard stare. "I'm serious."

My heart sinks because this would make an explosive story but a promise is a promise. No story unless I confirm this elsewhere. And yes, journalists do have ethics and I reiterate to Lindsey that I will not use this information with her as the source.

I have a few more questions but Lindsey looks at her watch and I hear movement in the office. She remembers something and digs through her pile for her day planner. "Since you had a run-in with Matt, you may want to skedaddle. This is his golf day and he always comes here first to pick up his check."

A raw panic rushes through me and I don't need to be told twice. I slip on my sunglasses, thank Lindsey once more — who waves me off — and rush out of the office. While I'm waiting for the elevator I glance around and notice movement in the adjoining office, a couple of women heading toward the ladies room and an overweight man panting and sweating as he exits the stairwell. I give him one of those nods and sad smiles that says, "You go, dude, understand your pain." He smiles grimly back and disappears into an office.

Seconds are ticking away and now I'm noticing my own perspiration beneath my arms. I tap my foot on the thick, boring-brown carpet and bite the inside of my cheek. What will I do if Matt appears? Will they call security, nab the spreadsheet, and haul me off to jail? I have no newspaper to call to bail me out, no editor or publisher to speak on my behalf.

I'm really starting to panic when the elevator bell jolts me out of my skin. I turn slightly so that no one exiting the elevator will see my face directly and in my peripheral vision notice three women and a couple of suits exit and head toward Lindsey's office. I quickly enter the elevator car but sideways like a crab. When I'm safely inside and the doors are beginning to close, I brave a glance at the two men. No Matt Wilson.

I exhale and push the lobby button.

"We're going up," the man to my right says and I nearly hit the ceiling one more time. I look over and it's a bicyclist carrying an armful of packages. I look to my left and there's a college-age girl pushing a mail cart. *C'est tout*, as they say in Cajun Country. So far, so good.

We move to the upper floors and both deliverers exit the car, then I push the lobby button and head south. Everyone's coming in to work so it's a straight route to the ground floor. When the elevator opens, there's a crowd of people waiting, so my anxiety ratchets up bigtime, I lower my head, push my sunglasses higher up my nose, and slip through the crowd. I swear I see Matt off to the right talking to another suit; Matt's wearing what looks like casual golf clothes. It might be my freaked-out imagination, I tell myself, but I don't waste time heading toward the front door and finally breathe when I hit the sidewalk. I glance behind me to see if I'm being followed and spot a security guard at the entrance. He looks at me, no doubt because I'm looking at him, so I smile and wave like an idiot, which makes him frown and stare.

"Stupid," I tell myself and turn and walk as fast as I can — without looking like I'm walking fast — toward the hotel. Time to grab my things and get the hell out of Dodge.

"Where are you going so fast?" Eric yells at me from the café when I haul past.

I look his way and think to politely explain that I can't talk right now, there's a posse after me, but I'm done with this man. I need to pack up and leave, make a few phone calls on the way home, and finish the job I was paid to do.

I get to my room and throw everything into my bag without caring if it wrinkles. I grab all the toiletries because I'm low at home, and leave a tip for housekeeping. I take one last look around the room, including one wishful glance at that delicious bed that was heaven to sleep in, then head out the door. When I slide my room key across the front lobby counter, I notice Eric's blonde waiting there as well.

She checks me out and frowns, then slips closer. "Do you know Eric?"

Before, I doubted that this Courtyard would suspect that Eric and I were reviewers, but at the moment I don't think it's a good idea to blurt anything out in front of them. "Why?"

She leans in close and it's now I witness the hurt in her countenance. "He's an asshole."

I can't help it. I laugh, and the pleasure it brings after an hour of espionage feels so good that it doubles in intensity and I can't stop. The woman frowns and steps back, muttering something about me being a jerk as well, so I wave to the front desk person, grab my bag, and take off for the parking garage, laughing all the way.

As I get to the second floor of the garage, my merriment ceases and I pull the sunglasses back on. When the elevator doors open, I glance around to make sure I'm alone. I am, but I still walk cautiously to my car. The windows are thankfully intact and I waste no time throwing my suitcase into the trunk, my camera and purse into the passenger seat, and light that baby up. I'm on Interstate 10 in no time flat, finally breathing normally.

The first person I call is TB.

"You will not believe what information I have dug up on Lake Lorelie."

I hear carpentry sounds in the background, remember that he's on the job in Lafayette. "You won't believe what *I* found out."

I can't imagine what my ex could have unearthed on a construction site, but I ask anyway. Instead, he asks me out.

"Do you know where Jefferson Island is?"

"The one with the pretty house and gardens down near New Iberia?"

"Yeah, Rip Van Winkle Gardens."

I've heard people rave about how beautiful this place is but the name always put me off, always imagined it like the children's section of City Park in New Orleans, with statues of little people and Mother Goose characters. A cloud settles over me thinking of that park of my childhood, under water for weeks along with the rest of City Park after Katrina.

I shake it off. "What's at Jefferson Island."

"Where are you?"

"Leaving Houston. Should be home in about four hours."

If Matt Wilson doesn't spot me and push me off the highway into the Sabine River.

"I'll be off work by that time; this is a half-day gig. Meet me at Jefferson Island and I'll buy you lunch."

"There's a restaurant?"

A man yells something in the background and TB yells back. "Gotta go," he says and suddenly my ex-husband with some important piece of information is gone.

The next person I call is Sirona and my car swerves into the right lane while I do, causing the car behind me to honk and yell something about cell phones. "Yeah, yeah," I say but know I shouldn't be calling and driving. I push the speaker button and prop the phone on the dashboard allowing me to focus on the road. Elijah answers on the third ring.

"Elijah?"

He recognizes my voice instantly for he becomes self-conscious. "Uh, hi Miss Valentine."

I try to sound like it's none of my business that he's at Sirona's house. Because honestly, it isn't. "I was looking for Sirona."

"She's not here." He still sounds like a child caught stealing a cookie. "This is actually my work phone. Can I leave her a message?"

I frown at that last remark; he's trying to sound like her receptionist, not her lover, and since when does she work at the library? I so want to tell him I don't care who he sleeps with but that would be worse.

"I have some new information. In fact, you need to hear this, too."

This perks up Guilty Boy. "I can arrange that. How about tonight?"

Tonight? I find that an odd suggestion but maybe they both have to work all day. "How about tomorrow? I'm heading home from a job in Houston."

"Tomorrow works."

"And maybe get Old Man Frederick. He should hear this, too."

Elijah laughs, and for the first time in this conversation he's not acting anxious. "I'll try but you never know with that guy."

"Whatever you can do. Where shall we meet?"

"My house." Elijah rattles off the directions. "Nine okay?"

"Nine in the morning?"

Silence follows.

"Elijah?"

I'm answered with a deep exhale. "You know, it's all good. We should come clean with all this anyway."

"Clean with what?"

"I'm off work tomorrow so anytime works."

I'm still in the janitor's closet wondering what needs a broom. "Clean with what?"

"I'll explain when you get here."

"And Sirona will be there, too?" There's something fishy going on and I imagine Sirona is at the center of it.

"Yes. Why don't you come first thing and I'll make us all breakfast."

This is sounding better but there's so much I want to know. "What did you mean by...?"

"Just come around mid-morning. You have my cell number, right?"

"Yeah."

"Gotta run. Have to be at the library in ten."

"I thought this was your work number."

In an instant, Elijah's gone.

So many things unraveling, so many questions still unanswered.

I drive east on Interstate 10, then head south once I hit the 49, otherwise known as Evangeline Thruway. When I first moved to Lafayette, I asked residents if that spelling was on purpose or did the highway department not know how to spell and all I got was confused looks. Later, I discovered it's a highway thing. Weird.

Another hour south and into a rural area where the blistering sun pours its heat down on grateful acres of sugarcane and I pull into Rip Van Winkle Gardens. There's a lovely road leading up to the main house and restaurant, both overlooking a lake skirted by live oak trees dangling Spanish moss that waves to me in the slight breeze. And I mean slight. TB's pickup truck is parked outside and through the front window of the house I see him chatting it up with a woman behind a counter.

I leave the comfort of the air-conditioned car, hit the wall of humidity awaiting me, and head inside what looks like a gift shop and information center — apparently you have to pay a fee to enjoy the historic home and gardens. The woman greets me while TB smiles like *he's* that child stealing the cookie, only he got away with it.

"You're never going to believe this," he tells me first thing.

"Believe what?"

Both he and the counter lady smile knowingly but the woman heads off to speak to a tourist couple gazing at brochures.

"Believe what?" I repeat.

TB grins like a hormonal teenager, a sight that always amazed me. The man could be one hundred years old and he will always be able to resemble an adolescent.

"I've been working on a property near here," he begins. "Hurricane Rita ruined this lady's roof and the scumbags that repaired it did a horrible job so Big Joe — you know the guy I've been working for through Fred Richard's brother — hired a bunch of us to replace the section over her kitchen because it's been leaking horribly."

Did I mention he also travels to Alaska before getting to the point?

"She has this adorable Acadian-style home. You would love it, Vi. Slopped roof, big front porch."

I love front porches, always wanted the wrap-around kind, but my patience is wearing thin. "What's the big reveal?" I ask a bit too harshly.

TB's smile fades as if I stole the joy from his story. "I'm getting there."

I put my purse on the counter and plant my feet so I'm comfortable. "Sorry."

His smile returns. "Anyway, I'm admiring her house and see through the front window that she has one of those old Victrola's, the kind you have to wind up to play. You remember how my Uncle Buzz had one down the bayou?"

We're probably in Wyoming by now but I just nod and take a deep breath.

"I tell this nice lady — her name is Miss Smith, if you can believe there's actually a Smith living in Cajun Country." He snorts laughter and it's all I can do not to laugh back, because it's TB that's funny. "The Victrola was her granddad's and he bought it from a traveling salesman back in the day when this area was so rural they didn't have but small grocery stores. Definitely no Walmarts."

TB laughs again and we're now in Seattle, so I veer him back on track. "This is what you wanted to tell me?"

He sobers. "No, but it's related."

A bell rings at the door behind me announcing an incoming tourist so TB pulls me aside while the counter woman greets them. I give TB an inpatient look mainly because I'm starving and I'm ready to head to the restaurant before it closes. TB gets the message and starts up again.

"Miss Smith invited me into her house because she wanted to show me her other antiques. She has a house full."

My stomach growls. "And?"

"And," TB smiles broadly, "there was this picture on the wall. Apparently, Miss Smith has lived in the area her whole life and she was a witness to what happened."

He pauses because, even though TB takes his own sweet time to tell a story, he knows how to prepare you for the grand reveal.

"Okay, I bite. What happened?"

TB keeps smiling as he grabs my arm and leads me to the back of the gift shop where an oversized photo hangs next to a couple of newspaper articles. I figured this is what he wants me to see so I look deeply at the black and white photo. It appears to be the lake outside our back door but without water. There are boats left listing in the mud while debris is scattered everywhere. At the top of the photo the owners have marked "The drilling disaster of Lake Peigneur."

I turn to TB for information.

"Miss Smith had a similar photo." He leans in close to make sure I hear every word. "They drilled into the salt mine underneath the lake."

I shrug. I've heard of salt domes occurring throughout Louisiana. The region used to exist beneath an ocean at one time so salt deposits were created. In fact, places like Jefferson Island are not really islands. The land around the salt deposits eroded so the domes protrude above the landscape making them appear as islands. I learned this visiting Avery Island, where Tabasco is made. The McIlhenny family produced the hot sauce using salt unearthed from their underlying salt dome.

"So, there's a salt dome here?" I ask TB, knowing well the answer.

"Yes." TB points to the accompanying news articles. "And in 1980 they drilled into the dome and punctured the roof."

A shiver runs through me because I'm finally getting the point. I look back at the photo and realize why the lake is empty. Behind me I hear TB say, "They sucked the lake right into the salt mine."

CHERIE CLAIRE

CHAPTER FOURTEEN

We stare at the expanse of Lake Peigneur, watching as the waters glisten and wink at us.

"Hard to imagine, isn't it?"

I turn to TB, still amazed at how my clueless ex-husband might have solved the mystery of Lorelie Lake.

"All of this disappeared?"

He grins, slipping his hands inside those tight jeans smudged with pits of dirt and paint. "All of it."

I have so many questions, not to mention so much to share, but TB grabs my arm and pulls me toward the restaurant which — we've been warned by the lady in the gift shop – will be closing soon. Just as well because I'm starving; been a long time since breakfast. And yes, I tend to skip breakfast to the detriment of my well-being.

The place is empty so the waitress sits us at a prime spot with massive windows overlooking the lake. I gaze out and watch a lone man cast his line off a small boat. Just before the waitress leaves after handing us menus, I grab her sleeve and ask for bread and an unsweetened iced tea.

"Carol in the gift shop said the special today is chicken fricassee," TB reports from behind his menu, "but the gumbo's to die for."

I give TB a questioning look when he lays the menu down.

He shrugs. "I've been coming here for lunch for weeks now." He pulls his napkin into his lap and makes himself comfortable. "The bread pudding's great, too."

Gumbo sounds divine so I place my menu on the table. "How many jobs have you had over here?"

He turns to look at the lake and the side of his mouth twitches, a sure sign he's hiding something.

"TB?"

"A few."

I suspect he's been taking these jobs in Acadiana to be

202

closer to me — and to offer the hotel stipend so I won't starve to death. I wonder if I hadn't been so hell bent on moving on from Katrina, on following Eric's lead in the art of bitching, I would have noticed TB's kindness and allowed him to help me. Sometimes I'm my own worst enemy but I don't want to think about that now. I'm too excited about the day's revelations.

"So, explain to me how this drilling accident caused the lake to disappear."

TB leans forward on his elbows, eager to share the story. He explains how in the fall of 1980 a Texaco oil rig accidentally drilled into the salt mine beneath the lake. What followed was akin to someone pulling the plug in a bathtub. The lake waters poured into the enormous caverns on the third level of the mine which had been emptied of its salt.

"Not only did the lake waters disappear but the drilling platform, barges, docks, boat, and other items fell into that hole, not to mention all the fish."

I gaze back on that fisherman and imagine him being sucked into a vortex.

"And the canal that connects into Vermilion Bay flowed backwards," TB adds.

The waitress arrives with a large basket of bread and my iced tea that I immediately gulp down. Did I mention it's frickin' hot here in summer?

"Are y'all talking about the lake accident?"

TB's eyes light up. "Were you here?"

The waitress is pushing twenty at best, so even if she were alive in 1980 I doubt she remembers. But I leave it alone.

"My parents worked here at the time," Chelsea Leblanc answers. (It's on her nametag.) "They say the backflow created the largest waterfall in Louisiana history."

"What?" TB asks incredulously and the waitress laughs.

"Did anyone die?" I pipe in, always the journalist thinking of the grim details.

"Three dogs."

Chelsea's face remains serious so I suspect she's not

messing with me.

"The workers in the salt mine got out okay," TB interjects. "And I think the crew on the drilling rig got off before it went under."

The waitress changes the subject to food and TB and I both order the gumbo. Lucky for us, the restaurant's closing soon so Chelsea offers us free bread pudding since the dessert made from day-old bread has pushed its limit on stale and won't keep.

"It'll just be thrown out," she says and leaves, bringing the menus with her.

I lean across the table. "Three dogs?"

There are so many times TB doesn't get my jokes and, I must admit, it's the kind of dark humor best served in a newsroom full of equally cynical and overly educated human beings. Today, he finds her comment funny as well and we both break into laughter.

Once the gumbo arrives and my iced tea glass is refilled, we get down to business.

"So, if I'm not mistaken, this is what happened at Lorelie Lake," TB begins. "Someone was drilling for oil or natural gas and punctured the salt dome underneath."

"If there is a salt dome underneath the lake."

TB smiles that adorable boyish grin, the one that got me into his dorm room bed after the LSU-Alabama home game. And a few times after that, which led to Lillye. I must admit, it's making me pretty hot right now so I take another gulp of iced tea and clear my throat.

"I called the geology department at LSU and spoke to this professor who studies salt domes." TB pulls a small paper from his back pocket and glances at some scribbles he made there. "He said there's a small salt dome on the side of Lorelei Lake, not too far from Fontus Springs. Gave me the coordinates, and when I checked the map, it looks like it's right where you said the bad smells were coming from."

Chelsea places two bowls of gumbo before us and I inhale the delicious smells of roux, crabmeat, and shrimp.

"TB, the Lorelie Lake incident was in the 1930s. The smells started last Easter."

TB's already breaking off pieces of French bread to dip into the dark soup.

"I know, Vi. The thing is, that piece of property was once part of the original Fontus Springs homestead but it's far away from everything. On the map, it appears to be the back part of the resort. I think no one went over there, knew what was happening."

I break off my own piece. "So, what are you thinking?"

He easily pushes that large piece of bread soaked in roux into his mouth and swallows and for not the first time I wished I had his metabolism. The man will eat anything and never gain a pound.

"I'm thinking that whoever owned the property in the 1930s allowed someone to use that section drilled for oil or gas and the company hit the salt dome. It wasn't directly beneath the lake like this one so only half of the water disappeared. Maybe the accident made that land unusable so now it's a dump site."

I look back at the lake, so serene and blue in the sweltering heat. "Makes a lot of sense. And I suppose the state knew about this and made people think it was their imagination as they were building the dam."

"Or, they built the dam because of it."

Now, we're heading into conspiracy theory landmines.

"Let's not veer into Fox News and stay with Walter Cronkitt."

TB pauses in his enjoyment of gumbo, mouth full of bread. "Huh?"

"We have to stick to facts. I'll do some research into when they actually planned the dam and when they actually built it."

TB continues eating but manages a few words between bites. "What news did you want to tell me?"

I smile because finally the pieces are fitting together. This time, I lean across the table in excitement. Through the gumbo, and then bread pudding, I explain how Hobart

Industries has been paying Matt Wilson to dump oilfield waste at Fontus Springs. At least, that's what the financial paper trail suggests. We agree that Matt or someone working for Bayou State Transport spilled something on Easter weekend to produce a smell discernable to residents, particularly Old Man Frederick.

"Still doesn't explain the ghosts," I add.

TB orders a coffee and turns pensive.

"What?"

"You can't drive up there tomorrow alone. And not in your car. It's not safe."

I had thought about that. "I'm getting a rental."

TB stares into his cup, stirring the sugar 'round and 'round with his spoon. That adorable boyish attitude has turned into a sulking child. Normally, his retreat into childhood annoys the hell out of me, but today, not so much. I really want the company. I really want *his* company.

"If you're not working tomorrow, do you want to go with me?"

He looks up, those brown eyes searching. "Do you want me to?"

Like I said, these circulative conversations used to burn up my spine and yet, at this moment, I understand why he acts this way. He loves me and I haven't loved him back in quite some time. TB wants me to throw him a bone so why wouldn't he behave like a pensive dog?

I take his hand. "Yes, I want you to come."

He gives it a squeeze and his countenance shifts. I was wrong in my assessment. TB isn't sulking at all, just being cautious to my feelings of separation.

"It's okay, Vi. I understand how you want your space. I just wanted to make sure."

This is new. "Honestly TB, I'd love to have you with me."

He smiles but it's half-hearted. He's not waiting for a bone at all. He leans back, coffee cup in hand, and drinks it slowly down. He wipes his mouth with his napkin, then stares at the tablecloth lost in thought, fiddling with his fork. I can't remember when I've seen him this serious.

Finally, he speaks. "I do understand, you know."

"Understand what?"

His gaze meets my eyes and there's a new man looking back at me.

"We married so young, didn't have much time to sow our wild oats. Most parents never survive the loss of a child, and for us, well...."

He looks back at the table and Chelsea arrives with the bill and a coffee pot. "Take your time," she tells us. "I have to refill the condiments and stuff."

TB pulls out his debit card and hands it over before I have time to object. Chelsea heads off with the bill and TB pours me another coffee. I want to say the three glasses of tea are about to blow up my bladder but I'm curious where he's going with this talk of wild oats.

"Anyway," he says, "I understand."

"Understand what?"

He looks up and a shiver runs through me.

"Understand your need to move on, to try on new shoes."

It hits me like a sledgehammer.

"You're seeing someone?"

TB's lips edge up slightly but it's not really a smile. "Seeing isn't the right word."

"Wow." I can't help it. This is the last thing I expected, although I don't know why. My ex-husband is a sweet, good-looking man that any woman would be lucky to nab. What's surprising is how this never happened before. Still....

"She's someone I met at one of those real estate open houses. I go to those on weekends to get designer ideas for the house." He shrugs. "And the free food."

I can't help it. The last bit, plus the surprising pain invading my heart, causes a laugh bubble to rumble through my gut and out my mouth. TB smiles, because it seems like he, too, is finding this whole conversation uncomfortable.

"Yeah, I go for the cookies."

We both start laughing at this point, but it doesn't feel

good. I worry a cry lingers at the other end.

Chelsea returns, I take a detour to the ladies room, and we head out. I pause at my car while I retrieve the keys, tears lurking too close behind my eyes. I avoid his gaze while asking if he wants to come back to my place.

"Unless you want to see Cookie instead."

"Who?"

I know if I look his way we'll only start laughing again which will most definitely produce other emotions. I'm grateful he gets the joke.

"Uh, yeah. I didn't know you were coming home today."

"It's okay, TB."

"Really, Vi, if I had known…."

I do look this time and he's the old TB, smiling at me like he cares. Does he still love me? And why, all of a sudden, does it matter? Maybe it's Lillye, I reason. He's the one person who understands, the remaining evidence that she once lived on this earth, the person who shares the memories of our child. Maybe it's just been a roller coaster ride of a summer, full of frustration and anger. TB has every right to move on and sleep with whomever he wishes, like I have with that asshole in Biloxi.

I cringe. Suddenly, being with Eric and driving that anger seems so far away and useless now.

TB touches my arm because, apparently, I have once again wondered off to lala land.

"I'll meet you at your apartment in the morning."

I nod.

"What time?"

I'm still thinking about some well-dressed real estate cookie, the kind with perfect makeup and heels, toying with TB's blonde hair, asking if he wants another glass of merlot while they relax on her chaise lounge by a pool. I hate merlot, so of course this bitch will have a bottle.

"Vi?"

I inhale, look up, and smile as if nothing's the matter.

"Sevenish. Elijah said something about breakfast."

TB nods and bends down to get a better look at my face. I keep offering that fake smile, then wave him off, turn, and unlock my car door.

"It's sweltering out here. See you in the morning."

He's still hanging around the parking lot as I drive off toward home. I spot him in my rear-view mirror standing there, watching me leave. That is until the vision blurs.

"Damn," I say to no one and wipe the moisture from my eyes with the back of my arm. It's summertime and I'm naturally wearing short sleeves so the snot goes everywhere. "Damn," I repeat.

I reach my potting shed around four and calculate I have an hour to check emails and pitch story ideas to editors. I need to push all these insane emotions aside and get back to work. Who should be waiting for me at my doorstep but two other adorable men: Reece Cormier and Stinky. I pick up one and hug him close and step up to the other, who's dressed in a Ragin' Cajun T-shirt, jeans — clean and spotless, the opposite of my husband, — and a tool belt.

"I heard you drive up," Reece says. "Is that your cat?"

I scratch Stinky behind the ears and the purring begins. "He is now." Then with an afterthought I add, "Is that okay with you?"

Reece waves me off. His post-Katrina guilt lets me do anything.

"Sure, no problem at all." He reaches over to pet Stinky, but my lovable cat lets out a hiss and Reece withdraws his hand.

"Sorry, he's usually not like this."

"It's okay." Reece puts his hands inside his jeans. "I'm not much of a cat person anyway."

An awkward silence falls between us and I get the impression that Reece wants to tell me something.

I'm right.

"Look, about us…," he begins.

I'm in no mood for another man I care about telling me he loves another. Even if Reece has only returned to his wife

209

for the kids, I don't want to hear it.

"No worries," I say quickly. "Families come first."

He looks sad and I know the turn of events have sent him reeling. We did have chemistry between us but that spark is long gone. I admire him putting the children first but not so much for letting it ruin his life, if that indeed is what's happening here.

"Piece of advice," I say as I prop Stinky over one shoulder — which the cat lets me do amazingly enough — and open the door to my tiny home. I drop the cat inside and he rushes toward the bathroom and food. I turn and gaze at those gorgeous Cajun eyes I have dreamed about, knowing that anything romantic will never happen. "My parents stayed together for us kids and it turned out horribly wrong. Make sure you also do what's best for you and your wife."

He nods solemnly, but removes a hand from his jeans pocket and lightly touches my arm. "Maybe soon we could...."

I definitely don't want to hear the end of this sentence or feel his seductive touch. I move back and cross my arms over my chest. Stinky begins crying — no doubt because his food bowl is empty — so I blurt out "Gotta go" and hurry away. Once inside the door, I lean my head back and close my eyes.

"So, this is what comes of being angry," I say to the hot stuffiness of my tiny enclave. "The good guys go away and you end up lonely in a potting shed."

Stinky cries louder this time, as if he's dying in the bathroom. Having to care for my stray feline thankfully gets my mind off self-pity.

"I'm coming, I'm coming."

First things first, turn on the A/C before I die in this sweltering apartment. Then I open the cabinets to pull out a can of food for my new roommate. Staring back at me are rows and rows of Science Diet, a brand I could never afford.

"What the...?"

Stinky cries again, rubs up against my legs impatiently. I pull one out, open the can, and dump the entire contents on to a plate.

"I don't know who brought these," I say to Stinky when I place the plate on the floor and he begins devouring the contents. "But aren't you one lucky cat."

Now, that I get a good look at the kitchen, I realize there's a new faucet, bright white caulking around the sink, and a fresh coat of paint on the cabinets accented by hip new hardware. On one hand, I'm thrilled that Reece upgraded the kitchen in my absence and someone — either he or TB — supplied me with high-end cat food. On the other, it feels like a guilt move, and I'm getting weary of the Katrina pity party. Still, it's an improvement I desperately needed. The spray in my eyes every time I turned on the faucet was getting on my last nerve.

I sit down on the kitchen floor next to my chowing cat and admire my new digs.

"Definitely looking up, hey Bud? Although it would have been nice to have my landlord share it with me."

Stinky stops eating long enough to wail, and it's a deep-throated cry.

"What?"

He returns to devouring his dinner but squeaks out another cry between bites. If I didn't know better, the cat doesn't approve of Reece.

"Well, no worries on that end."

I spend the rest of the night going through the box that Elijah gave me, reading about the town and lake's history, the legends of sirens and the miracles of the spring's waters and the German family who found it all. I explore what Lindsey gave me at Hobart's and find years of the company paying Bayou State Transport to "dispose" of "naturally occurring oilfield waste" at a central Louisiana site. I scour the Internet for more information about all of the above and find bits and pieces, mostly a fascinating account of the springs when General Eisenhower visited during his Louisiana Manuevers. Apparently, the good general found the waters soothing while training hundreds of thousands of men to be sent overseas.

"There's a spiritual component to these waters," Eisenhower relates in the Alexandria Town Talk. "With all the injustice in the world and the dark days that have befallen us, it's comforting to retreat to a spot where we can be renewed spiritually as well as physically."

I'm about to call it a night and watch Jon Stewart berate President George Bush on *The Daily Show* when Stinky waltzes in and lets out another cry. It's not as loud as his earlier demonstration but it's enough to get my attention.

"What now?"

He saunters over to the book TB left me, the one about Professor Emoto and his experiments with water. He pauses, then looks back at me and cries again, this time sounding more plaintive.

"What?"

I swear the cat gives me an exasperated look.

I lean over and pick up the book called *The Hidden Messages in Water*. It's been one I had meant to reread since TB brought it up but I had never found the time. I gaze back at my cat who's still giving me the stink eye, so I make myself comfortable in bed and begin reading about the power of thought and water.

TB arrives bright and cheerful just before seven and I know what lies behind that goofy smile. I offer him coffee in a traveling mug that announces an off-road attraction in the Tennessee mountains, but remind him that Elijah is cooking us breakfast.

"Then let's head out," he says.

I look back and Stinky's watching us both carefully.

"Hey Bud," TB says, following my gaze, and leans over to scratch his ears. But Stinky will have none of it, cries at the door until I let him out.

"Guess he's got a hot date," TB says with a grin.

I grab my purse and keys. "That, or he smells it on you."

I lead the way to TB's pickup and thankfully we never broach the Cookie subject. Instead, I relate all the things I had read the night before, including the ghost stories found on the Internet, Eisenhower and the Louisiana Maneuvers, and Emoto's book.

"And, I have to admit, you were right." I pull out the printouts on the history of Lorelei Dam. "According to this, they built the dam after a long drought caused the lake to fall three feet one summer."

"It's a cover-up."

"Maybe." I won't travel down a dirt road unless I have a reliable map; it's the journalist in me and yes, we do insist upon facts. "If that's true, then the state was involved."

TB huffs. "If Matt Wilson's an indication, there is a long history of the state being involved."

Matt is definitely hiding the fact that his company's dumping on private property but whether that means the State Department of Water Quality is also guilty is another thing. And whether the state built the dam to cover up any illegal drilling back in the 1930s is another story. Still, so many questions to answer and I wish with all my soul that I was researching this baby for a story and not to eliminate ghosts. While TB quietly drives north up I-49, I visualize writing this tale and having it printed on the cover of *The Times-Picayune*, later winning a Pulitzer Prize. I even rehearse the acceptance speech in my brain.

We pull up in front of Elijah's modest home an hour later and I made sure to place a handkerchief on TB's antennae. It was Frederick's request to do so but I'm not taking any chances, even though we're in the middle of a middle-class residential neighborhood. There are several cars parked out front and the old coot may be one of them — with that gun.

"Looks like a party," TB says.

"I told Elijah to bring Sirona and Old Man Frederick. He probably included Miss Bessie, too."

TB shuts off the engine, but pauses. "Old Man Frederick? You don't call him that, do you?"

Me and my big mouth. "Oh gosh, no." Again, an image of that gun comes into mind. "And don't you, either."

We enter the home that's a mirror of Elijah's grandmother's: everything in its place, no dust or dirt in sight, neat and tidy as a showroom. What's with these lake people, I wonder, as I gaze about the immaculate house.

Sure enough, Old Man Frederick and Miss Bessie are seated at the table, enjoying coffee. I introduce TB to Elijah, who then makes introductions all around.

"Want some coffee?" Elijah asks, heading into the kitchen.

I can never have enough coffee. "Sure," I tell him, but I head to Miss Bessie to give her a proper hug.

"Hey, sweetheart." She hugs me back without getting up. "Heard you're going to make these dead people go away."

Frederick huffs. "Good luck with that."

"Don't listen to that old fart." Miss Bessie pats my hand. "There's a solution to every problem."

Considering what's been going on at the springs, I'm not sure there's an easy solution to a toxic dump site, but hopefully we'll have a place to start.

Elijah brings in plates of scrambled eggs, wheat toast, homemade biscuits and fruit-based jam, a few slices of bacon and what he calls substitute sausage.

"Is that that fancy-smancy vegetarian crap?" Frederick blurts out.

Elijah pauses in his delight bringing us a multitude of goodness and his smile sinks. He's got that look most visitors to Louisiana have when locals shoot down their organic hospitality because it's different from our usual barrage of fried foods, sauces, and pork products, delicious though our carcinogenic cuisine may be. I saw that look many times when volunteers arrived to help with the storms. They wanted to feed locals something healthy to revive our bodies and spirits and were greeted with raucous laughter.

Then again…I gaze over at Old Man Frederick who's got to be at least eighty years old and living next to a toxic dump and he's loading bacon on to his plate. But I'm not taking any chances so I happily choose the healthy options and thank Elijah for his kindness.

"So, let's get down to business," Miss Bessie says between bites of biscuit, a few crumbs dribbling down her chin.

I let out a long sigh and then explain what TB and I have discovered. We're halfway through the drilling accident at Lake Peigneur that we believed also happened at Lake Lorelie, and how the dam came immediately afterwards, when who should waltz in but Sirona. I hear her apologize for being late as the front door opens and Elijah offers her a greeting, but what startles me the most is TB's reaction. He's staring at the door, jaw hanging open, eyes as wide as quarters. Before I can turn and greet Sirona myself, TB grabs my forearm.

"That's her," he whispers to me.

"Her who?" I whisper back.

TB leans in close so his lips are brushing my ear and the sensation sends goosebumps traveling through my body.

"The siren," he whispers.

I smile at his naiveté, at how my boyish husband will believe just about anything. I start to explain that I've met Sirona before, that she's as normal as I am, but when I pull back, TB's gaze is still wide-eyed. He motions his eyes in the direction of the door, urging me to look for myself.

"We've met before," I whisper to him, recalling the day Sirona and Elijah appeared on my doorstep and begged for my assistance.

And Stinky freaked out.

I don't know if it's the thought of Stinky's violent reaction to Sirona or TB's current amazement at the sight of her but the goosebumps rush up my arms. I push my chair backwards slightly and turn.

Sirona is standing in the doorway, wearing a long golden gown with the bright sunlight of morning pulsating from behind, causing a vibrant aura around her. She's paused on the threshold as Elijah reaches her side and greets her, giving her a chaste kiss on one cheek. Once again, I'm sure there's something between Elijah and Sirona but they mask it well, especially Sirona who appears uneasy being here.

"Oh, my God," Miss Bessie says to my side. "She's real."

Now, the goosebumps are going crazy. I look back at Sirona to discern what others are seeing and realize the aura isn't sunlight at all, but a glow that surrounds this woman and shoots out like stars. There's a rainbow of colors too — purples, blues, burnt orange — as if her aura is taking this opportunity to show off. Upon her forehead is a star-shaped diadem. And that cheek that Elijah kissed isn't dark-skinned or white but ethereal, as if her appearance is whatever I wish it to be, strange though that may sound.

I stand so fast my chair turns over. I hear Old Man Frederick saying something about "I told you so" and see Miss Bessie faint in my peripheral vision while TB catches her mid-fall. But I can't take my eyes off this vision of a woman, who's no woman at all.

Sirona Harmon is the naiad protecting Fontus Springs.

CHAPTER FIFTEEN

Everyone stops in their amazement to attend to Miss Bessie still lying lifeless in TB's arms, and when Sirona leaves her dramatic entrance at Elijah's threshold and rushes to help, the vision disappears. Suddenly, Sirona Harmon is just another woman in this group of Lorelei residents.

Except that most women don't wear golden gowns and place stars on their foreheads.

Elijah springs to action and he and TB carry Miss Bessie to the couch while I run for a glass of water and a damp dishrag. We huddle around the couch placing the rag at Miss Bessie's head, Elijah speaking softly in his grandmother's ear, and Sirona holding tight to her hand.

Old Man Frederick remains at his seat behind us, not about to forget what just happened. "I knew she was real. I knew it."

"Not now, Fred," Elijah says a bit brusquely, and it's obvious he's known who Sirona was all along.

TB stands above us all, staring at Sirona with those enormous brown eyes. I can't help feeling he's seeing something about this magical woman the rest of us might have missed ordinarily. Reminds me of that Bible verse about being child-like and entering the kingdom of heaven. For not the first time, I wonder if my simple-minded husband found the keys to the universe while the rest of us learned people keep struggling to find the door.

Miss Bessie opens her eyes and looks at each one of us before landing her gaze on Sirona. Thankfully, we're in a dark area of the living room and there's no sunlight behind our water nymph to create her goddess persona and scare Miss Bessie back to darkness. Sirona responds by squeezing Miss Bessie's hand and speaking in a language I'm positive none of us can understand.

Somehow, Miss Bessie does. She rises to a sitting position

and, to our surprise, smiles warmly and reaches her arms out to Sirona for a hug. The two embrace, while tears stream down Miss Bessie's face. I look over at Elijah who's just as shocked by the gesture.

Finally, the two unwrap themselves and Miss Bessie wipes her eyes.

"We were friends years ago, down by the lake." She looks up at Sirona who smiles in remembrance. "I was so lonely at the time, my dad working double shifts and my older brothers away at school. My mother spent most of the day cleaning other people's laundry so she would swoosh me out the door."

Sirona squeezes Miss Bessie's hand and tears once again pour down the senior's face as she utters through the emotions, "My mom said I made you up. Said you were an imaginary friend."

"She couldn't see me, so you can't blame her."

It's the first time Sirona speaks and her tone is lyrical, like a harp played softly, and I remember how lovely it sounded the first time we met.

"Why did I see you?" Miss Bessie asks.

"Because you needed me. And you didn't see me with the logical blocks that most adults have."

"I have logical blocks," Old Man Frederick says from behind. "But damned if I didn't hear you at night."

"How old were you?" Elijah asks his grandmother.

"Young. I went to kindergarten that fall."

Miss Bessie's eyes, once so full of light and joy, dim and I feel the sadness behind them. I've felt the same emotion from people who have seen ghosts but can't convince people otherwise.

"My friends at school didn't believe me either," Miss Bessie says. "And after my mother said to forget you, I stopped seeking you out and once, when I was at the lake, you were gone so I believed I really did make you up."

Sirona looks down at Miss Bessie's hand and strokes it gently. "That's the way it's supposed to be. I shouldn't have appeared to you in the first place, but you were so lonely that summer."

We all turn silent pondering this information. So much to take in, a childhood friendship begun and dismissed, the fact that a water goddess is seated before us, not to mention that this tiny central Louisiana outpost with a beer-drinking beaver-nutria atop the Hi Ho is a magical place worthy of ancient Europe. Go figure.

"Can we get back to the toxic waste dump."

Give it to Old Man Frederick to bring us back to center.

Miss Bessie throws her feet over the side of the couch, TB and Elijah help her up with Sirona still holding tight to her hand. I follow along as we regroup around the kitchen table and Elijah finds another chair.

"The eggs are cold," Frederick says.

We all look at Frederick in disgust but Sirona laughs and the sound of her voice lures us back to a happy place and we all join in, even Frederick. Elijah grabs the platter of eggs and heads to the kitchen to heat them up in the microwave, while Miss Bessie pulls an extra plate from the center of the table and begins piling up ingredients for Sirona.

"Thank you, Miss Bessie," Sirona says, "but I don't eat people food."

We all pause again, contemplating this information. Sirona senses we're all thinking about the poor fish in the lake, so she begins asking about what TB and I unearthed. TB's still in a trance so I repeat what we discovered at Lake Peigneur, and Sirona nods her head in agreement.

"That makes sense," she says. "I knew they were doing something illegal on the far side of the springs."

"Why would drilling for oil be illegal?" I ask. "If it was their property, they could do what they want."

"Not if they didn't have a permit and it affected the lake, or if they knew there was a salt dome underneath and something like this could be possible," Elijah says. "Several boats were damaged." He looks at his grandmother. "Docks were pulled apart, weren't they Grandma? My dad always said the damage was worse than they admitted to."

Miss Bessie turns solemn. "Two people were fishing on the lake when it happened."

This news takes us all by surprise, even makes Old Man Frederick stop eating.

"But, they didn't die that night," Sirona inserts.

Everyone looks her way and it's obvious that even Miss Bessie thought the accident was the cause.

"They told the authorities what they saw," Sirona continues. "And they disappeared."

We all turn silent until the beeping of the microwave brings us back and we jump at the sound. While Elijah rises to bring us reheated eggs, I look out the back window on to the placid lake, glistening in the morning sun as if tiny nymphs dance on the surface, their feet lightly touching. I glance back at Sirona and she smiles as if she knows what I see.

"Okay, so now we know what caused the lake to disappear a million years ago," Frederick says scooping eggs on to his plate. "Can we get back to the problem at hand?"

"Fred," Miss Bessie admonishes him. "I lost my son because of that accident, lost him to Chicago for the rest of his days."

"And I lost my land, Miss Bessie."

The two start arguing so Elijah rises, pushing two palms out to calm the fighting seniors. "Please, you all, we need to get back to solving our problem with the ghosts."

"You all," Frederick says in a huff. "Spoken like a Yankee. It's y'all, son."

Elijah rolls his eyes and I feel more arguing ensuing so I start explaining the connection of Matt Wilson and the smells coming off the site at Easter. I pull out the financial reports I nabbed in Houston and relay what I learned at Hobart while under cover. I feel like an investigative journalist but know that Pulitzer will have to go to someone else.

"So, Matt Wilson has been lying to us about the water quality while his company dumps toxic waste at the springs?"

Sirona asks.

"I've been telling y'all this," Frederick says while looking smugly in Elijah's direction, who rolls his eyes again.

"Is the state involved?" Miss Bessie asks.

"I don't know." I pull out the paperwork TB and I printed out at the department in Baton Rouge. "The state did find problems here but the department glossed over those facts. Maybe it was Matt acting alone or maybe someone higher up helping, but one thing's for sure, Wilson's probably acting illegally by dumping on the site, then covering it up at the department. This all needs further investigation."

"Probably?" Frederick says. "Matt Wilson is the devil."

"But why the ghosts?" Miss Bessie asks. "Oilfield waste doesn't cause the dead to walk the earth."

Sirona suddenly appears uneasy. She frowns and it's like a cloud passing over the sun. We all feel the sudden darkness and turn to look her way.

"I did it," she finally says.

Miss Bessie pats her hand. "Did what, honey?"

Sirona becomes antsy, rises and begins pacing the room.

"The first time worked. When they started bringing in prostitutes and the springs were suffering. I only meant to scare them and it worked pretty good."

We're all ears. Even Old Man Frederick gives up eating, pushing his plate away to devote his attention to Sirona. I look around and everyone appears clueless but I think I know what Sirona has done.

"You called upon the dead to help."

Sirona looks at me and nods. "It was temporary. I was hoping those horrible people who took over the springs from the Germans would be scared off and leave the place alone, but only a few of the staff members got frightened and left."

Frederick turns in his seat to look at Sirona head on. "Wait, you're telling me you called the town's dead to haunt Fontus Springs?"

"It was temporary," Sirona insists.

"How on earth?"

"I can't explain it. It's power that belongs to me that I'm not allowed to share." Sirona looks down at her feet. "I shouldn't be among you now, shouldn't allow you to see me, but I made a mistake and I'm not sure how to fix it."

"You called upon too many, is that it?" I ask.

Sirona looks at me and nods. "What they did at Easter, it's more than you can imagine. It's not only polluting our sacred spring but the lake as well." Her gaze follows those around the table. "It's poisoning your drinking water."

We all take in this last piece of information, Elijah gazing into his coffee cup, and Frederick shaking his head in disgust.

I'm still thinking about those ghosts. Now, it's my turn to stand and pace. "You asked the town's dead to scare Matt Wilson and the people who work for him, right? And more appeared than you imagined and now they're walking all over town at dusk?"

Sirona nods solemnly. "I can't make them go away. That's why Elijah and I approached you. We thought you could help."

It's one thing to face a ghost, find out why they're haunting this plane and help them move to the other side. Quite another to send a whole town packing, dead people who were on the other side to begin with.

"Honestly, Sirona," I begin, "I haven't a clue how to fix this."

We all begin discussing one idea after another, none of which makes sense considering what we're dealing with, but we act like they might, throwing intellectual thoughts right and left. While we're being theorists, TB rises and starts riffling through my purse. Usually, I hate when people do this; a woman's purse is her castle. Today, I'm curious as to what he's about, unless it's to find chapstick, and then I'll be pissed.

He pulls out Dr. Masaru Emoto's book and it's as if that proverbial lightbulb goes off again. Another Biblical passage enters my mind, the one about the meek inheriting the earth. TB looks my way and I smile, which gives him courage to enter the conversation.

"I think I know a way," he says.

Everyone pauses to gaze at my simple-minded husband, a man I never give enough credit for finding answers. TB sends me a look, waiting for my approval or dismissal. I smile and nod, all the encouragement he needs.

"But we need more people," he adds.

Elijah spent most of the day calling residents to meet in the back of the Hi Ho after work and by five-thirty almost two dozen people stand around asking questions while that skinny teenager pours them all coffee. More residents drift in by the minute and I wonder how we will all fit into the restaurant, but Elijah assures me we can easily bleed into the bait shop.

TB saunters over to my side and whispers, "What's up with the nutria?"

I look down and see the smiling mammal on his coffee cup.

"It's supposed to be a beaver, but the artist left off the tail."

TB scratches his head. "I don't get it."

He may understand the secrets of the universe but an artwork mistake not so much, so I leave it at that.

"Do you want to explain to everyone what you said at Elijah's?" I ask him.

TB shakes his head. "You do it. You're good at these things."

We wait another thirty minutes until Elijah feels that everyone who said they were coming is there. Those who were sitting rise and make room for more people to file into the restaurant area, and once we have the crowd organized and within hearing distance of me, we start.

"Some of you have met Ms. Valentine, and some of you may know why we asked her to come to Lake Lorelei," Elijah announces.

There's a titter through the crowd, and I sense a few

223

people think my ghost-hunting skills lack merit, or refuse to believe in the apparitions haunting the town, mainly those men who have never spotted one. Overall, however, the crowd appears curious and I feel the warmth of their gazes upon me.

"She knows about our problem and she has an idea on how to fix it."

Where's Sirona? I wonder. As Elijah introduces me and asks me to speak, I gaze around to spot my illusive goddess but she's nowhere to be found. Does she not want to be recognized? In all our preparation, we failed to ascertain that little fact.

I look up and realize Elijah has finished and everyone is waiting for me to speak. I clear my throat, pull out Emoto's book and begin.

"Fontus Springs is sacred. I'm sure you've all heard the stories through the years and know that waters pouring forth from miles underground bring special healing with them."

"Not according to the American Medical Association," says a thick southern accent in the back.

"True," I answer, knowing that owners of springs are not allowed to boast of their attributes. "But y'all live here and y'all know how important these waters are."

A few nods and murmurs of agreement.

"Fixed my arthritis," says an elderly voice to my left.

"Great for eczema," says another.

This starts a host of exclamations, like witnesses in a church. Elijah raises a hand and brings the crowd back to order.

"Water makes up seventy-one percent of the earth," I continue. "And our bodies are mostly water. So, if there is a vibration happening throughout the earth, one that Native Americans believed in, one that perhaps the Hilderbrands understood, then it's likely to be felt in water most of all."

Now, I've lost a few, so I hold up Emoto's book.

"Masaru Emoto was a Japanese scientist who studied water. He believed that words and thoughts were vibrations called 'Hado,' which means wave. If the energy of a place was negative, people would say that its Hado was low. If a place emitted good vibes, people would say it had a powerful Hado."

A few glazed eyes, so I open the book and show them photos of the water crystals, explaining how positive thoughts and words created beautiful water crystals in the water while negative thoughts and words created distorted ones. I pass the book to TB and he begins walking through the crowd, showing them the photos.

"Emoto believed that these vibrational waves of thought, words and consciousness can change things, even at the atomic level," I continue. "If all energy is vibrating, then we can change anything by changing the vibration."

Shifting of feet.

"He also believed that vibrations exist in a middle world, so to speak, and that water is the first to detect it."

"What are you getting at?" says a woman to my right and others begin talking.

"Sounds hokey to me," says another.

"If this is some of that hocus pocus stuff they talk about in California…."

Within seconds, I'm losing ground.

Elijah whistles. Loudly. And the crowd comes back to order. I'm amazed at how such a soft-spoken man can command attention like this, but then, he is the mayor. I quickly continue so as to not lose the group again.

"For instance, at a dam in central Japan, a Shinto priest repeated an incantation and cleaned the waters. And there was a lake in Japan that was heavily polluted. It smelled bad, had a horrible algae problem, thick reeds everywhere and the water was dirty. One day, hundreds of people came to the lake with Dr. Emoto and offered good Hado and what Emoto calls Kotodama, or the spirit of words. They asked for world peace. The lake cleared up."

"Our lake isn't polluted," Southern accent says. "It's just filled with ghosts."

Several people laugh, but it's a nervous one. I understand what Dr. Emoto meant when certain feelings create specific vibrations. Right now, an uneasiness and confused vibe streams through the room.

"The ghosts and the pollution of the springs are connected," I try to explain.

Several people question this statement and the murmurs continue. I look at Elijah for help but he's as clueless as I am to explain what Sirona has done. If only she were here.

"Matt Wilson has been dumping toxic waste at the springs," TB says, and everyone stops talking and looks his way. "He's been bringing in oilfield waste. There was an incident at Easter, we believe, which hurt the ground water and the lake."

"I knew it," says a man next to Elijah. "I kept seeing those trucks going in and out of there and knew nothing good would come of it."

"Are you sure?" someone else asks.

Elijah relates what we discovered about Hobart, Bayou State Transport and Matt Wilson. He shares how I lost my car window, what I found in Houston, and how Old Man Frederick — he doesn't call him that — has received constant threats over the years. He even mentions the disappearance of the lake in the 1930s and of the two men who reported that incident and were not heard from again. The crowd becomes eerily silent at that news.

"One was my father," Elijah states. At this, questions start flying. Elijah holds up a hand. "A story for another day."

"But, I don't understand," the woman to my right says. "What's this got to do with ghosts?"

Once again, I'm stymied. Dr. Emoto's theory is hard enough to explain, but a water goddess who calls to the dead? The crowd titters again, and this time I'm not sure Elijah will be able to control them. I look at TB and he's just as concerned, especially as the crowd noise rises and questions are asked everywhere.

"I did it."

I close my eyes and thank the heavens, for Sirona's voice rises above them all and a silence falls upon the room. She doesn't arrive with the magical aura of before, considering she's entering a double wide at the back of a bait shop, but her presence stuns the crowd regardless, that lyrical voice and glow making everyone ponder who this majestic woman might be. Her star remains on her forehead but this time she has a golden snake coiled about her lower arm.

"I called those ghosts," Sirona says. "I wanted to scare off the men polluting my waters and I went too far. It's my fault they are here, but I believe that Viola can help us make things right again."

"Who are you?" whispers the woman at my elbow.

Sirona inhales and lets out a heavy breath. "I'm a naiad, a spirit or water nymph, if you will, chosen to watch over Fontus Springs."

I'm expecting some laughter or huffs, but the crowd remains silent, watching this goddess in awe. Maybe it's that snake on her arm or the crystal on her forehead that's silenced this group. Still, ghosts, Emoto, and now a naiad is a lot for this small central Louisiana town to absorb. I look over at TB who appears equally stunned at this reaction.

"In the early days," Sirona continues, "the Fons Perennis or the eternal spring came forth in this area, bringing life-giving water. I was assigned to watch over the spring."

"I've heard you," the skinny teenager says and I notice she has tears in her eyes. "You speak to me."

Several people murmur in agreement.

"I've seen you in the woods," a man utters, and I notice that he, too, has moist eyes.

"I hear you at night," says the woman to my right. "Your singing lulled me to sleep after my husband died."

I finally understand. This woman, the subject of myths and legends, has been real to these residents for years, only no one was able to speak of it without being chastised or labeled crazy. As I gaze around the room, people stand smiling, enchanted, some even crying openly, and Sirona absorbs their love and gratitude openly.

"I love you all," she says softly, and I swear I can hear harps playing.

After minutes of Sirona greeting people and spreading that brilliant aura, she turns to me.

"We need to do what Ms. Valentine suggests. And we need to do it tonight at sunset."

I don't have to convince any of these people to follow me now. They are all on board, even those men who insisted the ghosts were the subjects of women's imagination. I motion for us to head out to the lake's shore and everyone follows behind, a circle of energy surrounding Sirona. TB rushes to my side but I can tell he is as enchanted as the rest of them.

"Go hang with Sirona," I tell him.

"Are you sure?"

I smile. "I've got this."

He moves to leave, but I grab his sleeve. "Bring back some of that magic with you, though."

We make our way to the Fontus Springs property, through thick woods of pine and live oak trees. Old Man Frederick leads us to a hole in the fence, one no doubt he created. We're trespassing because this land, once a part of the Fontus Springs resort, belongs to the Parker family, but none of us pause in our actions. We arrive at the tiny stream composed of spring water, the one that trickles from the capped spring and rolls down the hill to the lake's edge.

"Now what?" Elijah asks me quietly, and I look to find him by my side.

I start to suggest holding hands and silently freak out because I really don't know what to say next. Dr. Emoto offered prayers and declaration for world peace but I haven't that wisdom to impart. Thankfully, I see Sirona moving forward and raising her hands to the heavens, speaking words in that language I heard at Elijah's cottage.

I take Elijah's hand and he offers his to the woman to his left and the crowd immediately gets the message. In no time at all, we are all holding hands in a circle around the stream of spring water, and looking to Sirona for guidance. The distant lake glistens in the setting sun.

"What the hell is going on here?" a voice calls out from behind.

I turn to find Matt Wilson and three men coming through the woods. One man has a rifle and the other two shovels resting over their shoulders.

"This is private property," Matt says when he gets closer. "You have no business here."

Elijah breaks the circle and faces Matt. "You don't own this water."

Matt doesn't miss a beat, smiles smugly and crosses his arms about his chest. "Mayor, we've had this discussion before. I own this land and everything on it, so you and your prayer circle, or whatever the hell this is, needs to go back to where you came from."

"Actually, you don't own this land." Frederick steps forward and walks within feet of Matt and his men. It's now that I notice Frederick has his own set of tools.

"If it isn't crazy Old Man Frederick," Matt says, and his men laugh. "Gosh, Elijah, I hope you're not listening to this insane old coot."

Frederick raises a crowbar and is about to show Matt what an old coot can do, but Elijah puts a hand to Fred's chest.

"Brock Parker's heirs own this land," Elijah says. "Not you, Matt. You think you have us fooled. We also know about Bayou State Transport and the illegal dumping, not to mention the accident that happened on Easter weekend."

Matt's eyes enlarge and I swear I can see him grit his teeth.

"I'm one of Brock Parker's heirs, Elijah, and I have no idea what you're talking about."

Now, it's Elijah's turn to smile smugly, only he does so on the side of right.

"No worries. I have lots of documentation to prove what you've been doing, plus I'm sure the other heirs would love to know how you've decimated their property to the point of it being worthless. In fact, I have their numbers right here. Want to call them and see what they think of us trespassing on their property?"

For the first time since I've met him, Matt appears worried. He doesn't say anything for the longest time, then turns to his men and nods for them to move off.

"I'm going to the authorities," Matt says softly. "And we'll just see about this."

Elijah doesn't falter a bit. "You do that."

Matt, also, doesn't back down. "Your days are numbered, Mayor."

Elijah laughs. "Considering these nice people here vote for me, I'd say you're probably wrong there."

Matt huffs and heads off, but he has the last word. "I'll see you in court."

As we watch the men walk off into the woods, everyone cheers. There's laughter, the patting of Elijah's back, nods in my direction. But after a few moments, we all turn serious, no doubt wondering what the future will bring. I look at Sirona to start the ceremony once again, but she looks back sadly. And suddenly, I realize there's one more action to take before we bless the waters.

"Hey, old coot," I yell to Frederick. "How about we use that crowbar on the springs?"

Frederick doesn't miss a beat. "Why did you think I brought it?"

We head over to the spring head where a round piece of concrete marks the spot. Frederick hands off two other tools — a pickaxe and a shovel — to other men and the three begin tearing the concrete apart.

"Hurry," the skinny teenager says, gazing at her cell phone for information. "Sundown is almost here."

After ten minutes of hard work, the men finally break the concrete and others rush over to begin pulling apart pieces. There's more blockage underneath and I can almost feel the collective sigh as we spot this.

"We need to hurry," Elijah says.

Everyone picks up the speed and the pieces are thrown every which way, while one of the men shovels dirt out from underneath. More pickaxe and crowbar delivery, followed by removal of dirt, concrete and metal. As the sun slips below the tree line, I wonder if we're going to make it. We're so close.

Just as darkness settles and I expect to see dead Confederates greeting us, someone yells and water comes pouring forth from the ground. Frederick holds his crowbar to the sky and howls, the other men splash the water on to each other, and the crowd descends to the springs for their own baptismal. We relish the clear water like thirsty travelers in a desert, even though there must be toxicity in its composition. It's our springs, and we own this moment.

Finally, Sirona holds up her hands to quiet the crowd.

"We still have to bless the waters and ask the departed to return to their resting places."

Everyone forms a circle and we all hold hands once more.

"But the work here has only begun," Elijah says before we begin. "We have to fight this. We have to make the responsible parties pay for the damage done to our springs, our lake, and our drinking water."

"I have a friend who's a lawyer in these kinds of things," a man offers. "I'll talk to him about pro bono."

"We need to do a title search," another suggests. "I can help with that."

"I have all kinds of documentation on the property, including how my grandfather was cheated," Frederick inserts.

"And we must hire someone to do an independent water assessment," Elijah says. "It's all going to cost money. Are you all with me?"

There's nodding and agreement all around along with a few "hell yeses," and I'm warmed by the collective optimism. Without logic seeping in, I'm convinced this small group of people will put Matt behind bars — or at least stop his destructive actions and put Bayou State Transport out of business. In time, this lovely spring will return to its sacredness, offering people healing powers and solace.

TB approaches me and smiles, seemingly as happy as I am at the turn of events.

"You see how the collective consciousness can move things?" he asks me as I take his hand. "There's so much positive energy now. I'll bet we clean up this water right here today."

He's beaming with hope. I'm not convinced our thoughts and words will heal this toxicity, but heck, it's worth a try. I do know that love, gratitude, and hope are as powerful as the anger and meanness Eric had taught me, but the end result brightens the world instead of promoting shadows. And dang, it feels so much better.

We all hold hands again, and Sirona moves to the center, raising her arms again to the skies and speaking words none of us comprehend but understand nonetheless. The words and the hopeful thoughts running through our consciousness vibrate deep into our souls.

As the sun sets over Lake Lorelei, named for the German siren who sang love songs on its European shores, we pray for the return of the departed, thank them for their assistance, and ask them for peace in the afterlife. With one last thought, we bless the waters that run through us all.

As dusk settles around us, no ghosts appear.

CHAPTER SIXTEEN

"So, what's supposed to happen?" Elijah asks me as we join the crowds gathered on the shore of Blue Moon Bayou.

I explain again the myth of falling in love with the first person you see upon the rising of the blue moon. I know I've told Elijah this when I had called yesterday and invited him to join me.

"But, there was one earlier this summer, right?"

"In May," I answer, which seems so far away considering everything that has happened. "Despite the fact that most people think blue moons happen infrequently, hence the term 'once in a blue moon,' they occur every two to three years or so. Sometimes, like this year, they happen twice in a year. And yes, we had one earlier this summer."

"Cool."

I love odd Southern traditions, and I gaze around at the crowd of people enjoying family, tradition, and, *bien sur*, fabulous food. I smile at myself for remembering a French expression from my LSU days, something to impress residents in my new home in Cajun Country. But who am I kidding, I speak French to these people and they roar with laughter.

I look over at Elijah, who's not enjoying the moment as much as I am. I slip my arm through his and give him a friendship squeeze.

"You think I'm crazy, is that it?" he asks me. "For falling in love with an immortal woman who lives inside a lake?"

"Well, now that you put it that way."

We both laugh but it's a half-hearted one. After our communal prayer at the springs, Sirona disappeared. Elijah threw himself into hiring the pro bono lawyer and working through the information I gave him, so he routinely claims he's too busy for anything else, including a love life. Of course, I know better. And, I know something he doesn't.

"She does travel, you know."

Elijah looks at me questionably.

"Remember when the two of you came to visit me?"

As if on cue — maybe goddesses can do that — Sirona takes the opportunity to join us, sitting beside Elijah on the ground and smiling. Gone is the crystal on her forehead and that awful snake on her arm, but I feel happy just being in her presence. Elijah, on the other hand, lights up like a fire. He may be mortal, but his aura is shooting out beams like a god.

I quietly excuse myself. Who knows where that relationship will lead; I've had friends in worst situations. Well, maybe not as tricky as loving an immortal with fins, not to mention one who can change her appearance. But really, love is all about the here and now. If there's one thing I've learned seeing ghosts is that life's too short. Grab all the happiness while you can.

I head over to Annie Breaux's tent next to The Mortuary B&B where my family has gathered for the event. For once I was right that my mother would love this crazy tradition. She insisted on coming back, interviewing residents, and writing a paper on the phenomenon. She and Annie are deep in discussion.

"I can't believe mom likes this nonsense," Portia says to me as I approach. She's got a plate piled high with corn macque choux, smothered chicken pieces over rice, potato salad, and barbecue ribs.

"Sorry, you're having such a bad time," I reply, gazing down at her plate.

She shrugs. "Have to entertain myself somehow."

"You might want to pace yourself. Annie's wild blueberry pie and pecan tarts are to die for."

Portia has already started shuffling Cajun goodies into her mouth, but she manages to utter, "Good to know."

Sebastian couldn't make it, but I'm not surprised. He's on to a new adventure, this one in Santa Barbara, California, at some swanky farm-to-table restaurant attached to a winery. He invited me to come visit — even offered to pay for the plane ticket — and I'm so there. I'll do anything to escape the oppressive heat of Louisiana in mid-summer.

Still, life is good. The dam holding back my paychecks from clients finally broke and I've paid this month's bills, including putting new brakes on the Toyota, plus have savings in the bank — a tiny savings but at least there's something in there besides air. A press trip to Florida looms on the horizon and I picked up three travel assignments this week alone. If it wasn't for the orphan on the banks of Blue Moon Bayou, I'd say even the ghosts are leaving me alone at present.

Portia pauses in her culinary enjoyment and swallows hard and I have a feeling where this sudden change is going.

"Don't worry about it," I say, more because I hate having heart-to-heart talks with my sister, who I'm sure doesn't have one. "I know you didn't mean what you said the other day."

She exhales and gazes down at the bayou. "I really didn't, Vi. I'm just so angry these days."

This makes me laugh because one, my sister always appears aggravated and obstinate and two, for once I know exactly what she means.

"I'm sure it's the stress of Katrina, the constant unknowns regarding New Orleans, and now mom has Parkinson's. We've had enough anxiety and trauma to last us a lifetime."

Portia nods and resumes eating, but between bites she manages to appear almost sweet.

"Still, I'm sorry I said it. I can't imagine anything worse than what you've gone through."

An acknowledgement of my pain. Miracle of miracles. I look to the sky to see if it will snow. Usually, I would act the typical little sister and make light of it, gush about how I'm sure she has gone through similar hardships, but the truth is, I've been to hell and back and it's nice hearing my sister admit as much.

"I'll be right back," I tell Portia. "Have to say hi to someone."

Portia grabs my sleeve and looks around to make sure

mom is not within hearing distance. "Okay, but come to New Orleans soon, will ya?"

I sigh because I thought we were done with this argument. "I've been coming in more often and spending time with mom." And seeing way too many dead people in my hometown. "I'll be in again soon."

"It's not that." Portia takes a sip of her beer and burps softly. "I need to talk to you alone."

This worries me. "I thought mom was doing well."

She waves me off. "She is. It's about dad."

A dread travels from the bottom of my feet to the top of my head and my look must have mirrored that for Portia waves me off again. "Don't worry about it. It's not as bad as all that. Just come in soon, okay?"

I think about what news Portia could possibly impart about our absent paterfamilias as I make my way down to the bayou's edge. Abigail waits for me there, still wearing her trademark overalls. Of course, what else would she be wearing considering she's dead?

"Are you all right?" she asks me, something I'm not expecting.

"Yes." For the first time this summer I am, despite whatever news Portia has waiting for me. "But, I have to ask, what do you need?"

"Me?" Abigail looks surprised.

"Do you need help getting to the other side?"

Abigail acts like she doesn't know what I'm talking about.

"You know, not be a ghost. Enter heaven."

Abigail spits. "Hell no. I never want to see my sorry excuse for a mother again. Or those horrid farmers who took me in." She looks around at the bayou and the happy people waiting for the blue moon to rise. "I like it here."

I smile and nod, and am also grateful there's nothing crazy I need to do for yet one more apparition. At least not this week. "Good. I wish you well."

Abigail is fading but she asks again. "Are you sure you're okay?"

"Yes, why?"

I can barely make her out now.

"She just wanted to make sure."

"She?"

Abigail fades and I wish she were real and I could grab her sleeve like Portia did me.

"She?" I practically yell.

A panic fills my chest and I have trouble breathing. I must know what Abigail meant.

"Abigail?" I call out too loudly.

"Who are you looking for?"

I turn and find TB at my side, the last person I expected to see today. The surprise of him being here allows me to exhale and resume a steady breath.

"What are you doing here?" I ask, but this time without the terse tone because I'm happy to see him.

TB slips his hands into those ragged jean pockets and I can't help noticing how that denin stretches over just the right places.

"That lady I was working for when you came to Lake Peigneur, the one with all the antiques? She called me back to do a bunch of odd jobs."

"That's great." I find myself smiling broadly. "Stinky will be pleased," I add, hoping to cover up the excitement building inside of me.

TB shrugs. "Mrs. Smith loves to make me apple pie and lemonade, show me her old photos. I'm not even sure she needs all that work done."

I can imagine how much Mrs. Smith loves TB, a sweet man who will sit and listen to old people's stories and honestly show interest. He's really a great guy.

"Portia called and told me y'all were meeting here so I thought I would come and say hi."

He's unsure of my reaction, I realize, and I hate that TB feels that way around me. Despite everything, including the fact that he may be in love with a real estate woman who loves merlot, he's my best friend. The announcer calls out that the blue moon is about to rise so I link my arm through his and TB and I head over to Annie's tent, where I make introductions all around. After some small talk, the announcer yells out that we're seconds away so we all get comfortable in lawn chairs facing the bayou.

"I thought you'd be in New Orleans with Cookie this weekend." Dang, I really didn't mean to bring her up. Not today.

"Who?"

"The real estate lady."

TB does a smile-frown and I'm sorry I asked. I have no right to mention women he's slept with, make him feel guilty, girls throwing rocks at glass houses and all.

"It was nothing, really," TB says. "It was, what did you call it? A moment where liquor was involved."

"Oh, there was wine with the cookies?" Stupid me trying to make light of this. "You must like her, though, since you spent the night before Lake Lorelei with her."

I didn't mean to get that personal but deep down I really want to know. TB starts rubbing his palms on his knees and squints as he gazes out over the bayou. Either I'm making him uncomfortable or he's not telling me something.

"She lives in New Orleans, Vi."

"I figured."

"Did you think I drove to New Orleans and back before we went up to the lake?"

Honestly, I didn't think about the logistics of that five-hour round trip. All I was focusing on at the time was TB in love with some woman with a well-paying job and no baggage. At least, I assumed as much.

"I don't understand," I say, because I hope to God that Cookie wasn't waiting back at TB's hotel. In my head, I admonish myself. I have no right to TB. In fact, if the man had any sense he would run screaming from having any business with my sorry ass.

"I didn't know you were coming in that day so I let my boss get me a hotel room for the night." TB's still looking guilty.

My heart drops thinking that Cookie drove over from New Orleans. That would mean something solid is between them.

"Well, you don't want to waste a good hotel room." I cringe, not what I meant to say.

TB picks up a long stretch of Saint Augustine grass, the kind that snakes through the lawn and is as tough as rope. Sebastian and I used to pick these and make crowns out of them, pretend we were magical twins.

"I didn't want to tell you."

I look over at TB who's still not meeting my eyes. I dread hearing the truth but I ask anyway, "Tell me what?"

"The LSU Cable Network was running highlights from the fall season that night and the hotel carried it. You always used to make fun of me for watching old football games, since I had seen them already and knew how they turned out. So, I didn't tell you."

The eighteen-wheeler parked on my heart pulls away. I can't help but grin broadly. TB thinks my wide smile is because of the stupid LSU games so I pull my arm through his elbow and lean slightly in his direction. I still don't know how he feels about Cookie but for now, he's here, and all is right with the world.

Without thinking, I say, "I thought you left to go see Cookie."

TB grins but it's a hesitant one. "I kinda wanted you to think that."

There's a buzz happening at the bayou, kids run down to the stage, and the musicians stop playing. It's close to the rising of the moon.

"Your landlord's here," TB whispers to me.

"What?"

TB points to my right and I look over to find Reece and his two kids playing at the bayou's edge. He's wearing neat and pressed jeans and a Polo shirt, a little too preppy for my tastes. He's always perfect like that, I realize, reminding me of

Eric.

Reece notices me and waves. I wave back.

"If you want to head over there, that's fine."

I look back at TB. "What do you mean?"

The announcer begins the countdown, starting with ten.

"I've seen the way you look at him, Vi. I get it."

Nine.

"What way?"

Eight.

"I've seen the way he looks at you, too."

Seven.

"He's married, TB."

Six.

"Last time I spoke to him, he said it wasn't working out."

This is news.

Five.

I shake my head. "You're mistaken."

Four.

"I told you before, I understand."

Three.

"Vi, the moon is rising."

Two.

"So, it is."

I stare at my ex-husband — who's really not my ex — as the announcer counts down to one. I smile tentatively. And the blue moon rises.

AUTHOR'S NOTES

Blue Moon Bayou and its Blue Moon Rising festival honoring the rising of the blue moon is completely born of my imagination. "Blue Moons" are real, however, an extra full moon within a calendar year. Since lunar months are 29.53 days, there will occasionally be two full moons with a calendar month. Despite the saying, "once in a blue moon," blue moons happen frequently, usually once every two to three years. Sometimes, they occur within a couple of months of each other, which is what I used here. In 2018, for instance, there will be two blue moons, on January 2 and 31 and on March 2 and 31.

I base Blue Moon Bayou on Breaux Bridge, a delightful Cajun town that's home to boutiques, restaurants, antique shops, and Café des Amis, which, until recently, hosted a zydeco brunch every Saturday morning, in addition to fabulous food. Today, Buck & Johnny's of Breaux Bridge offers the zydeco brunch.

I mentioned Curley Taylor and Zydeco Trouble, both of whom are real and worth notice; check them out. The Mortuary Bed & Breakfast next door with its plethora of ghosts does not exist (except in my fictional town), but you'll find this unique establishment in forthcoming books.

Lorelei Lake and Fontus Springs are also figments of my imagination, although I got the idea after reading about Hot Wells, Louisiana, a hot springs resort in the center of the state. Hot Wells, located near lovely Cotile Lake, experienced periods of growth and decline, but as far as I know the mafia wasn't involved, nor was it haunted. General Eisenhower did participate in the Louisiana Manuevers, which trained men and women in the center of Louisiana for combat overseas, but he never visited the springs nor offered the quote to the *Alexandria Town Talk* newspaper that I have included in this book.

To read more about this real-life ghost town, I recommend *Hot Wells: A Louisiana Ghost* by Larry Jorgensen.

Likewise, there is no Hi Ho bait shop and café, there was never a salt dome accident at Cotile Lake, and I fabricated the Louisiana Department of Water Quality.

Grapevine, Texas, is a real town and home to many hauntings, including several at Cross Timbers Winery. The Diamond Grill in downtown Alexandria, Louisiana, exists, an elegant restaurant inside an art nouveau/art deco building that used to house C.A. Schnack's Jewelry Store. It wasn't opened at the time of Viola and Elijah's visit, so I took some liberty there; it opened a few years later. The TV series *Ghost Hunters* visited the Diamond Grill in 2011, searching for a former employee named Stella who likes to hang out in the dining room. The show's staff members experienced high electromagnetic readings behind the bar, moving doors with assistance, and a dark black mass during their investigation in Season Seven, Episode One.

In the nineteenth century, the New York Foundling & Orphan Asylum, run by the Sisters of Charity, sent New York orphans throughout the country to Catholic homes. In Louisiana, more than two thousand orphans arrived, including at Lafayette, Opelousas, and New Orleans. The system ended around the time of the Great Depression, but the Louisiana Orphan Train Museum in Opelousas tells its story.

Peigneur Lake at Rip Van Winkle Gardens in South Louisiana did disappear one fall day in 1980 when a Texaco oil rig drilled into the side of the underlying salt dome. As far as I know, there is no salt dome beneath or beside the waters of Cotile Lake.

For more information on Japanese scientist Masaru Emoto and his experiments with water, I'd recommend reading his *The Hidden Messages in Water, The Healing Power of Water,* and *The Secret Life of Water.*

Finally, I've had three family members suffer from Parkinson's Disease, my father, my brother and, most recently, my dear husband Bruce. It's a neurological disease in desperate need of a cure. Portions of this book's profits will be donated to my brother Quentin Dastugue's Team Fox Louisiana, part of the Michael J. Fox Foundation's grassroots community fundraising program.

ACKNOWLEDGEMENTS

It takes a village to write a book, although in the most unusual ways. Most people never realize how important they are to the lonely business of novel writing.

Thanks to Barbara and Jim Lambert for the use of your lovely lakeside home for a writer's retreat. The experience not only gave me quiet time to start this novel, but fodder for Fontus Springs and Lorelei Lake. I appreciated the visit more than you know. And thanks to Jan Risher for inviting me to participate.

To my sister-in-law, Penny Dastugue, for explaining to me complicated property transfers in Louisiana. I hope I did you proud.

To David and Christee Atwood, for giving me an ear to vent and for always making me laugh. Y'all keep me sane.

To Andra Paitz, an awesome editor.

To the three greatest critics and fans, my mother LilyB Moskal, and sisters Danon Dastugue and Roxane Moskal Berglund. You all kept me going with your enthusiasm and support. I can't thank you enough.

And to the men I love more than life itself, my husband, Bruce, and my sons, Taylor and Joshua, the water on which I stay afloat.

ALSO BY CHERIE CLAIRE

Viola Valentine Mystery Series
A Ghost of a Chance
Ghost Town
Trace of a Ghost

The Cajun Embassy
Ticket to Paradise
Damn Yankees
Gone Pecan

The Cajun Series
Emilie
Rose
Gabrielle
Delphine
A Cajun Dream
The Letter

Carnival Confessions: A Mardi Gras Story

ABOUT THE AUTHOR

Cherie Claire is a native of New Orleans who like so many other Gulf Coast residents was heartbroken after Hurricane Katrina. She works as a travel and food writer and extensively covers the Deep South, including its colorful ghost stories. To learn more about her novels and her non-fiction books, upcoming events and to sign up for her newsletter, visit her website www.CherieClaire.net. Write to Cherie at CajunRomances@Yahoo.com.

CHERIE CLAIRE

Made in the USA
Columbia, SC
29 February 2020